WILDERNESS WHISPERS

C.K. Haworth

WILDERNESS WHISPERS

C.K. Haworth

Wilderness Whispers by C. K. Haworth.

While based off some factual locations, and natural occurring landmarks, this novel is a work of fiction. All incidents, dialogue, characters and locations, are either products of the author's imagination and/or used in a fictitious manner. Any resemblance to real persons, living or deceased, is purely coincidental and unintentional. Although real locations and public factions are mentioned in this novel, the goings on, incidents and situations that occur within or around them, are fictitious and do not depict reality.

For

Bob. You were the good boy.

C.K. Haworth

"Dogs are better than human beings because

they know but do not tell."

-Emily Dickinson

C.K. Haworth

Chapter 1

The gravel crunched louder this time of year, the Alaskan temperatures not yet waving the white flag for spring. Chief of Police Frank Brown edged up the long driveway and watched Samantha Shaw exit the old brown bronco she never gave up on, throwing her hunting pack on the familiar deck of her cabin before greeting her favorite dog. She had many, but Roy, he was always number one since the day she'd rescued him.

Given the fact that he was waiting for her, Frank deducted she must have just returned from running a bounty. Roy went everywhere with her unless she was driving predators back into unpopulated forest; poor dog didn't have the legs for it and was a bit too plump for his breed.

The Chief threw the patrol truck in park and waited for the piss and vinegar he knew was rocketing through her veins to simmer out a bit. Based on the way her eyes searched the moose antlers above her door following the exhale that loosed from her back, it was a fair amount of piss. She knew it was him. Still, he stayed in the truck until her hand eased off the butt of the gun strapped to her thigh.

Frank was the only one brave enough to come up here unannounced, Sam knew it. Only one reason to come sniffing around after the Iditarod, something she also knew, and was already seething about.

"Chief." Her voice was cool, best anyone deserved for stopping her from the warm fire awaiting her frozen bones. And she was hungry as hell. Dangerous waters. She faced him tensely.

Jesus, she looked more like her mother every day.

"Hell of a way to greet your old man, kid."

He tipped his trooper hat towards her gun as he slammed the cab closed to keep the heat in, lowering himself to greet the giant, tail-wagging shadow approaching. Roy never let anyone near her, short of a select few; Frank was one of those few.

"Traitor." The brindle coated Saint Bernard mix merely blew his nose at his mom and positioned himself so the police chief could get a better scratch on his backside.

"I had nothing to do with that mess Frank, alright? I'm cold and I'm starving." And was clearly not in the mood for small talk, not that she ever was.

"You hungry was always thin ice." Frank rose and looped his hands in his belt.

He'd filled out around the middle as you'd expect a man to do pushing sixty years, but the signs of his glory days were not completely gone, and he'd take on a bear if he had to. He was a deep Native through and through, though not in blood, his family tracing back over a century on this island when a traveling fisherman found himself in love and sent for Frank's grandmother to join him from Washington. The town respected and loved him, and Shavila was all he knew.

"You haven't missed an Iditarod in four years Samantha. No one sees you and two top dogs go missing on the last leg. Given your reputation…" He grunted slightly and shifted his feet. "I have to do my job kid."

"Didn't stop Bradley Oliver from winning again, did it?" His name came out like a hiss. "Probably ran his remaining team into the ground, bastard." Frank raised a prompting brow. "You need to hear me say it old man?"

His eyes shifted guiltily.

"Ah, I see. You just came up here to appease the rich prick did ya?" Sam fisted her hands. "I didn't take those damn dogs, happy? Nice to know our history doesn't outweigh the golden boy, Frank."

"Your history with Brad raised the possibility is all."

"His treatment of his dogs raises more."

Frank grunted, knowing he would get nowhere trying to dodge the obvious, she was smart as whip, and just as painful when she proved it, even when she was little.

"Who's in the back Sam?"

"Just Snow White and the seven dwarves."

One might laugh, except she'd literally named her sled team after the seven dwarves, and her best breeder after the dame herself.

Her dark green eyes shifted in the direction on the large barn, where she kept her team and a slew of enclosures for fostering abandoned dogs, hidden far back behind her rural cabin.

"Why don't you look for yourself, because I'm done being interrogated." She began to kick the snow off her boots.

"Sam… honey." The pleading in his voice irritated her, before softening the glacial walls she kept around herself, in the way only a distant father figure could do. "Come on baby."

"Haven't been your baby since I was twelve Frank, so cut the crap."

He winced. She'd feel bad, if the wounds he'd left her weren't far more painful than her tongue lashing.

"And I was banned from competing ever again, remember?" She kept her back to him, hand on the knob like it was the only anchor to her spite she had left. "Apparently, Brad didn't like his nose broken last year, but his pain matched the splits in his dog's pads. Wish I did take those dogs."

Frank scowled at the incident he risked his job to make sure she didn't do time for, again.

"I sold Snow White's last litter in Anchorage this weekend, then I came home on the train. James has my times on the flight log, he took me, like always, stayed for the Fur Rondy. I just ran a bounty for Doc."

"James would lie for you in a heartbeat and would go down for you even faster. We both know that."

He would, but this time, he didn't have to.

"I have the receipts, the name of the mushers who bought them." She squeezed her eyes, knowing damn well he had every reason to question her, but she didn't have to like it, or let go of the hope her good intentions would someday mean more to him than that damn badge did.

Lord knows her mother didn't, nor did the badge Sam once wore herself.

"I didn't take that blue blooded asshole's dogs Frank, but I hope whoever did is treating them better than he does." She wanted to slam the door behind her, but she remained, hoping for something… anything. She had a hole in her heart labeled 'Daddy Issues' and it ached.

Frank leaned on the hood of his truck and folded his arms. "A new recruit is coming into the station kid."

Her belly clunked like a bucket reaching the bottom of a dry well. Frank was reaching retirement, the whole town knew it, but even though that badge should be hers, Frank couldn't- wouldn't, give it to her. She didn't want it anyway. That wasn't her legacy anymore. Still, a new deputy was bad news for her… hobby.

"From the lower 48. I'm just trying to save you the trouble by dealing with the questions myself, less he come up here out of boredom or running the outlander's backgrounds."

Outlanders where all who lived outside of Shavila; the small fishing town and seasonal tourist craze they called home. About a two-hour train ride from Anchorage -or a solid day's mush across the ice highway in winter- and a cool forty-five minutes from the base of Denali mountain, a popular climbing challenge many inland idiots attempted each year. One school, two grocers, lots of fishing boats, a few cheesy shops for the moose-lookers.

Given that she was the furthest from town by seven rugged miles, she was sure to be top on the list, and her record, or the rumored record rather, was sure to raise an eyebrow for a hot shot looking to make a name for themselves.

She whipped around to face him, her concern bringing height to her meager five-foot five frame.

"I'm getting old Sammy." He shrugged. "You knew it was coming."

She winced. Her tension with him never dampened the love for this step-in father figure she'd adored since using crayons, but he'd left her, and the scars made sure she never gave anyone a chance to do it again.

"We need a new chief kid, and we outta start training one to handle this island and all its quirky residents sooner than later, I chose sooner." He took his hat off and burned his eyes into hers. "That's why I came really. I know you didn't take those dogs. You're too smart to pull that shit again." Their matching gaze attested to them both knowing otherwise. "Just had to say I looked into it, give you a heads up."

"You hired from the Outside?" Her lip curled. "You're kidding right?"

Frank fitted his hat and rubbed his face, as he'd done many times when she would send her mother into a fit by getting dirty before they went into town.

"Unbiased, fresh faced. We need a sharp set of eyes Sam, not ones clouded by local favoritism or familiarity. We're small but get a lot of foot traffic during tourist season. Theft, vandalism, poaching, animals missing." She swallowed hard. "And they just voted to lift the booze ban in town."

That was definitely going to be an adjustment. It'd always been a dry town, on paper anyway.

"He's good, a solid performance record, ex-military, special ops. Damn good cop. Thirty-five, physically top of his squad. From Idaho. He can handle the snow." Sam scoffed at that. "He'll adjust. Arriving tonight. The first line of duty for a new trooper in a small town is-"

"I have no designs on getting to know anybody beyond those I already know." Sam bit. "So, tell him to stay off my property unless I break the law." Or get caught doing so.

The door on his patrol truck creaked loudly as it opened. "Take care of your mom Roy." The large dog barked happily at Sam's feet in response. "Give Kallik my best."

"Pa hates you, Frank."

"Yea well…" The truck rumbled to a start. "Happy birthday kid."

She turned to watch him back down the long driveway off her forested property, a small package where his front wheel had been. Ripping her beanie off and slamming it to the ground, her black curls flowed wildly around her jacketed elbows as she gathered the package and fondled it.

"Don't look at me like that Roy."

He picked up her beanie and promptly pawed the door, as if his fat feet had had enough. She gazed at the tree line and sighed heavily to the song of his pleading whine.

"Yea I know. He's alright, I'll get over it someday."

Stripping down to her leggings and flannel, she noted a smell foreign to the cabin unless she'd been the culprit. It drew her towards the kitchen; the gift abandoned by her boots. It wasn't a huge home, but it was perfect for her and Paw, although it'd once held so much more.

Slider from the kitchen made a huge deck accessible, one bedroom downstairs that housed Paw -as he couldn't manage the stairs any longer anyway- with enough room for his endless fly-tying hobby. One huge master upstairs, one she'd blessed with a huge sink in bathtub her grandfather still couldn't understand the need for. It'd once warmed her parents, but that had been only blips of time with gaps too large for any amount of love to fill in.

Paw was the only one who'd ever been consistent in the house he'd built, and now it seemed, so would she.

Her socked feet slid along the wood floor hallway following the lure of baked goods. She smiled a little.

She'd redone the entire house, repairs and all, in a fit of necessity, and pure need for painful distraction, a few years back when she'd returned to Shavila. Paw still hated how much the wood shined, but she was not about to skimp on the polish when she'd milled those boards herself. Every.single.one.

She paused by the opening that led to the living room.

An amber glow from the fire illuminated the logged walls of the largest room in the house. Antlers dancing shadows of arms reaching out for you across black and white photos of Paw fishing, or family doing something else very Alaskan cliché. One TV in the room that collected dust more than anything, and more books lining the wall than the town library held.

The long-legged man sat asleep on his recliner; one he'd protested when Sam had bought it but hadn't seemed to rest elsewhere since. Silver graced his hair, but even at 81 years old, he was a picture of pure blooded Native Alaskan beauty.

Her father Liam had received most of that beauty as well, at least what she'd seen in photos, and she remained grateful that she wasn't as pale as the Irish woman her father decided to breed with, less she burn the way her mother did. She got the jet-black hair and tone to her skin, but the wild curls and green eyes were all her mother. Arguably the only good thing she received from a woman who simply could not cope with Alaskan life without drugs, or blaming her for everything.

Sam rubbed her face, certainly smearing the eyeliner she obsessed over, and veered right to enter the kitchen. Maybe she could drown out the shit memories that made her so bitter with whatever sweet scent was beckoning.

"I'll be damned." She exhaled, staring at the very ugly cake sitting on the stove. "Guess the solar panels and 'useless oven' finally sucked the old dog in."

"Don't tell anyone." She all but jumped having not heard him rise. "The old fishing crew would never let me live it down."

Sam moved towards the frail elderly man she loved more than any living thing and embraced him, partially holding him up. "They'll have to wait till you join them in hell old man."

"Not today."

No. Not today. But every day she woke up wondering if it was the day.

She jerked her head towards the message on the cake, having no idea what it was written with. Not exactly a house you'd find icing in.

"Thirty huh? Told you I'm twenty-five. Dementia is getting you."

"In your dreams kid." He patted her shoulder, insulted she felt the need to help support him. "It's a big enough deal to warrant a cake." He lowered himself to the table they'd made together when he was still strong, and Sam noted the sorrow in his eyes.

Her father hadn't made it to thirty. Weak ice claimed him when she was a few weeks old, and she hadn't known her mother a sober day since then. Paw swears she had been when they married.

Bright eyed and college bound, Liam brought her mother here to Paw and G-maw when Elizabeth had found herself pregnant. The severity of her addiction made many question if Elizabeth had hidden it from Liam or if Paw just wished it to be known it was the despair of Liam's death that did it, out of pride. Pride ran thick in Alaska, rightfully so. Sam's own was foolish and sharp on the best of days.

Her grandmother had gone a year after her father, and Paw had reared Sam as best he could in between fielding her mother's outbursts, disappearances, and his own sorrow over their losses.

Sam drug her eyes over his sharp, tired features, cradling her head in her palm. She didn't know how he did it, with so much loss and sorrow, but he did it well. There was nothing Alaska, or life, could throw at Sam that she couldn't handle. Except maybe losing him or letting anyone else close to her heart.

She rose and grabbed some plates, turning at the huff Kallik made. "What?"

"I never said you should eat it."

"You stood long enough to make me a…cake, I think it is." He idly scratched his brow with his middle finger, sending her to a barking laugh. "I'm damn well going to eat it."

"Your funeral." The corner of his mouth curled. "I'll pass."

"Comforting Paw Paw. Real comforting." Roy shoved between her legs optimistically. "None for you fatty. Nice try though."

"After you bite into it you may find yourself sharing. We don't have any eggs, I made it work."

"I'll risk it." Sam sighed heavily as she sat down, sliding the second cup of coffee she'd brought over to him. "I'll hit town in the morning. I need to fill the gas cans anyway, last storm coming soon I bet. Not like I want to be anywhere near there with a target on my head right now."

Kallik took a shaky sip. "I hate to admit it, but he's a decent man Samantha. He must do his job."

"You heard that huh?"

He paused to encourage her to remove the scowl from her face, which she promptly did.

"You have a habit of... what do you call it?" She scowled again. "Ah yes... 'liberating animals from their questionable owners'. Given that tussle with Brad last year, it was the right place to start."

"Nobody ever seen me with an animal that wasn't mine. Hearsay." She grumbled into her mug, damn near spilling it when his palm hit the table.

"Because Frank made sure nobody ever did." He had her there.

Frank had also seen her load numerous dogs that had 'miraculously' shown up in her barn, into James's bush plane to rehome them safely. Roy was the only one she never could let go of.

"He let his love for you risk his job, and his reputation, and still you don't stop when he's begged you to. You owe him your freedom and lucky your arrogance only cost you your badge. Regardless of how much I'd like to knock his old block off for breaking your mother's heart, and yours; he showed up when it counted."

Sam stirred uncomfortably and forked the cake she had yet to brave biting into.

Not a single resident of Shavila hadn't heard about Frank peeling into Anchorage four years ago and saving her from doing time in exchange for her 'retirement' from the state troopers. She'd had a sharp eye on her after many folks known to harm dogs had somehow found said dogs missing, 'Lost Dog' reports rising ferociously when she'd begun her patrol. Never quit enough to peg her, until she busted a dog fighting ring and the owner found himself on a collared chain with a ball gag in his mouth surrounded by very angry bait dogs.

The photos were leaked to the news, pleasing Sam to no end, because she'd leaked them.

Frank's argument was based on lack of witnesses, evidence, and her stellar score card of shutting down drug houses and educating school children on her days off. Frank's fight damn near cost them both their badges, so she threw down hers to save his and came home. Just in time for Paw's health to begin its gradual decline.

That decline had since become an avalanche.

"I still maintain a disgruntled bookie did that to him and I needed to wait for backup." While taking the photos.

"Killing me little bear." He did not manage to hide his smirk. "Not one damn resident in Shavila didn't celebrate your grit, as we hold animals sacred even in use to feed and serve us." His voice was reminiscent of the spiritual lessons he taught her as they'd hunted, fished and trapped through her youth. "But even you cannot deny you abused the hell out of that badge on your chest and continue to push your luck."

"I regret nothing."

Kallik slid an arthritic hand to clasp her shaking one. "Neither do I, but maybe Frank does, and that's why he keeps looking the other way."

He took in the tell-tale signs of his little bear shutting down. Blocking out the anger, the pain, in the only way she knew how.

Kallik did have one regret, that she had never had someone who could teach her to cope with the vulnerability that comes with feeling, to learn that love was worth the pain, every damn time. He himself had to block out the pain of losing his son and wife to raise her, and it influenced her, clearly.

Plan B then.

"You gonna eat that or just make it uglier?"

Chapter 2

Landing in Anchorage had been shell shock enough. Alaska was a different kind of cold, but the train had been warm enough to make him think he could handle it, and this bitter bite was the onset of Spring. God help him. As Deputy Lucian Rose stood at the station waiting for one Police Chief Frank Brown to pick him up, he decided whatever tourist-priced clothing store Shavila had was going to get a good chunk of his money once he found it.

His ears were a throbbing drum making him question why he decided his obsession with Alaska had to be made a reality, with every beat they banged into his head. One man walked by in a light sweatshirt and lifted a small bundle of child into the air, both seemingly unphased by the cold that had him longing for a hot shower and a deep check into his sanity.

With no family to check his decision, he supposed it wouldn't be the last time he made a questionable choice.

"Trooper Rose?" Frank waved him to the patrol truck, rounding it to shake his hand once he met it. "Chief Frank Brown. Welcome to Alaska kid."

Lucian gave him a firm shake the military had deeply programmed into him, smiling tightly. "Luke. Nice to meet you Chief. Some Spring."

"I'll humor you by saying it's balmy for this time of year." Frank threw the truck in drive and peeled off like they weren't on numerous inches of snow. "But no Alaskan bothers talking about the weather son. It just is, and we just do."

Luke white knuckled the door slightly, but not hard enough to insult his masculinity, which he coveted.

"Noted." He ground out when Frank whipped into a turn. Even on the lightest snow days in Idaho, the most arrogant officer didn't drive so confidently. "I've got a room at the local lodge. Rest of my gear should be there already Sir."

Frank lazily held the wheel with one hand for most of the journey, sipping coffee at the light near the Welcome To Shavila sign they just passed. The only light Luke had noticed and didn't pick up any others. This town was smaller than he'd originally assumed.

Good. Small, stable, controlled. Exactly what he wanted.

"Nice enough place, but we've got you set up in the apartment above the station." Luke showed obvious signs of surprise, and slight annoyance. "Your stuff is already there. Tourist season is coming, and we need the rooms. You said you wanted this to be a permanent position did you not?"

"Indeed." Luke swallowed the chalk in his throat as he took in the lines of scattered square houses, and docks with fishing boats that turned into a general store, a little touristy museum and some other local joints on the main strip, including a sign that said, 'Big Johns Bar coming soon'.

The beauty of the wilderness had him gawking out the windows worse than he had on the train.

"I just never heard of an apartment above a station is all." Sort of.

He was actually hoping for room service and not having to wash his own sheets for a while. Not that he'd never roughed it, but this was a far cry from the desert tour.

"We're always on call trooper. A small, tight community. It would be good to have someone there again." Frank reached over and turned off the heat much to Luke's dismay. "I did some good time in that joint until Darleen married me up and moved me in with her sister in their family home. You'll meet D in a minute, though you may wish you never met Anita. They're both our dispatchers. Can't get away from either of them and I only married the one!"

Luke forced a smile at the older man's humor.

Even though he was close to his thirty sixth birthday, he could not imagine marrying, let alone one with her sister in tow like a shadow. He'd go insane. He moved all his adult life, joined the military to do just that, after raising himself in a flurry of an addict mother and wife beating, locked up father. Becoming a cop after the fact was just a natural choice after he'd had his fill of sightseeing and action, seemed the logical thing to do to make sure he didn't turn out like either of them.

Still, he wasn't surprised he'd chosen to take root in a small town after growing up in one. He liked order, consistency, a solid plan. Knowing his day before it was started, something a small town could offer that he'd been robbed of growing up. The lack of stability in his youth had him chasing roll call, chow time and orders in the Marines, and he'd learned as he aged that he wanted control, of everything. Not to wake up wondering if he'd have breakfast or have to call 911 because he found his mother on the carpet.

Here he could learn the locals, have a small bachelor pad, and not have to worry about some storm making a mess of his life. That storm died with his mother, with the end of his service in the Marines. Short of a rogue moose or vehicle collision, he imagined not much would stir his temper.

A temper that had been far too tempted dealing with the amount of scum that hurt women and slung drugs, both in the military and on the streets.

"No storms." Luke absently sighed out loud as they pulled into the station, a second patrol truck in front.

"Oh, it's coming." Frank hollered over the truck door slamming. "We always get one good slap in the face to remind us Alaska is boss before Spring hits, so I hope you know how to snow mobile son."

"Can lace my own boots and everything boss." Luke slung his coat on the hooks, the station's heat up far higher than Frank kept the truck.

"Like Satan's sauna in here Darleen!" Frank bellowed as he disappeared on the other side of the cold room door.

"Stuff it Frank! You keep the house cold enough! I will not work in a parka!"

Luke scanned the small station.

The main room had four desks butted up to one another through a large doorway to the right, paperwork scattered and a table boasting a coffee pot, and arguably an entire elementary school's bake sale.

He tugged his belt on his taught abs and remined himself he didn't keep this fit by touching anything on that table, ever.

A hallway off that, clearly holding cells given the lack of anything to grab onto or fuss with on the drunken walk down. A seating area to the left for any inquiring locals, and a private office next to it currently holding Frank and too other officers he could only see the backs of, discussing something lazily.

His eyes landed on the middle, a large U-shaped desk with too seats and monitors, a smiling face waving off the need to call the station over a bear in the trash.

"Cheechako." The dispatcher huffed as she slammed the phone down. "Damn Air B and B business bringing idiots to the bush that belong in a hotel."

Darleen was short and warm the way you hoped your great aunt would be and could have passed for Reba McEntire if she dressed for it. Her eyes met Luke's boots and traveled up, way up, very slowly as if a grizzly stood before her.

"Well, I'll be." She tugged her shirt as if the heat suddenly was too much. "Anita! Come look at the trooper Frank just drug in! He's about the tallest tree on the island."

19

Anita came out of the bathroom near the officer's desks, looking similar to her sister, but with a few years on her and black hair, letting out a low whistle.

"Well, your name and record certainly gave no warning to your stature young man." She shot her eyes to Darleen. "I call dibs."

"The hell you do!" Darleen cackled.

"Ladies, Jesus Christ we're on the clock." Frank rubbed his tired face as Luke gagged down the flush rising to his cheeks. "Will you please make some fresh coffee for the man you just embarrassed while I get him his bearings?"

"You're no fun Frank." Anita grumbled. "Angry old piss-ass."

Luke slid as quickly as he could -without looking like he was running- into the office, Frank mercifully closing the door behind them. Luke went to introduce himself then paused, blinking.

"Twins. You'll get used to it." Frank mumbled.

They both held out their hands at the same time, and Luke shook them.

"Willow and Forest Jenkins." The slightly taller one said. "Welcome to Shavila, Outside. Staying long?" They asked the last question together, their voices harmonizing.

Outside. A term he knew would be coming for him, being from the lower 48. He'd pick his battles later; he wasn't chief *yet*.

Both deputies were no more than twenty-five, twenty-six at best, had long, straight black hair to their ears, sharp features and a lean build, coming up to Luke's shoulders, putting them at about 5'10", give or take. Neither looked too pleased to see him, one or both possibly wanting the position he'd been brought in to take, Luke assumed. They were too young to have it, but that didn't seem to lessen the wary vibe he picked up.

Lucian Rose straightened as if his height might take the edge off their expression. It didn't. So, he tried verbal combat.

"You two always speak in unison?"

"No." So far, that was proving to be a lie.

Luke cleared his throat, determined to start off on the right foot, by keeping one out of their asses and hopefully in good graces, as he wasn't going anywhere.

"Nice to meet you both. Hopefully I can count on you to show me how things are done around here, so I do it right."

The humility seemed to soften them a bit, as if they were expecting him to throw his weight around right away. He saw no need to, at least not out the gate, though he had no problem doing so and had many times. His jaw ticked.

Stability, consistency. No storms.

Willow clapped Luke on the shoulder, startling him slightly. "Awe just jiving you Outside!"

Forest chuckled and plopped into a chair while Frank eased behind the large desk. "We have too much fun left to take old man Frank's job. You're doing us a favor!"

"Seriously bro." Willow belched and chowed down on one of the many sticky things by the coffee machine in the office.

So many sweets. Luke swallowed the desire to eat one. He was strict with his regimen and wouldn't be caught dead sporting the gut those pastries had earned Frank over the years. Maybe just one a day. No.

Luke took the coffee Darleen poked in and grinned awkwardly at the wink she shot him before leaving.

"Their big brother Tig owns the general store with his wife Charlotte. You'll meet them soon enough." Frank grunted to a seat. "Not much on the books today boys. Storm about to hit in a few days, so I want you both to remind the most arrogant of our residents to prepare, and make sure nobody gets into too much trouble beforehand. We won't be getting to Anchorage for a few days, and we don't need any serious injuries Doc can't handle here."

The twins nodded and rose.

"I'm going to show Trooper Rose to his apartment, and around town where he can get provisions, meet the fire marshal, give him the storm protocol, yada yada, before I head home."

"Big John is doing a local's-only soft opening in few nights Lucian." Forest chattered. "You outta come by and meet some folks." He waved a hand towards the main strip. "The bar?"

"I saw." Luke nodded. "Made short work of getting that place loaded after they lifted the dry-law huh?"

Willow laughed and shook his head as he followed his brother out. "He's been the biggest advocate and has waited a long time for it." He gave Luke a wry grin as he closed the door. "Can't wait for you to meet Big John."

Luke turned to Frank. "Big John someone I should be concerned about?"

"Not unless a sharp tongue and bitter taste concerns you." Frank walked them to a door behind the deputy desks and up and flight of tight steps. "He's a damn good mechanic and has lived here all his life. He just doesn't think anyone outta mind anyone's business except their own, so he can be a bit touchy with the law. Likes his privacy. His honest and fair, just an asshole. He's the closest Outlander, but mainly so he can earn by doing auto work. Dry town or not, he's spent a night or two sobering up in the cell, much to his dismay."

"No charges?"

"Waste of time." Frank gave him a serious look. "If it ain't a big problem, we don't make it one, Lucian."

Interesting. "Luke, if you please." He dropped his bag next to the few boxes he'd had shipped to the hotel that had clearly been brought over for him, roughly. "How many people live outside of town?"

"About twenty or so, scattered cabins. They all know what they're doing and do just fine, but there is a file in the office. We like to give them a heads up if any real nasty weather is coming through. Many have radio but not much else. Sometimes we drop a house call to the truly off grid folks."

Frank watched Luke eyeball the small galley kitchen that opened to the living room they walked into, and the door that lead to the furnished bedroom. "You could start getting to know the locals by hitting that file after I give you a lay of the town, make some house calls. They'd like to know the new badge they'll be seeing on their rare trips in, just mind lose dogs." The Chief cleared his throat. "You can skip the Shaw's. They know weather better than the weather itself, and you'd no doubt get lost trying to find it."

Luke turned with inquisitive eyes. "Samantha Shaw does live here?"

The Chief's eyes darkened in a manner that told Luke he should tread very lightly, and that everything he'd read as speculative, was possibly true.

Frank was irritated. Hoping he could deter the newbie, finding himself blindsided that Deputy Lucian Rose was as good a cop as they said he was, and had learned his team.

"Tell me son, how's a kid from Idaho know about a random trooper from Alaska?" Frank took his cowboy hat off to allude comfort that was, in reality, interrogative. "Did your homework did ya?"

"Innocently, sir. I assure you." Luke unbuttoned the top of his uniform and leaned on the counter, matching his play.

He would do his job regardless of Frank's obvious connection with Samantha Shaw.

"I looked into my new team, as any smart cop would do coming into a small joint like this. Your name was connected to her in an interesting incident on record. She has many notes on that record, and an oddly early retirement from the force that followed."

"Speculative and closed."

"Regardless Chief, I found it interesting and only discovered her name when looking into my new boss. She keeps her nose clean; it'll be no skin off my back who she was or what she may or may not have done."

"You don't mind that girl." His tone was riddled in warning. "She lives well and doesn't need that bullshit brought up. Especially with her grandfather on his last leg. You just leave her be. She's a good kid."

Luke decided to take the dare, the look on Frank's face making it almost impossible not to pry. "Yours?"

"Might as well be." Frank grunted, before sighing in defeat and tossing his hat on the counter. "Small town word gets out eventually, so I'll give you the general facts before the sewing circle gets your ear, clucking embellishments that'll have you questioning my title, which I won't have." His eyes narrowed. "On the grounds you leave my baby alone."

Luke squared himself up and crossed his arms. "I have no designs on some woman who stays out of the dispatch line. I do my job. I fell upon the information." He took the edge off his tone. "I meant no offense."

"You'll find it easy to offend around here deputy. We're a small community, we matter to each other. Even if we don't like the other, we take care of our own." Luke opened his mouth and snapped it shut as Frank continued. "She never had a Daddy, you understand? I dated her mom for quite a few years when she was still a snot nose. Damn that woman."

Frank yanked his belt up and crossed his arms. "She liked the pipe you feel me? I tried to get her clean, helped here through detox so it wouldn't be on hospital record, less they rip Samantha outta her home. Destroying her stash, only to have her slip out and get more when I was on duty. She never gave two squirts of piss about that girl after Liam, Sam's father, died, but she gave a whole lot about the pipe. I still fell for her. She was wild and impulsive with a seductive spirit that any man would... She was my drug... and she was good at hiding hers."

Luke locked his aching knees. So was his mother, for a while.

"Chief I didn't mean to-"

"I booked her myself."

Luke stiffened. "Excuse me?"

"Elizabeth, Sam's mother. I couldn't help her, and Kallik refused to admit his daughter in law was beyond help, more because she was a part of the son he'd lost, so I did the best thing I could to keep her bullshit from screwing up Sam's life, and mine. I cuffed the woman I loved and booked her myself, as she screamed at me, as Sam cried, covered in the bag of poison she'd found in her mother's purse. Sam had tried to flush it, and her mother smacked her around, ripped it out of her hand, dusted her own kid with that filth." He rubbed his neck. "Jesus she was... eleven? Twelve maybe? I thought she'd get clean and come out after doing her years. She overdosed in the pin; the same day Samantha was sworn in as an Alaska State Trooper in Anchorage."

Holy hell. Luke stood silently and schooled his face neutral.

This was certainly not in the reports he'd read, and no amount of writing could put into words the pain on that man's face. This was more complicated than he'd been originally told.

"Finally found Elizabeth's supplier and shut it down." He cleared his throat. "So, there you have it." Frank grabbed his hat and headed to the door, pausing. "Sam was a good cop. She just had some dark moments. So, leave that girl alone, that's on the record and off deputy, you get me?"

"As long as she walks a straight line, I have no need to think twice about her Chief."

"Nobody walks a straight line out here kid."

Luke ran his hands through his dark brown hair and lowered matching eyes to his boss. "I understand family, but I will always do my job, period. You clearly believe that also, or you wouldn't have brought Elizabeth Shaw in."

Frank put his hat on, grunting an agreeable noise. "Suppose that's why we hired you Trooper Rose, because to be honest, sometimes I wonder if I did the right thing, and so does Sam." His boss shut the door and left the deputy rattled.

Luke dug through his bag and slapped the file on Samantha Shaw onto the counter. It'd been quite the talk during his layover at the Anchorage station, in between getting jabbed for his improper gear by every trooper in the place. Given the recent stint at the Iditarod, he couldn't help but agree, to look in to her further, when prompted by the Investigator that had come in from Fairbanks.

Luke adjusted his pants. That had been an interesting evening.

Detective Harley Scott had caught his attention when she'd slid that tall pant suit out of the office in Anchorage. Fair to say she had set her hook in Luke before he'd blinked, having no plans to throw him back until she'd drained him. She had chestnut hair pulled into a tight military bun, striking blue eyes and after casually avoiding the new deputy from Idaho, the bags at his feet, for over an hour of calls and files, had made her way over to where he waited in the station.

After the expected recognition that they were both ex-military, a normal exchange practiced because military could usually sense the other, it'd come out that his train wasn't due to take him to Shavila until the morning. She'd managed to convince him a drink was a good idea; she'd like to brief him on the Iditarod dog case and see if he could keep an eye on the locals for lip slips.

Detective Scott had all but jumped him in the parking lot and rode him home like a bat out of hell in the back seat of her car, before barley slowing to a roll to let him out at the station, not failing to remind him that Samantha Shaw was a suspect, in her eyes at least, and to keep an eye on her.

The rest of the station had mumbled quite carefully behind the Chief's back, that 'Sammy' was missed, and had been a ruthless cop. One they needed more of. 'Above the law' was said more than once, and fondly. It had turned his stomach sour.

Luke was a stickler for the law. Upheld it tightly, if only to compensate for the frayed ends he saw in himself, and the corruption of many badges he'd worked with. Strength. Stability. No storms.

He grunted down his attentive male appendage. He was a man after all. It had been a long time since he'd taken the edge off, and he didn't mind Harley Scott using him quickly and tossing him out. He preferred the safe pattern of the one-and-dones anyway. She was easy on the eyes and tall enough to rack him, but it had been empty, as always. A basic load and fire he'd practiced all his life, having little time, or desire, for much else.

Alaska was a big place, and he was fairly resigned on not having to see Detective Scott again. The way it worked best for him, with all women. If Samantha Shaw was involved, and Scott came to bring her in, well he had a year out before he assumed the role of Chief, so Frank would handle it. Luke would only have to bite his laugh back at the sounds Detective Scott made as she'd worked him, for a short time till they left the island.

It had almost made him go soft. That woman sounded like a damn rabbit in a bear trap.

The raise he was offered if he got enough to put Sam in, was nothing to shake a stick at, and he could afford to get his motorcycle shipped out, buy a cabin. He upheld the law regardless, and no law stopped him from digging deeper into the locals, especially one that had a hushed reputation of stealing animals and bloodying the ones she took them from.

Two top dogs go missing from the first Iditarod she'd missed after she'd run every year since turning in her badge, highly suspect. To add to it, Samantha Shaw had busted the running champ's, Bradley Oliver, nose, on the last leg only a year prior, the same man whose dogs were in question... That's no coincidence.

Luke strapped on his gun and took one last look at the file. After this little tour and God, a hot shower and night's sleep, he'd have to pay Miss Shaw a visit, for the sake of storm safety, of course.

Chapter 3

Sam regretted not removing her coat when she'd come in the station the next morning, wanting it clear this was a quick stop. She didn't want to be in town any longer than she had to, not right now.

"The knife was beautiful Frank, thanks. Really."

"Never mind it. You always lose them."

"I still have the one you gave me when I was sworn in."

Frank leaned back in his chair and managed to hold the water threatening to show in his eyes. "How's Kallik?"

Sam blew out a breath. "Stubborn. Slow going Frank. He's got a few weeks maybe. I still can't figure out how he managed to be on his feet long enough to make that cake." She rubbed her stomach. "Or what was in it. I haven't had an appetite since yesterday."

The pause was long, no doubt brought on by the sound of Darleen's voice approaching.

"Well, I have a few things to grab, and I better get back to him. I want to check on him before I run a bear from the campgrounds."

"Storm is coming is less than 48 hours Sam. Don't run him too far."

"Roger that Chief." She gave an exaggerated salute, failing to hide her deep aching.

"Sammy…" She swallowed lead and hurried to the door. "I'll be here for ya honey, when his time comes, don't go it alone." She wouldn't reach out, but he needed her to know.

"I know Frank." She whispered, quickly leaving the station, not bothering to acknowledge Darleen as she passed her.

"Still no manners on that one." Darleen snipped as she plunked a file on Frank's desk.

"Her grandfather is dying Darleen, and she got nobody." His wife rolled her eyes. "And thanks to you she hardly has me. So, if you can pull the stick out of your ass for just a short time for the girl, it'd look good on you. Kinda like that black nighty."

"If you want dinner tonight, you'll watch how you speak to me." She shoved the file, before the expression on Frank's face sent her back a nervous step. "I'll do my best, for you." Darleen kissed his forehead and ran to get the phone.

Anita was off today, and the coming storm kept Darleen busy on dispatch. She watched Samantha jump into her Bronco and head towards the general store as she lazily listened to someone squawk about some local kids throwing snowballs at cars.

Darleen didn't have anything truly personal against Sam, she just never got over how much Frank fussed about the child of a woman he'd loved so deeply before her, and probably would still be with, had he not hauled her druggy ass in. Darleen loved Frank long before he'd even noticed her, not that anyone could compete with the exotic beauty that red headed wild cat Elizabeth, had brought to this island. That same beauty mixed with Shaw blood had Samantha looking just as stunning, but deadlier, and the reminder just rubbed her the wrong way.

Darleen knew it was her problem, and beyond time she got over it. Perhaps if she'd been able to give kids to Frank, she'd have been better about it. It infuriated her that a doting mother couldn't bear children, yet a neglectful addict had been blessed with such a strong and stunning one.

"I'll send Forest over to nab the kids by the ear ma'am. Some proper flashy lights and all. Alright." Darleen hung up the phone and loosed a long breath.

She really did need to get over it. At fifty-nine years old, she felt high school level petty at current, and Sam didn't deserve it, but the fact that Sam had almost made Frank lose his job, Frank's choice to get involved or not, well she could hold onto that spite a little longer she supposed.

"Another pastry for the woes it is." Darleen rose to circle the counter towards the goodies, pausing when she saw Luke staring out the window at Sam's dimming taillights. "Close your mouth honey. Swing-it-Sam will knock her fist into it before you get a word out anyway."

Sam's eyes had met Luke's for a split second as she'd peeled out of the driveway with the determination of a wolverine.

Not today trooper, or any day after, you overgrown tree. Damn she hated coming into town.

Luke snapped straight and headed to Frank's office, his insides stirring without permission. Her uniformed photo had done nothing for what the deputy had just seen get into that beat up Bronco. Those lengthy, wild curls, that seemed to defy gravity and frame her face perfectly, had spun an evil web of curiosity, tantalizing a man's thoughts with what could be under all that gear. Her hair had been pulled in a tight bun in every photo he'd seen, and now he wasn't even sure if he'd seen the same person.

27

But those eyes, there were no mistaking those eyes. Angry, hard, emeralds heated in warning. But wild, and untamed, and they had murdered him without hesitation when they'd met his.

He grunted down his foolish physical response to her and chalked it up to basic biology. Something an evening in an Anchorage bar with a willing, faceless bar-bunny, would fix easily for him. Soon, he nodded.

His sex drive had always been somewhat of an issue; his hand and he were good friends. Getting too close to women was not in his life-plan. He was better alone. Everyone was, they just didn't want to admit their fear of it.

Frank was grabbing his coat from his chair when Luke lumbered in. "Heading out Chief?"

"We're out of coffee and I'll be damned if I'm dealing with the pre-storm nuttery without it."

"I'll get it." Luke said almost too quickly, sending Frank to pause. He recovered painfully. "I met the schoolteachers and Mr. Buckowski when I set up my bank account, but I haven't met the owners of the general store yet. I need some provisions myself anyway. Especially if the townspeople get as jumpy as you say they do before a storm. Gotta stay fueled."

It'd been more than he'd said in one breath since he'd arrived, and with prepubescent spark. Frank picked up on it.

"Caught Sam did ya?"

Shit. Good cop. "Just the glare she gave me."

"She'll give you more than that if you corner her."

"Just need coffee." He said casually and slipped out the door.

"God help him." Frank shook his head and opened the file on Bradley Oliver's missing dogs.

They'd been found, slaughtered and hung from the trees of the Iditarod champ's home when he'd returned last night. The home was the largest on their coastline, arrogantly so, and it'd been one hell of a night locking that down before the sun came up, the days getting longer. He'd have to send it in to the big britches in Anchorage soon, but he didn't want to.

Frank knew Sam could never hurt dogs like that, but the Anchorage Chief wasn't so convinced, so much so, they'd hauled in a tight-assed detective, go the call this morning, and he was sure they had a certain chief in training sniffing her out. He didn't tell Sam, hoping she wouldn't notice the curious looks that may come her way once the rumor mill started.

Most of the town knew her better than that, he hoped. Frank rubbed his brow nervously.

It was going to be a long Spring.

Sam made her way to the general store and whistled for the young lad to load her up with dog food before heading into Charlotte and Tig's place for eggs and coffee. Maybe a few of Paw's favorite snacks. Anything to keep him happy.

Charlotte met her friend's eyes and waved Sam over to an unopened register to ring her up. A beautiful native woman with a chin tattoo that not only signified her wisdom and culture but made her outright sexier every time her lips moved. Sam often resented the bottle never landing on her when she'd spun it during their sleepovers in high school.

"Everything the old man used to come get himself." Charlotte mused as she scanned the ridiculous number of snacks. "How's he doing Sammy? We're all kinda... well on edge ya know?"

Sam took her beanie off and ruffled her curls, sending them swishing across the lower back of her jacket. "You're sweet Lotty, it's rough. He refuses a hospital. 'Born here gonna die here I built this house' blah blah." Charlotte giggled at Sam's perfect rendition of her grandfather's ruffled feathers. "It'll be soon." The pain returned to her face. "A few weeks maybe. He doesn't eat much and sleeps almost always. I'm so..."

Charlotte reached over the scanner and grabbed her shoulders. "Don't shut us out, ok? This town loves you, every icy, shitty edge of you."

"That's comforting."

"I mean it Sam. Nothing you do or have done is going to leave a Shaw alone on the mountain, you got that?"

"Gross stop." Sam squeezed her hand before dramatically swiping them off. "I need a break... release. I'm so anxious all the time. Maintaining his meds, making sure he will be ok when I work and all. I know it sounds selfish, I simply will be destroyed when his time comes, like my life will end with his... I can't even think about it..." She gagged back tears. "All the same, the bounties I'm running just aren't cutting it-" Sam palmed Charlotte's scheming face. "No, no. Not a chance in hell. The last time you tried to get me laid I had a 45-year-old ass clown from Yukon bringing me old fish as a mating call and trying to park his snowmobile in my yard. No."

Charlotte shrugged mildly offended. "Well since Tig doesn't like to share..."

"Don't tease."

"You can always lean on James. That was aways a good ride for you, ya?"

Sam laughed out loud. "Yea, damn good ride, but that had to stop, has been for over a year now. He wanted more than I could give. I don't want that with anyone, besides, he's really not right for me, not like that. Nobody is."

Sam bit back the ache saying that out loud gave her. James was never going to be it, but it was a jagged pill to swallow that nobody ever would be.

"Anyway, I like being alone. James wants a helpless housewife and is insufferably arrogant. The friendship is enough to manage."

"So? You already made all that clear; James knows it. Just get laid for god's sake! You are under so much pressure, and from what you've told me, he's got a huge-"

"LOTTY!" Sam threw her head back as she covered Charlotte's mouth, laughing wildly.

Luke almost dropped his armload. Christ that short little thing was even more stunning when she laughed. Given the daggers she'd slung at him earlier, he wasn't even sure she could do that.

Suspect Luke. Break off buddy. Futile. Do not pass go, do not collect two hundred dollars.

He was so hooked on that warm look she gave the owner, who was clearly a longtime friend, and those dancing eyes, that he couldn't peel his own away from her, even as he tried to talk himself down.

He slammed right into Vanessa Eska, the darling elementary school teacher he'd met on his tour yesterday.

"Oh, Chief hi! Preparing for the storm?" Vanessa was Sam and Charlotte's age, an old school mate, and was every bit as warm and bubbly as you'd hope a young schoolteacher would be, packed into the tiniest frame you'd ever seen, and he'd just about knocked her to the ground with his broad, lumbering stature.

He needed to get his shit together or the entire town would peg him a baby-huey moron before he'd answered his first call. He flipped his operator face on and locked himself down.

"Not chief for at least another year Ms. Eska. I apologize. I was distracted." Bewitched really. No, jet lagged. Casing his surroundings. Not distracted.

"Oh no mind, I have littles running me down all day!" She shrugged warmly, her arms overflowing with dinner preparations and baby formula. "It is so crowded in here; some early tourists didn't account for the last storm we usually get. Let me see…" She scanned the lines, landing right where his eyes had been. "There! Follow me." She nudged. "Friend perks, and Charlotte owes me for bailing on babysitting last night. Tamar was furious and proposed in the living room!"

Tamar Richards was the high school teacher, a tall man Luke had met as well, who'd come all the way from south Africa to experience a climate he'd always dreamed about. Like so many others who visit Alaska, he fell in love, not only with the land, but with the tiny schoolteacher leading Luke straight towards blistering green eyes that were already planning his funeral.

Shit. He'd wanted his approach to be a bit more official than an armful of coffee and more protein bars than any man should eat, regardless of his muscle mass. Given the way Samantha Shaw's face fell when she noticed them approaching, he was in for a very cold greeting.

"Congratulations on the engagement honey." Sam smiled at Vanessa, ignoring the uniformed ox behind her. "Soon the be Mrs. Richards."

"Thank you. Wasn't as romantic as it should have been but…"

"I know I know I'm sorry!" Charlotte flapped her hands. "You see this place? It's been like this for two days! I don't mind the money, but somebody outta tell these moose-lookers to wait until May!"

Sam tucked her wallet in her back pocket and grabbed her bags.

"You meet the new, well, soon to be chief yet, Sam?"

God dammit Vanessa. You polite, sweet, pain in the ass Vanessa. Sam would kick her if she wasn't one of the only real friends she had.

She forced herself to look over Vanessa's shoulder and realized she had to look up much, much higher. Holy hell he had to be at least six-five or more, rare around here. His eyes were shadowed by his trooper hat, but those lips curled in a half smile that seemed genuine and curious all wrapped in one delicious corner.

Not today, Satan.

"Well, I have now." Sam shrugged boredly, snapping her eyes to Charlotte. "Bet you can't wait to tell Tig bigfoot *does* exist. He's going to never let you live it down."

"Samantha!" Vanessa stifled a laugh in the sweetest way she could muster.

Sam marched out the doors and struck up a conversation with Tig as he finished helping the store hand load the last of the dog food bags into her truck.

Luke blinked blankly. "Well, that was the most unique greeting I've had so far. Big john didn't even insult me yet." He dumped his ridiculous hoard onto the belt as Vanessa paid for her goods.

"Oh, wait… he will." Charlotte chuckled. "And don't mind her, she's a local, with the personality of a glacier."

Vanessa clicked her tongue. "Char… come on."

"Oh, I love that jagged ice block." She smiled at Luke. "Just trying to warn the man early. Save ya some trouble. She's just wary of newcomers. She'll come around when she realizes you ain't going anywhere." Maybe.

Luke made an agreeable sound. "Suppose we'll see how I fair this storm."

Sam waved Tig off. "I got it Tig. On my way after I check on Paw. I'll make sure that bear doesn't come back to the campground for a while."

31

"$300 says you will. Fire marshal has your Benjamin's Hun. Maybe kill it this time Gunner?" Tig ruffled Roy's fur in her passenger seat.

Tig Jenkins had called Sam 'Gunner' since he took her and Charlotte shooting when they graduated high school. She was a crack shot, but he'd had his eyes on Charlotte and was just biding his time until she turned eighteen, having ten years on her. He was a good man, humble and sweet, but it wasn't long until after that birthday that he was in Charlotte's living room promising her dad he wasn't a dirt bag.

Lucky for them all, he wasn't, or Shavila would have been short one Tig and old man Wilson would have been in the pen for murder. And that was if Big John didn't avenge his baby sister first, Tig's best friend or not. Tig owning the General store worked wonders on Charlotte's prospect for security though, and she had a ring on that finger before she was twenty. Big John got over it eventually.

"Not my style Tig, I'll run him back good. Tell that overgrown deputy in there he better get those idiot campers out of there and into the hotel before the storm hits. Frank is running the off-grid memos, and the twins are doing what dumb boys do on their day off."

"So, the Mercado twins?"

"Probably!" Sam laughed and drove off.

Big John sniffed and casually flipped Sam the bird as she drove by, which she enthusiastically returned with a mumbled holler Luke couldn't make out over her dog's vicious barking out the window.

Big John then nodded arrogantly at the deputy before sticking his head back in the engine of the car broken down by the bank across the street.

"What was that about?" Luke nodded towards the butt crack John was now proudly displaying as he tinkered.

Regardless of the grizzly bear sized man he was, Luke was sure even he could find pants that stayed up, and noted he never wanted to go head-to-head with him either, no matter how much he worked out or what military training he had. Big John, was quite literally, BIG.

"Chief Lucian Rose you are a tall fucker, aren't you?" Tig wiped his brow and shook Luke's gloved hand after he'd lofted his bags into the window of his assigned patrol truck.

"Luke, and not chief for a good year yet. They cross?"

Tig laughed and lit a cigarette. "I'd say so. Sam took a tree branch to the side of his head last year, sighting he was hitting deer intentionally and leaving them on the side of the road. We got a lot of families that struggle round here Deputy, so she don't take kindly to wasted meat. None of us do."

"So, she bashed his head in? Are you yanking my balls?"

"Nah, just rattled his grill a little." Tig waved his hand like the stern eyes on Luke's face were ridiculous. "She's a buck and some change soaking wet, Deputy. Strong as hell Sam is, I wouldn't want to fight her, but Big John can take a hit from a bear, let alone an angry Sammy. My boy wasn't doing it, she just has a hot head about animals and jumped the gun. He didn't press charges, just made her pay for the dental work, and it was water under the bridge."

"Apparently not."

Tig took a long drag and blew it out, eyeballing the tall newcomer with warning. "We handle a good deal on our own here. His car was bashed up like he'd been swatting game with it. Claimed it was stolen and returned, which we found out later it was. Some tourist's bratty teenagers. But that's a hard sell to a loaded pistol like Sam, my guy. She's got a temper on her period, worse when it comes to animals, and her buddy James claims he saw Big John doing it. He saw Bj's *car*... not him, but she'll take James's word over most. They're close."

"Close?"

"*Buddy* buddy." Tig wiggled his eyebrows.

"I see." Luke ignored the wasp that burst into action in his gut parading around as jealousy.

He had a job to do and not one design on the mysterious battle ax that just drove away. That woman was more than likely a vigilante criminal, being very well protected by those who knew her. His interest was purely job oriented, his distraction simply the adjustment period and need for a good lay.

"Either way champ, seems to me they both avoided trouble by shaking hands once Frank showed up and peeled Sam off him." He let out a low whistle. "Swing-it-Sam, she'll grab a tree if it ain't her fist first!" He chuckled like that was adorable, and not a woman who had a history of assault.

"Big John had a thing for Sam, being Charlotte's older brother, he suffered greatly on those sleepovers in school. So, I have no doubt his pride was more wounded than his jawline. Not the hit he wanted from her aye?" He slapped the deputy on the back, breaking Luke's stare down with Big John. "They rouse each other from time to time, but civil. Everybody went home happy, no paperwork. You could learn a thing or two from the locals pal."

"Indeed."

Big John gave a wide bearded grin as Luke drove by, tipping his hat in what Luke was sure was a come-and-get-it dare. He rustled into the bag and ripped a giant chunk off a protein bar as he eyed the sky.

Sam had a few hours to run that bear off before dark, which meant he had less to warn the campers and get back to the station to possibly sleep before the last day of storm prep tomorrow, which would be nuts given the number of tourists who'd jumped the gun on their Spring trips. Frank let him know about her bounty earlier that day, so Luke wouldn't

33

be alarmed if they crossed paths at the campground, as she'd be armed to the hilt.

Who runs off predators for a living? And in the dark possibly? A psycho. A certified… stunning psychopath. Red Flag deputy. He took another bite and caught Big John watching him out his rear view, the protein bar turning to chalk in his mouth.

He was going to have to tell Big John to postpone his soft opening tomorrow night until after the storm. A bunch of locals stumbling around drunk in a blizzard was too dangerous. Not the best way to start his new job.

"Ah hell."

~

"Speak of the devil" Sam smirked as she drove past James Porter's yellow bush plane, parked on the last shore landing, before the turn to her winding private road. If he wasn't already at the house, he would be shortly. He must have just gotten back from sleeping off the Iditarod hangover, one she was happy she missed, spending it repairing the damage Snow White had done to her pen while she was away.

Snow was cruel to her puppies after they reached a certain age, but the initial shock of them gone always spun her up. It was her last litter. One sought after by every musher statewide. Now she could retire, and Sam could sleep well knowing every single one of those puppies had gone to amazing dog lovers, modest families who needed them for transportation in the rugged bush, and not a single one to Bradley Oliver, no matter how the zeroes on those offered checks had tempted her.

It still blew her mind he was allowed to race after she'd blown the lid off his dogs bleeding feet, and the one dog he'd left to die when it couldn't run. Something that had clearly been ignored for the sake of his glory boy status until she'd begun to race. Or maybe she knew Sully was sick and was just angry because that dog had been her baby. Either way, the rich dog abuser could burn in hell.

She dumped the bags on the counter after reminding Roy to use his thumbs and close the door, which he certainly didn't do. Stripping her gear, she walked into the living room and paused, exhaling when she saw Paw's chest rise and fall under the blanket.

She always had a satellite phone on her, taught him how to use it, but she knew he wouldn't call, and would slip away to G-maw in peace, and in pride. She had to work, but Sam silently wished each day that she'd be here when his time came. Paw wouldn't want her to be, still, she hoped she was.

He grabbed her hand as she drug the blanket up further. "Creator forgot about me."

"I'm glad he did today Paw." Her words were strained. "And I'd appreciate it if he forgot about you until I got back." She kissed his forehead and placed a bag of pork rinds in his hands.

He lifted his head slightly, smiling as he rested back again. "If he doesn't, you have made sure I die a happy man."

She really wished he wouldn't talk like that, it killed her each time, but she knew he was tired.

"Bounty?"

Sam nodded. "Bear hassling the moose-lookers at the campground. Gotta run him out before some trigger-happy city boy hurts him cuz he was too stupid to lock his bacon up. Big storm coming tomorrow night, but I should be back before sunup." She patted his shoulder. "Pain?"

"Pain reminds me I'm alive."

"Paw..."

"I took the pills little bear, go run your brother back home."

"Yes sir. Little bites old man, no dying dumb."

"I know the rules. Mind yours."

"Gun on the hip, head on a swivel. I'm going to check on the dogs then head out." She placed the phone closer to him despite his grumbling. "Makes me feel better, even if you don't use it."

She jogged down the back steps, leaving Roy to watch Paw. Leggings and a flannel weren't enough for an extended jaunt, but a quick check of the dogs didn't need much, and the barn was warm.

Footprints too large to be her own confirmed her suspicions, and she had a snowball ready when she slid into the small door on the large barn slider.

"Whoa hey!" James laughed and rose from Snow White's kennel, an eruption of yips and howls from her team a soundtrack to him shaking the snow out of his collar. "Nice to see you too birthday girl."

"You missed it mountain man."

"Yea well." He pulled a brown bag out of his pocket. "Hopefully you'll forgive me, I had to sleep it off."

She grabbed the bag greedily. "Get laid?"

"Not yet." He winked.

"Knock it off." She blushed mildly.

James was just a friend, but in high school, they'd been knocking boots like it was their job. She was rebelling from growing up without her parents, but James had been falling in love. When she resigned and got back to the island, and a bad relationship had sent her reeling, James had been there.

She didn't have anyone, and they occasionally rolled around in the barn, out of pure biological necessity and familiarity, but she had to draw the line with him, repeated it too many times, and yanked the plug on the physical bouts over a year ago.

He was a good guy, and no lack of attraction. How could you not enjoy a broad built man with a clean-cut beard and the body of a rugby player? But it was no more than a distraction and primal need for her. She'd broken off whatever they'd had to go train to be a trooper after graduation, and no amount of his pleading stopped her. She was just gone one day.

When she came back, shivering from the wary avoidance the rumors had brought from the town, he'd been there. When her heart got broken by a pompous prick, James got her through it, even if his methods were backwards and not all that noble. Beggars can't be choosers.

He still had eyes for her but had accepted long ago she did not want what he did and was even married for a few years while she was on the beat. Sam was grateful their friendship endured the heartbreak that was his alone, and tried not to take it, or him, for granted.

"Ugh… you smooth Canadian bastard." She groaned eyeing the mountain of maple candy in the bag, her absolute favorite treat.

She popped one in her mouth and almost forgot about the dogs squealing as the flavor threatened to be better than the sex she'd gone too long without.

"Fed the dogs for ya too. Heard you had a bounty."

He sauntered over and looked down at her swallow the last of the melted maple slowly, her throat beckoning him. "Thought I'd help while I waited." His dark hair pieced across his forehead as his blue eyes danced over her.

"You really are trying to get me into bed aren't you J?" She might.

He was a sure bet for fast and hard and since she needed little else, she was tempted, but it felt selfish, and she didn't need his head getting a start on her again.

"How about a birthday smash Sammy?" His hand slid around her hip and threatened to cup her rear. "I bought you a little time, I work quick."

"Yea you do." She laughed and dodged his lips. "James, shit I got so much on my mind man, we've done really good for the last year." She nudged him back. "We don't need to mess it up."

"I know where we stand Samantha." He pulled the bag from her hand. "How long has it been for you?"

She scowled and it was answer enough for him, lifting her to wrap around him, which she didn't fight, stupidly. He walked her to the feed room of the barn, that conveniently had a couch she occasionally came to cry alone on so Paw wouldn't hear her. It'd also seen numerous sweaty nights with both of them last year.

He trailed his mouth down her neck and every yearning she'd been ignoring for months ignited like a fever pitch.

"Friends can help each other out can't they?" He set her on the couch and knelt between her legs, pulling her face up to his. "Don't I always help you out?"

"Mmm." She pondered dramatically. "You do. Just looking out for me huh? Noble of you."

He cupped her firmly over her leggings and the warmth made her suck the cold air violently through her teeth.

"Given what I've done for you, you know damn well noble is not a word for me." He pressed him thumb into her most sensitive craving and began to circle, holding her gaze to his. "But I know you Shaw, and you need this." His hands were strong, and he didn't waver from his mark.

"James, we shouldn't. Stop." She gasped through her words. "Don't ruin it. I have... I have to run a bounty I- oh god."

"You'll end up swinging on someone if you don't soon." He clasped his huge hand around her neck, tilting her gaze back. "You know me. Relax." He felt her rising. "Atta girl."

Her knees shook and she grabbed his arms. "We don't need this. It's not ri-" She moaned a quiet groan of release, the wet warmth seeping through her leggings to his hand as she writhed against it.

She was in worse shape than she'd thought.

He groaned satisfyingly. "There it is." He exhaled as she went limp, flopping back on the couch as he set to yanking his jacket off.

"You're an asshole J."

"One who is about to fuck the shit out of you."

Sam couldn't argue she was a flesh and blood woman who needed this, and he was a reliable source of it. They'd been here before, and even though she had nothing emotional to give, Sam surrendered to the simple physical need they both had and followed James hands to his pants. He was always fast and hard, greedy and taking, but it would quell the demon well enough she supposed.

Roy's vicious barking set the entire sled team off, and she jolted up, palming his groin to a still.

"Please tell me you want this before I glove it." He gripped the back of her head. "God your lips."

"No shhh!" Roy's barking grew more violent. "That's an alarm J. Someone is here who shouldn't be." She tugged her flannel over her leggings, covering her readied state and bolted through the barn.

James ripped his coat on and raced after her, zipping his jeans, pissed as a wet cat.

Her mukluks skidded around the side of the house in time to see Roy descend the stairs in a low stalk. Her eyes finding his target as James spun the corner behind her.

Luke put his hands up and backed towards the patrol truck. "Easy pal. Friend."

"What the hell are you doing here!?" Sam saw a blur and barked Roy's name, following with an order in a native tongue Luke would probably be unable to look up later.

One hundred pounds of fury slid to a stop and immediately bolted to her side. Taking to lapping James's hand instead.

Luke tried to ignore how tousled the two looked, following her flushed cheeks down the frame of her body. He'd yet to see it out of snow gear, and seeing her now, in black leggings and a thin flannel, suddenly made his other brain a far bigger problem than her eyes and wild curls had already done.

She was a tank of muscle, with a softness only a feminine energy could balance. Those hips. Her flannel did not hide much, but he was a leg man, and had a thing for a simple handful. She wasn't a traditional beauty, in society's terms, but Jesus she was… something. Exotic. Odd. No woman had ever flustered his militant regimen so much, and she was too short. Then again, women were usually the flustered ones around him.

A tether snapped inside him watching those pupils burn and widen in disdain. A lifeline that had kept him walking his carefully plotted straight lines, popped and flailed like the sea ripping a ship from its mainstay. She was pulsing a force field of fuck-off energy and it set every determined cell in his body into conquering overdrive.

He would have to figure out the new sensation of this heated shot of heroin, another time.

"Hey asshole." She snapped her fingers to wake him up. "Care to explain why you're on my property sasquatch!?"

"I, uh." Luke grunted and dropped his hands, clicked his Marine face in gear so quickly it had Sam take note.

She had a hard-ass on her hands. Good thing she wrote the book.

"You named the dog Roy? Really?"

"Wrong answer, uniform."

Damn she was rough. He'd never had any woman speak to him like that. His physical reaction was questionable, to say the least. He was clearly more fatigued than he thought.

"I have to clear out the campers before the storm. Figured I'd lend a flashlight if your bounty ran late."

James snorted.

"City boy thinks I need a damn escort? You every run a bounty before, *deputy*?" The way she dug into the last word pinched his ego a bit. "Sun don't all the way this time of year, genius."

"Way to make an entrance slick." James laughed and headed to the door, Roy trotting his happy fat ass right behind him. "I'm gonna go check on Paw, no doubt the dogs woke him up. James Porter boss." He tipped his head. "A pleasure. You owe me a lay."

"J, stuff your hole!" She was quickly reminded why he needed to stay out of her pants, and mildly forgave the deputy for the needed interruption. Mildly.

James looked the brick-walled deputy up and down. "I'm sure I'll be seeing you again."

Luke did not appreciate the threat in his voice but kept his focus on the brewing hailstorm to his right. Storm. She was a pulsing storm of unimaginable chaos, destruction and unforeseen depth in those angry eyes, and he'd driven right into the nexus.

No storms. Control. Stability.

He rested his hand on the butt of his gun and lifted his chin, locking himself down. "Deputy Lucian Rose. Luke preferably. I-"

"I don't give two squats of piss, Outside. Why are you on my driveway and talk fast. I have somewhere I need to be."

Luke let a deep breath leave him before he continued. Meeting her fire would have them both combusting, and it's not what he wanted, not vertically anyway.

Focus Deputy, and get to Anchorage and get laid, sooner than later. Day off in a week.

He watched her wave her hand like he was slow and locked his face stone cold. Who the hell was this woman, besides a raging b-

She marched up to him and penetrated his space. "Let me help you then. Ex deputy Samantha Shaw, but I bet you already knew that. I didn't touch pretty boy Brad's dogs, but I'd like to know who did. I have run over fifty bounties in the last four years and I don't need you or any other uniformed man with a hero complex to babysit me."

He swallowed as the scent of her maple breath blurred his vision.

"Side note, nobody lives out here to be bothered unannounced, and it could cost you your life ya know? Everyone is packin' round here. Some locals don't have the kind of control over their dogs that I do, but they all have dogs, deputy. Big ones." She caught herself, he'd knocked her off her axis and she was compensating. She turned to walk away and snapped back. "You got huge nuts you know that? Where do you get off!?"

"Inside a woman if I can help it but..." He shrugged and eyed his palm humorously.

He'd thrown her again. She'd always had her fire fought with fire, and he was throwing daisies on her flames. The side of her mouth betrayed her, and she finally slipped a small chuckle.

"Son of a bitch." She threw her hands in her hair laughing.

Luke about died.

He might have pissed his pants, had he not stared down the enemy in combat. Man she was... he didn't know what she was, but she was mucking up his form. And he did not like his feathers ruffled, ever. He had to be in control, at all times. No exceptions.

He put out his hand and tilted his head. "Can we start over Miss Shaw?" She hesitated, finally grabbing his hand and shaking it. "I stopped to meet the Fire Marshal on my up. Tiny station. Guess I'll have to look into that, we need more resources. I have never seen such a small station." He was babbling, an unfortunate side effect she'd caused twice now. "Anyway, he heard I was coming up here, gave me this."

Luke held out the three, one-hundred dollar bills she was being paid to run the bear back.

She snatched it up and stuffed it in her sports bra, glaring at his dumb, useless, sexy smile.

Now she noticed. The dark brown eyes that matched his hair, that stupid dimple that showed up when he smirked. The body he spent way too much time on about to come right out of that uniform. That sharp jaw he kept taught with hard focus and determination. Ex-military. You can smell em. Show off, get a uniform that fits, you ape.

Alright deputy. Not bad. Not a chance in hell, but not bad on the eyes. The eyes were all he was going to get. The last thing she needed was a law pusher sniffing around her... comings and goings, as it were. No, Sam settled, that would not be good. She needed to drive this problem right back where he came from, and fast.

"I'm sorry I came up suddenly." Luke pulled his shirt tight. "Not my intention to interrupt anything Ma'am."

"You didn't." Her response was far too fast to be casual. "He helps me with my dogs sometimes. Friend from high school."

The flush in her cheeks and the tone he caught from her 'friend' earlier begged to differ. Luke put a pin in that to use later.

"Not like it's any of your business, Cop."

Jesus. Getting close to the suspect was going to be harder than he thought. Redirect marine.

"I heard of bounty hunters, never known one. What do you do with the kill?"

Sam curled back. "I do not kill them. Many do, but they're just chasing water, food, and don't deserve to die because they find it."

So she did love animals with a vengeance, the glow in her eyes a testament. Luke pinned that as well.

"I use my top two dogs, drive them back into the bush if they are too close to civilization. Saves them, helps the townspeople feel safer." She stepped back suddenly, realizing she was still looking up at him, uncomfortably close. "It pays decent, keeps me free from the 9-5. Too much structure freaks me out. I ride my own wave."

There it is. What he needed to steer clear of this deadly siren messing with his code of conduct. He knew he'd find it. That little nudge he needed to remind him he was pursuing a case, and to keep his damn head on target.

He ignored the part of him that was disappointed and clung to his final decision like a lifeline. If he could knock that chip off her shoulder, maybe he could find out what she does when everyone is sleeping, and what that hard structure is hiding. Her attitude, not her body, Luke...

"Care to show me how it's done? I'm heading that way anyway. First official assignment."

She laughed in a way that was certainly meant to be insulting. "You want to run a bounty, Outside?"

She whistled in a high pitch one might have missed and two large, white huskies -that should have been labeled timber wolves- came barreling around the side of the house to run circles around them.

"Saddle up city boy. Tonight, your first assignment in Shavila, might be your last." She gave him a threatening grin. "If we're lucky."

Chapter 4

If they ever threw someone in a volcano, he imagined the animosity blistering through him was a very real simulation of what it'd feel like. His mind was a battlefield. What the hell were they thinking bringing in a newb to become Chief? It had seemed like no big deal at first, necessary, but the deputy was already proving to be a bit too nosey. The only good use for non-locals was their money and watching them leave at the end of the season.

The cops here new to leave well enough alone when it mattered, and this new tight ass didn't seem like one who would, given that he was already trying to get to know everyone around here like making friends is what he's paid for. Despicable how trusting everyone was being. Grayson Hunt handed the tommy-tall-pants Sam's money like he was one to be trusted already. And nobody chooses to just park their ass in Shavila having never been here, especially a lower 48 douchebag. That should have been a red flag. What's his angle? He'll be sorry if he doesn't watch his step. Scratching his beard, he took a swig of his flask and swerved into his driveway.

They should've handed the job to Sam. He shook his head. Yea they had their history there, but he'd rather live under her, than some flatlander who had his tongue on the law's balls. He slammed his truck door and kicked the snow before taking another swig, letting the burn fuel his plans for the evening. He'd seen that look in the upstart's eyes… he gets too close to Sam, he'll blow the lid off something that doesn't need to be blown off, even if he didn't always agree with her tactics, they were noble in intention.

Stupid girl. Snot nosed deputy wants to postpone the bar opening too, according to word around town. Fucking pussy. He lifted his head to view the northern lights and grunted decisively. After loading the cages into his truck, he drained his flask. It may prove to be the distraction he needed to pull of his plans… but Lucian Rose doesn't belong in Alaska, or anywhere near *her*.

~

Luke was going to die. As soon as he hit the bed, every muscle in his body was going to liquify and they'd simply find a puddle of skin and decaying organs in the morning. The beaten deputy fumbled his gun on the counter, too tired to unload it, something he could never admit before and had never done. If someone found it and shot him before he could get to it, good. It'd end his suffering.

He tripped out of his boots while simultaneously tearing off his uniform and stumbling to the shower. It was the size of an airplane shitter, but so long as it had hot water, he didn't give a damn. Knees shaking, he pulled his head under the water and groaned deeply through the rushing expansion of his tense muscles. God they were screaming.

In the military, he'd gone days without removing his boots, weeks hiking the toughest terrain with a load on his back. He'd waded through swamps and run miles through the dessert. Had bodies blown up beside him and carried many a two-hundred-pound man on his shoulders. He could even attest to being lost in the snows of Idaho overnight as a teenager.

Still, nothing had ever tested his fitness level or hung him out to dry like running a bear back into the Alaskan bush with a simmering tsunami of a woman had. Everything hurt.

Samantha Shaw as insane. Utterly off her rocker. Epitome of psych-ward material, not that he thought a straitjacket could hold her. First, she did not have enough layers one needed for hours of activity in freezing temperatures. To be fair, after she had him running for a while, he understood why. Even ounce of his body was drenched in sweat. He just a soon burn that uniform than think he'd get it clean again.

Second, she let those dogs disappear into the abyss like they knew what they were doing. GPS collars or not, who trusts dogs to just find their target, their way, or come back like that? Oh, but they had. On command, after running that poor bear right up a tree, post playing tag with it for miles. Only someone raised by damn wolves could train a dog to obey with such loyalty, and after the way he saw her jet down a steep bank like she was immortal, he'd thought maybe she was part wolf.

Luke had stopped to tell her they could die if they went down it, and her response was so steady it ricocheted a flame of challenge right through him.

"We could stud, but imagine how invincible you'll feel if we don't." She'd purred those daring words, right before leaping over it and joining her dogs in the chase.

His descent had been less graceful and wrought with tumbles and rolls he'd only survived because he'd been taught how to bail out of a convoy and not die.

At one point, the bear decided to try his luck, and turned heel on the dogs, going after them. That crazy wilderness woman hadn't hesitated one blink to run straight for it screaming. The gun in her hand did little to deflect from the fact that this petite woman had charged towards six hundred pounds of teeth like it was a stuffed toy.

She'd handed him water when he'd clearly needed it, yet didn't touch a drop until they'd returned to their vehicles. Yea that had been fun. After running yogi ten miles up, it'd dawned on him they'd need to hike back, and he'd considered just lying there and letting hypothermia claim him. It would have been easier. He fought like hell to pretend he wasn't hurting, but no ego nor masculinity could compensate for his stumbling and her insufferable sighs when he lagged.

She even giggled at him, *giggled* damn it, when one of her dogs shot out of the bushes and made him yelp like a little kid spooked on Halloween. Then, to put the icing on the cake of shame he'd already eaten, she stripped down to her underwear and sports bra right outside her bronco and pulled on dry sweats and a hoodie, like he wasn't standing *right* there, and like it wasn't the north pole outside.

She was an untamed animal, and nothing he'd even experienced in his life.

He rolled his neck around under the water, palming the wall for support. She had a death wish. What the hell else made a woman so damn…

The shower curtain ripped back, causing him to bang his head into the far too low spout and stumble against the back wall, before his military training kicked in and he had his hand firmly around the wrist reaching in.

"What the F-"

"Easy deputy." Her voice was soft, for the first time since he'd met her. "Just brought you something for the pain."

His eyes noticed a small bottle of red liquid with a cork in the top, held in a hand that looked far too lovely for the lunatic they were attached to.

"I knocked." Sam kept her eyes locked on his dilated pupils. It was not the easiest thing she'd done, considering.

Luke clapped his hands over himself. "Jesus Christ!" He yanked the flimsy shower curtain to cover himself, sending the rod tumbling to his feet.

"Little modest for a military man, are we?" She let her gaze fall just a hair, for effect of course, before setting the bottle on the sink and sauntering into the tiny living area.

It took him a moment to gather himself, before grabbing a towel and wrapping it around his broad hips and charging out. "What the hell are you doing in my apart-"

She had his gun in her hands, running her fingers along the barrel.

"You need to put down my weapon immediately." His voice was sharp as a trooper's orders should be.

It amused her.

Sam moved quickly, and he'd barely taken a step before she had slid the magazine out and popped the bullet out of the chamber, placing the gun gently on the counter with the slug still spinning at her feet.

God help him.

"You outta lock your doors deputy." She pocketed her hands and met his floored expression. "Somebody could get hurt." She kicked the bullet towards his dripping feet. "Banger in the slide deputy? Shameful."

He swallowed hard. "Samantha Shaw, I need you to leave my residence promptly." He cleared his throat and tightened his towel. "I am not dressed appropriately, and this is... right weird is what it is."

She paused, pondering. His insistence on being prepared for anything, was kind of cute, and outright unhealthy. She shook her head smiling.

Not many could handle her boldness, so she had to hand it to the deputy, he was rather composed. She was lucky he hadn't laid her out flat honestly, and he'd recovered quite well. How very interesting. He might last longer than she thought. She straightened.

That was not a good thing.

"Take that bottle within the hour, or it won't do jack." She was out the door before he could ask what it was.

He moved, and the door suddenly swung back open, his hand snapping to his gun, dropping the towel.

"It's just a shot a moonshine and turmeric stud, I don't need to poison you to get rid of you." She deliberately ran her eyes over him before shutting the door.

What the hell was that? Why? *What!?* Luke had never in all his years dealt with whatever the hell just walked out of his dwelling. She was a chaos-spinning nightmare. One he was afraid he'd spend more time in once he closed his eyes.

~

Sam drug her tired body up the steps and through the door after she'd made her rounds in the barn and locked up her runners. All dogs accounted for, warm and relaxed. After holding her palm on Paw's chest long enough to feel it rise and brush off the pork rind dust, she all but crawled up the steps to her room. That was one of the largest runs she'd had in a while, made more so by the third eye she'd kept on Lucian Rose all night.

He'd impressed her, and not just by the hard body she'd gotten a glimpse of, although that was a nice show. No matter which way she zigged, he zagged. She dove, he leapt. He only slowed down towards the end, and the only reason she didn't was because she'd had an audience, and too much pride. She was whooped. It'd been a cloudy day, and as she pulled her sweater over her head, she prayed with everything in her that the solar panels had enough charge in them to squeak out a hot bath.

"There is a Creator." She moaned in relief, watching steam rise a moment before sinking into the filling tub.

She dumped lavender buds in the water and spun them with her fingers, trying to keep her mind off that tall oak that'd burnt his build into her corneas. It was like leaving an old T.V. on pause for too long before turning it off, the image just glowed there like a taunting outline of what you'd just been watching, threatening to never truly go away, continuing to show faintly even when you turned it back on or changed the channel.

He could use a bit more squish on those sharp cuts, nothing a few of Anita's sweets couldn't handle, but God had he ever taken a day off from working out? She slid her hands down her body as it beckoned to be stimulated. He was… Trouble Sammy, that's what he was.

She slapped the water and sneered at herself as she clutched the sides in reserve. Every trooper from here to Fort Yukon had their ear pierced by what had happened at the Iditarod, and if he was half the cop they said he was, he'd be looking right at her for answers. She kicked the water.

Those dogs showing up at Brad's house hung from trees had made her ball like a baby once she was out of town. Tig said it was bad, and that Brad was certain she had something to do with it, squawking in Frank's office for justice. Her and Brad had been… something once, and he should know better. She could never hurt dogs like that, and the son of a bitch knew it. He just wanted someone to go down for it and she…

"Well Sammy, you haven't exactly left yourself looking too good here given some past moves."

She sunk down deep in the steamy tub. She wished she knew who hurt those dogs. It had to be someone local. Who else could get here unknown before he left the race, or skirt past Brad's cameras, let alone know he had any, if they didn't live on the island? Brad had plenty of enemies, so that narrowed down nothing.

She'd find out and wouldn't sleep much until she did, the thought of someone doing that to her dogs making her body chill.

Sam dipped her head back soaking her hair, wondering if Lucian knew anything, was looking into it. She felt a tightening in her belly and clunked her head back on the wall. Fresh meat. That's the only explanation for him parading around in her mind again. It was a small island, many of them grew up together. New options were probably exciting for every un-hitched female on this rock, with no doubt some of

Charlotte's young cashiers were already putting in a betting pool on who'd bed the new deputy first.

Have at it ladies. The further away he stayed the better. She can't do what called to her with the law sniffing around, and she'd be damned if she had anything left in her to chance on anyone anyway.

Everyone in her life always left. Distanced. Polluted their body. Expected her to be something she couldn't be. That's what James wanted. Kids, white picket fence, a happy little wife at home. It wasn't her. She didn't want kids and she didn't want to be caged. She'd never been enough for her mother, and after Frank had cuffed her, he'd slowly faded back too.

Paw never did, but he was about to, even if it wasn't his fault. He'd never gotten over G-maw and her father's death, leaving him the greatest mentor and rock, but not one to be very affectionate. Vulnerable? Forget it. She was allergic to those things too she supposed.

Dogs were safe. Dogs didn't judge you, expect things from you, hold grudges. Dogs were loyal and forgiving to a fault, and she'd protect them always, the way she'd wished someone had protected her, from everything in her life that had left her broken and unworthy.

Sam tried to swallow the rock in her throat, before clasping her knees to her chest, finally letting herself cry. Roy nudged the door open and promptly began licking her face.

"You and me buddy. I don't need anything else."

Chapter 5

Bradley Oliver stood up and paced Frank's office, for the second time in two days. Lucian followed him with speculative eyes from his lean on the wall, more to keep his sights off the recent round of sweets Anita insisted on pumping into them. His stomach growled.

"Brad, son, I investigated it. She only has her team, not even a foster in her care right now. The flight log was valid, as was her train ticket." Frank rapped his knuckles on the file to signal he had copies of such in it. "Tell me how she got two dead dogs off the train and stashed them before dragging them to your house without being seen kid?"

Brad swung around and palmed Frank's desk. "Don't 'kid' me Chief." He shoved the file towards him. "This doesn't get closed until someone pays for the death of those dogs, or I'll have your badge. They had a few good years left in em and I'm not one to let shit go."

"Threatening my job Mr. Oliver? Not the best move if you want resolution."

Brad leaned over the desk. "Neither is protecting that conniving bitch!"

Luke lifted from his lean and squared up as Frank slammed his palms down and stood quicker than Luke had ever seen him move.

"You can threaten my job all you want, you little shit, but you watch your god damn mouth. Get the hell out of my office."

The door clicked open, Brad breaking his stare down with the furious chief to find Willow and Forest puffed up and ready for a scrap. Brad eyeballed Luke who had shifted to tower over him by a good two hands.

Brad sniffed and chuckled slightly. "So much testosterone for little ol me? I'm touched." He pulled his jacket down angrily and glanced at his Rolex. "Maybe my lawyer is awake. Clearly, I'm getting nowhere with you snow-pushers."

Willow snarled as Bradly dared them not to move out of his way.

"Boys." Frank waved his hand, the twins begrudgingly parting like the sea to let him pass.

"Oh hey new blood?" Luke met Brad's arrogant gaze and he walked backwards towards the exit. "Watch yourself now. I know it's tempting. But speaking from personal experience, Sam never hesitates to screw over anyone she's fucked. Better skip it."

A half-eaten cinnamon roll smacked into his fine snow jacket, clinging slightly before tumbling its sticky mass to the floor.

Frank had the collars of the twins before they could lunge, but Luke had managed to pry past like a snake.

Brad shrieked like he'd just watched his stocks drop. "Did you just huck a pastry at me!?"

"Your god damn right I did." Darleen snapped. "And I got a whole plate waiting for ya, if you don't watch your mouth in my station, you little brat!"

Anita palmed a tray of scones smirking, tossing one in the air repeatedly, in gleeful anticipation to loft it.

"Save them." Luke growled. "I want one." He snapped up Brad by the arm and shoved him out the door like he weighed nothing.

"Assault! This is corruption! I'll have all your asses!" Brad was wailing as Luke closed the door and straightened his belt.

"Frank. I want a divorce." Darleen swooned.

"After that move Mama, you'll wait till I'm done with you tonight before you file." Frank shot her an appreciative wink and she plopped into her chair flushed like a teenage girl.

Luke leaned over her station and picked up one of the cinnamon rolls. "Nice shot D."

She got even redder and answered the buzzing call board with a shaky tone, Anita grumbling about kids these days as she grabbed a mop.

Back in the office, the Chief and his deputies stood quiet for a moment before Frank filled his cheeks and whooshed a heavy breath.

"It's hard to remember we're wearing badges sometimes." His tone was tight with concern. "We need to watch it with that one, boys. Money talks."

"Then I'll take it off before I kick his ass." Forest spit, meeting Willow's fist bump.

Frank waved a deflecting hand, noting Luke's frigid stance. "I know you're a stickler for the law kid, but I appreciate the assist." Luke jerked in acknowledgement.

"It may be a bit loose for you around here Luke, but when it comes to serious shit like dead dogs hanging from trees, we take it seriously. Accusing Sam of something when we got nothing on her… Well that could cause some town wide rumors and rubber-necking that could rouse big trouble. We don't have anything on her."

49

Frank's eyes glanced at the file warily. "Storm prep today. I handled the off-grid folks, campers have been moved to the hotel. Good few feet but nothing Alaskans can't handle. Just keep the peace today boys and get everyone home in one piece. Should hit around midnight tonight. Town will be shut for the next day I reckon."

Luke crossed his arms. "We should postpone John's soft-opening for the bar until it blows over chief."

A symphony of moans that rivaled middle schoolers getting a pop quiz, whined out of Willow and Forest.

"It's locals only." Frank looked distracted. "We'll have him shut around eleven. Folks know how to handle a few flakes."

Willow laughed. "Better than nothin! But who's telling Big John, cuz I ain't dying tonight."

"Not it!" Forest grabbed his hat and hustled to hit patrol, Willow on his heels.

"Good as time as any to meet him." Luke shrugged, grabbing hit hat. "You alright Sir?"

"Fine." Frank spun a pen in his hand, lost out the window, before he got up to leave, stopping by the door. "Want me to hit up John with you before I run the coastline?"

"No Sir, I got it." Luke picked up a mug. "Think I'll grab some coffee first, you go ahead."

He waited a good few beats for Frank to leave before he leaned over the file, flipping it open. He found photos of the dogs, alive and how they'd ended up. Gruesome. Addresses and a list of suspects. Big John Wilson. Samantha Shaw.

He raised his brows. "James Porter?"

Some random poacher that hadn't been in town for months, and Bradley Oliver. Suspect in his own dog's killings? What the hell was going on around here? Frowning, Luke flipped through the thin file, slapping it shut and securing his hat firmly.

There was no flight log, no train ticket. Frank hadn't verified Sam's alibi, and Luke needed to find out why, and what the actual hell was going on in Shavila.

~

The last place Sam had wanted to be, was in town before a storm. She had everything she needed for a good month in the sticks, but Paw's pain had ramped up, so here she was. Waiting in the town's tiny clinic to pick up pain medicine to make sure if the storm decided to linger, she could help him through it.

When the Doc came out, James was behind him holding a bandaged hand. He nudged his head to meet him outside as the Doctor approached Sam.

"Here ya go Samantha." Doc Marshall placed a bottle in her hand and squeezed it shut, lowering his voice. "The yellow ones are for you. Xanax." She went to protest, but he patted her hand to silence.

A warm, round man, Doc Marshall looked a bit like Santa Claus, and was the kind of guy you wished was your doctor.

"I know how you feel about it honey, but there is no crime in taking the edge off your barbed wire occasionally. He needs you strong, try to get some sleep."

Sam shrunk slightly with a whispered thank you and pulled her wallet out of her back pocket.

"Don't insult me." Doc leaned in, to whisper. "After all the money you gave Star for the vet clinic, this ones on me."

She shook her head, overwhelmed, as he pulled it in to kiss her forehead, quickly calling back a young kid who'd clearly taken a good spill on the ice, given the arm he was cradling.

She'd given half the money she'd raised on Snow White's litter to help pay for the surgery room they were rallying for. She really couldn't afford it, so she made it anonymously, but wishful thinking in this town.

If the injury was serious, most animals were put down, they just wouldn't make it to Anchorage in time. If they could pull this off, many families would have their pets for longer, and wildlife would get an extra boost when they could manage it too. It'd put her in a tight spot financially, but she didn't need anything, unless Paw needed it. She didn't have much to fight for once he was gone anyway.

She had people who appreciated her here, cared some, but she went home alone, and almost never got invited to anything. Something her introverted ice walls had done to herself she knew. Still, even if she wasn't going to go, it was nice to be invited once in a while.

Stupid.

Sam knew damn well she kept everyone away to spare her the pain of them deciding she wasn't good enough. Even James couldn't get passed her refusal to stay barefoot in the kitchen, it disgusted him really. She did it plenty, just didn't want anyone telling her when and where.

There was always something. Her hair was too long, she laughed too loud, ladies shouldn't talk with their fists...

She shook her useless thoughts to silence and found James leaning on her Bronco. At least when it came to friendship, this one was a keeper, most of the time.

"Stick your hand in the plane prop again?"

"Har har." James lit a smoke, ignoring her dramatic hand wave against the cloud he exhaled. "Paw okay?"

"Yea. Just sleeps more and more. Pain kicked up a bit, but nothing too scary." She grabbed his hand and turned it over in hers. "Trap? Seriously?"

He coughed on his drag. "Could never fool you." He shoved the injured hand in his pocket. "Should come with me next time to run the lines."

"Jesus J, ya gotta make sure they're sprung first." She narrowed her eyes. "Trapping season is over."

James put his hands up. "Just cleaning up the last round, a bit late is all."

"Better be."

A raised voice caught her attention.

"You know better Sammy, I'm straight." James turned to see what the fuss was. "Oh boy. Looks like the new deputy decided to drop the bar bomb on ol' John finally. This outta be good."

They made their way over to the front of the bar. Not much happened around here, and Sam needed to stop by to see Star Ansley, the town vet, at the clinic next door anyway to pick up some salve for Roy's feet. Fat boy wasn't built for Alaska.

"Eleven!?" Big John shouted. "You think just because *you* can't handle a little storm that we need babysitters now?"

Luke crossed his arms and tilted his head. "John, I don't doubt any of you. It's just been a dry town for a long while, and we need to keep everyone safe."

John threw his head back and scoffed like Lucian Rose was the weakest man alive. Sam watched Luke strategically shift gears, not that she was paying attention.

"This is pretty exciting stuff man, and you know everyone is bound to have far too good a time with what's on tap. I'd hate to have anything bad happen and put a cloud on all the hard work you've put in."

Sam smiled faintly. Clever cop.

Her smile turned to a sneer when she saw Bradley Oliver jovially jog across the street to stick his rich nose in the drama. She really wouldn't mind watching Lucian, or John for that matter, put his ass on the ground, and silently hoped he'd act up enough so she could watch it happen. Anybody with a beard styled like a boy band, belonged on his ass anyway, on principle alone.

"If it helps give it merit and save the evening," Luke added, "Frank thinks eleven is better than nothing. Nothing was my original argument."

Big John's edges softened slightly, eyeing the carved sign he'd made himself, quite beautifully, before turning back to Luke.

"Alright Deputy." He put his hand out to shake. "Eleven it is; last call ten-thirty, but I'm starting at six instead of seven then."

"Fair enough." Luke clasped his massive hand. "Appreciate it, John. We'll make sure you have a good, safe season to make up for it."

"Pound sand Outside." John's tone was a rare playful one, something that shocked Sam tremendously. Took a wizard to get that venom out of the beast. Not bad deputy, not bad.

"Six? Sounds like a plan to me." All eyes slid warily to Bradley Oliver brushing invisible lint off his stupid pea coat before lifting his menacing expression to Sam. "Sam's always good fun if you get enough in her."

"Don't you have dogs to count Brad?" Sam gritted, pulling her keys out of her pocket to leave.

She had no interest in this BS today. Brad was about to retort when Paw's pills tumbled from her pocket to the ground.

"More meds for Paw?" Everyone tensed as Brad picked them up and held them out to her. "Surprised you haven't done him in like you did my dogs."

"Oh fuck you!" She lunged. "You lying piece of shit!"

James had his arm around her waist and was hauling her back, curls and feet flying, before her claws made contact with Brad's face.

"Easy Sammy easy!" James wrestled her like a rabid squirrel. "Cool it Sam!" He pinned her to the car, whispering. "Not in front of the badge honey, he ain't worth it."

"Oh ya Sam!? One of my runners took a chunk out of somebody last night! And Sam looks pretty scratched up to me! Explain that!"

"I ran a bounty you prick!" Sam lunged against John's firm grip. "You know better Brad!" Her eyes welled. "You know me!"

Brad rubbed his overly groomed beard. "I know you, Sammy. All the dirty parts." He licked his lips.

Onlookers gasped as John ripped the pills from Brad's hand and sent him jogging back a couple steps with an angry shove. "Dirty play rich boy."

Brad opened his arms in challenge, one Big John was sure to take. Brad would bleed in the streets, but ruin John's life in court. Big money brought in big lawyers.

"Alright enough!" Luke's deep rumble had everyone halt in shock. He'd been rather soft spoken until that point. "Everyone go about your business, or nobody sets foot in this bar tonight, you get me?"

The small crowd murmured as it dispersed. John slammed the pills into James's hand, the other still wrapped around Sam's fury. John gave her a quick nod before locking himself in the bar to brood.

The reigning Iditarod champ smoothed his perfectly cut blond hair. "Ain't worth more than the floor I took you on anyway." He spit at her feet and turned to leave.

"One more word Brad, and I'll haul you in for harassment. You're being a right prick Oliver, and you know it." Luke's tone sent a chill down

Sam's spine, even as her eyes burned with tears, she didn't want to give Brad the pleasure of seeing.

The jerk didn't even turn around, laughing at the Deputy's warning as he sauntered towards to general store. She snapped her head into James's sleeve as he shoved the pills in her pocket and steered her across the street.

Luke watched James tuck Sam into her truck and her tires peel out to disappear towards the woods. Something was between her and that pompous prick, more than just a busted nose last season, and it smelled like a possible motive. He intercepted James as he headed towards the vet clinic.

"Told Sam I'd get Roy's foot stuff."

"Ah." Luke formulated his approach. "Brad seems to like to dig at her, more than he does the rest of you. Is that a problem I should keep an eye on or is he harmless?"

James paused his hand on the vet's door. "Interesting you take notice. Most the town has him on a pedestal."

"I haven't been here long enough to give damn about either of them," But he did, her, even if he didn't know why yet. "Or said pedestal, just the risk they pose to each other in town, or in the bush."

James rested against the wall and lit a smoke. "What exactly are you asking Deputy?" His stance was protective. Luke pinned it.

"Is there reason to believe she has motive to hurt his animals, or he to pin something on her that she didn't do?" James lowered his brows. "It'd be a real help to keep her out of the line a fire, assuming she didn't light it, James. I'm just trying to do my job."

"Suppose that's something you'll have to ask Sam." He flicked his cigarette and pulled the clinic door open. "But maybe you should ask him if he lynched his own dogs first."

Luke's jaw dropped and went to call after him.

"She's got reason to cut that man's dick off and feed it to the pike, Deputy." Luke spun around and found Big John casually locking up his bar. "And there a few of us who, even on days when we can't stand that girl's attitude, would like to see her do it."

"Some old race beef or something?"

Big John shifted a crate in the bed on his truck as the wind kicked up. "He took advantage of her. Hurt her."

Luke felt his shoulders lock up. "Meaning-"

"Yea Boss, that, but the physical would have been easier for her to recover from than the rest of it."

Luke grabbed John's driver side window stopping him from pulling out. "Why the hell weren't charges pressed?"

"Because she loved him." He started his engine. "And that girl don't let nobody close. Mother fucker broke her."

Luke watched John pull away and ran his eyes down the road Sam had disappeared on. The sky was darkening, the wind carrying in snow clouds. In a couple hours the bar would open up. He'd better get back to the station and get the plan from Frank.

He nodded a hello to a couple local teens and pivoted towards the station distracted. Nothing was quite what it seemed in this place, including the people who lived here, yet the way his blood moved around that woman seemed to make the rest seem, hell he didn't know. She was doing something to him, and the change made him, uneasy.

Chapter 6

He knew it. Nobody just picks up and drops their ass in Shavila on a whim. The big britches in Fairbanks and Anchorage got together and decided to send a scout; pretty-boy Rose over here to sniff out Sam, and all the other things linked to her. Well, he'll be damned. They may not agree on some things, but one thing was for sure, neither of them needed this. He was playing his roll well enough, and she'd understand later why he had to do what he's been doing. Nobody was going to get pegged for this, except the one who deserved it, and Sam wasn't it. She'd been through enough. He'd put her through enough. She just had to deal with the suspicion long enough for him to complete his plan.

After killing his lights, he pulled his truck up along the bug out road Sam had whacked out after a fire scare hit the town last year. He saw her reflection pacing in her upstairs window, curls a frantic mess, book in her hand, lost in some adventure she couldn't give herself. Idly chewing her thumb nail and grinning through some love scene she'd never let herself have.

God she hadn't deserved it, what he'd put her through. It wasn't that he didn't care how his choices had affected her, it was just some things simply had to happen. There were some things that needed to take place in life that she would never understand why. He had a plan, a vision, and it was a beautiful one, until others messed it all up. He didn't want it to end up like this, it was supposed to be better. He'd make it better for her.

He just hoped the few things he did say had steered Luke in the direction he wanted. He put the truck in neutral and silently crept back to the main road, grateful the wind had kept his comings out of her dog's ears. It could have been a good time to scope the barn, but soon. He had time. The bar would be opening soon, and it looked like she had no designs of showing up. That gave him an all clear to keep an eye on that overgrown jarhead. Maybe get him laid so he didn't sense the next hit coming.

~

The twins cheered and jogged out the door, Darleen hollering at them to stop being animals as they dumped their reports on her desk, knocking over her flowerpot pen holder, stealing a pastry before they bolted towards home to change.

Luke strapped on his gun anyway. "Are you sure Frank? I don't think it's a good idea to have only one trooper on beat when this town hasn't seen a bar in over twenty years."

Frank rested back and put his hands behind his head. "Its locals only, everyone is tucked in for the storm coming. You need to meet them on their turf, out of uniform. It will do wonders for their cooperation in the future and might just save you some trouble."

Luke hipped his hands and tried not to sound pathetic. "I don't mind. I literally have nothing else to do."

"You met Star Ansley yet?"

"The Vet? No. Suppose I will eventually."

Frank rubbed the growth on his face and grinned. "I imagine if you find her, you'll find something to do."

"Jesus Frank."

"Ah hell kid get outta here. Have a beer. And don't deny me much louder or the wife will hear. If I'm forced to sit and watch Darleen and Anita's romance movie Friday night marathon, I'll have your ass doing crosswalk duty for a month. Don't screw this up for me."

"Well Sir, I just can't do that to you, so I guess I better go change."

"Shower too. Once you lay eyes on Star Ansley, you'll be glad you did. Not that she'll give you much choice once she lands hers on you." Frank pushed him out of the office. "Good luck."

That was awkward. Luke jogged up the narrow steps to his apartment and decided he'd definitely skip the shower. A good security measure for his screaming loins. Bedding down anyone before he knew who they were connected to was suicide in a small town. He already knew too much personal details about the residents and he'd only been here a hand of days. He'd just have to take a trip into the city on his day off and take care of it then.

He pulled on dark blue jeans and a black V-neck, slicking his hair back with water and calling it good. It'd gotten a bit longer than he liked, but nobody ever scolded James Dean, so he'd get to it when he could. He needed to shave, but it'd only been a day, he figured a shadow was another good measure to keep his dick in his pants.

He liked everything sharp and tight, especially when taking a woman, so being off his game would keep his proper head in control. A black jacket should be enough, he imagined the bar would be warm, and he was taking his patrol truck out.

The snow wasn't falling yet but the twins had helped him put the plow on the front of his vehicle earlier that day. Said it was self-preservation, so they didn't have to come save his ass when they were half in the bag later. He liked them. Young and rowdy but good deputies. Great with the high school kids. They could get anything out of them if they needed to and the locals loved them dearly.

He could hear some lazy country playing as he pulled across the street. A chill vibe sauntering across the windows in the shape of flannel and beards, ponytails and beanies. The ridiculously shiny truck next to his didn't seem to fit. He was about to head in and hesitated, before grabbing his phone and texting. He clearly wasn't done making questionable choices.

~

Sam had just finished letting her team wreak havoc on the grounds to get some energy out when she came to check on Paw. They hadn't been run much, as Sam didn't like to be away from Paw longer than something that made her money required. She'd dove into a book after dinner and decided sleep was the best thing to keep her from going stir crazy in her mind, regardless of it being the bedtime of a toddler. One last check.

"You should go."

"Paw, I'm away enough. Take this." She handed him the pain pill and watched closely.

James had dropped off his meds earlier and mentioned the bar's soft opening to Paw but hadn't asked Sam to go. He'd known she wouldn't. She'd been grateful not to have to shut him down. She did that often enough. He did suggest staying with her and finishing what they'd started a couple days ago; that she did shut down. She owed one deputy a thanks for stopping that from happening.

"You do not need to walk with me in my dreams, little bear. Go be young. Find you someone to be young with."

"Gross Paw." She squeezed his hand and plopped on the floor against his recliner. "I'd rather be here with you anyway."

"What about that new deputy? Give him hell yet?"

Sam chuckled. "Not if I can help it. Best he clears out."

Paw dropped his hand over the recliners arm and cupped her cheek, idly stroking it. "Perhaps he has come for a reason." He stopped when she tensed. "You need to walk a straighter path wild one; he may be able to help you do so."

"Yea. By putting me if cuffs."

He gave her cheek a swift, but gentle tap. "By showing you ways to do what your heart is driven to do, without doing things that could one day stop its beating." Sam grinded her teeth, prompting another gentle tap. "Stop it. Go. Be young. It is a gift."

"I'm off to bed Paw. That mess isn't something I need right no-" Her phone pinged.

Paw lifted it from the side table, opened it and slowly slid it down to her hands, Deputy Lucian Rose's message proudly displayed.

"I'll be right where you left me kid." She spun to her knees and gave him a ruffled look that made him chuckle. "I never said I couldn't use them granddaughter; I simply said I don't like them." He winked, grabbing his own phone and tucking it in his lap, feigning sleep.

"Sneaky old man." She snatched it up and shook it at him. "I'm taking this upstairs with me, so you know I'm *not* going."

A half hour later, Kallik held his smile flat when he felt the phone gently placed in his lap, a fresh spray of lavender emanating from her. Sam hushed Roy to watch over him, and the door clicked shut.

"Go get em, little bear."

~

After a round of jabs flying from all directions at how clean his jeans were, and a demanded dart game with the twins before a female set was dripping all over them, Luke had finally found himself a seat at the bar to observe.

Vanessa and Tamar were taking turns juggling their infant and showing off Vanessa's engagement ring. Luke didn't want to mention how unacceptable it was for a baby to be in a bar, assuming it would be the opposite of a good move when trying to make better local connections. He was off duty, it was mellow-about twenty people or so-and Tamar hadn't touched a drop. They were being responsible, doting parents, but it was still on the top of his 'strange sights' list. Small towns hit different.

Frank had popped in to see that all was well before slipping out again, and Tig and Charlotte had brought food for everyone before bullying the jukebox into some sort of back beat they began dancing to. Raine Buckowski from the bank, had stopped in for a minute before hurrying home at his wife's demand, and a handful of young cashiers, he begged to argue were not twenty-one -maybe it was the water here- were giggling around the joint and squealing anytime his scans landed on them.

Despite being at least in his mid-thirties, Bradley Oliver had pulled the one with the least amount of clothes on, onto his lap a few minutes ago. She was alert and willing, but Luke kept a side eye on it.

Big John slid a bottled light his way. "On the house Chief."

Luke lifted in thanks before he took a long pull of the first drink he'd had. "Not chief yet my man."

59

Big John Wilson slapped a towel over his shoulders and elbowed the counter. "Thanks for not shutting it down. This is exactly what this town needed before the tourist clog it up. Look at em. Happy as a walrus."

Luke noted the gathering. They were all content and easy, something he'd never really witnessed. It really was… something special.

"No James tonight? You cross?"

John began to absently wipe the clean counter. "We've had our run ins." He shrugged. "But nothing too heavy. Suppose he's banging on Sam's door like always. Fool."

Luke rose a brow. "How's it?"

"Ah hell it's not my business, but he can't let go that she ain't wanted him since she was a kid. She thinks she's got a good friend, but I think she's got a man trailing her who's waiting to be her only option. Seems it anyhow."

Something about that turned his nerves. Maybe it was he cop in him. "Meaning?"

John huffed a laugh and leaned closer. "Means what it means Chief. I took the hint a decade ago when she didn't even know my name after growing up with my baby sister." He jerked his head to Charlotte. "The tree Sam busted across my face helped." He pawed his beard chuckling. "But that man is around a woman who don't want him a bit too much to be healthy. Even after her spin with Brad-blue-blood over there. James is a stage five clinger, for a grown man. Just sayin. Maybe I just don't know how to be friends, can't say I like many folks much."

Luke tried to read Big John's face and got nothing. He was just, collected. Cool about it. Perhaps a bit too much.

"He'll show, but until then." John eyed the door. "The view ain't half bad."

Luke spun around and shifted in his seat uncomfortably. It was not who he expected to see, but damn if she wasn't something that would stir the blood of any living man who didn't prefer his own sex.

Legs that held a frame at least five ten and a dress meant for a cocktail bar -not an Alaskan dive- that left nothing to the imagination, balancing a huge set of breasts barley hanging on and a heart shaped face with blue eyes and blonde hair in waves. A walking playboy bunny who stuck out like a damn Ferrari in this crowd. Frank was not kidding.

Shit. Luke turned his back to her quickly and sipped his beer in desperation. He was in no position to fight that one off, it'd been too long since he'd sunk into something warm and female. The weak resolution residing in his loins began to taunt the feral green-eyed woman plaguing his thoughts, having no rhyme or reason to be doing so, into a war to see which one would win. The way his heart pounded at the thought of her, made him almost forget the blonde beauty approaching.

"She's not hitched boss." John grinned. "Kinda makes ya wish you were a sick cat, so she'd work on ya don't it?" He chuckled and slid down the bar to a beckoning Tig.

Star Ansley slid into the seat next to Luke after hugging Brad -far too long for the girl he'd been working's liking- and tilted her perfect head. "Deputy Rose I presume?" She offered her lean fingers for a handshake.

He shook it. "Not tonight. Just Luke."

"Well then it's just my night." Her hand landed on his thigh, too high, and he tensed. "Easy trooper. I don't bite unless ordered."

Son of a bitch she didn't waste any time, did she?

"You're the vet I presume?" He sipped his beer as steadily as he could, given her hand had shifted up slightly.

Down boy. Not a good idea.

"I am. Guess word gets out quick huh?" She thanked John for the beer and sipped it far too seductive to be normal.

Luke dropped his eyes to her hand and back up. "You give humans checkups too?" He put an edge to his voice he'd hoped she'd heard.

She did. "Only when it's wanted." She lifted her hand and a red tint hit her cheeks.

Better. Oh he'd definitely take a woman like her down hard normally, and love it, but something about Star's sureness that she could grope his thigh five seconds after shaking his hand, irritated him. The fact that he was juiced up for a woman who'd rather knock his block off, should be more concerning.

"Nice to meet you Ms. Ansley. What brought you to Alaska?"

She straightened her back as if alarmed he was being so neighborly as opposed to dicking her down. He went limp in his pants, which surprised him honestly, but maybe he was just tired or… her eyes weren't green…

"Oh, ya know." She threw her hair back and turned up the flirt, back on the ball. "Got all caught up on a mountain man who decided to crash his plane five years after he drug me here from California. Left me all alone." Oh she was laying it on thick. "But I love this town, and had my practice, so here I am." Her hand returned to his thigh. "Keeping busy."

"Tourist season must be great for you." Fuck. That was rude.

She snapped her hand back and was about to pop off at the insult when Luke glanced at the door and choked on his beer. Holy.Wild.Hell.

Star began to rub his back and all but put her tits in his face, seizing her next opportunity. "Are you alright, oh my goodness." She fussed ridiculously over the massive deputy who had just involuntarily aspirated his beer.

"Damn Luke you good bro?" John laughed and then followed his line of sight. "Ah. Yea man, that'll do it."

Luke kept his eyes on the door as he coughed. God help him.

61

Samantha curled her face playfully at Charlotte's squeal and shared a hug after Tig took her jacket.

Oh, Christ please put that back on. Luke wiped his mouth and waved Star back, still coughing.

Sam had piled her dark curls on her head loosely, a few framing her face and tracing down her neckline in a cruel way. She must have painted that black tank top on and it showed the tone in her chest between her, god damnit perfect handfuls. Her angry green eyes were lined with black that could cut glass and why was that paw shaped pendant around her neck the cutest thing he'd ever seen?

Luke had turned away when she'd stripped down by the cars after running the bounty, but he'd caught a glimpse. Still, something about her casual air, her no fuss beauty in this moment, knocked him on his ass. He'd never seen anything like her, *felt* anything like her. She radiated promises of the best high of your life, like a damn drug, thorns covering the nectar she guarded so fiercely.

Tamar spun her off her feet and Luke was no longer lose in the pants. Thank your mother for what is in those jeans woman. Luke decided he must be more exhausted than he thought when Sam took Vanessa's baby and his gut punched itself. He didn't even like kids.

Nothing affected anyone this quickly. This was bullshit. Chaos. No. He needed to go home.

Luke ran his hand through his hair and assured Star he was fine, needing her perfume out of his nose and a minute to inhale without risking sucking in her hair. When she turned to see what he couldn't peel his eyes from, she sucked her teeth.

"Fair enough. Sometimes malibu barbie has to yield to the bush babe." Star grabbed her beer and slid off the stool. "Watch that sexy smile deputy, she'll knock her fist in it before you can explain why you kissed her."

"He knows better." James took Star's stool and pulled her down on his lap. "But I don't."

There he is. Guess he gave her a ride, but judging by how Star was wiggling on his lap, James hadn't had Sam in his before they got here. Friends. Or he was trying to work the jealousy angle.

Luke rose and downed his beer. Not his monkey not his circus. Still, he'd text Sam, so he had to go say hi before he left. He thought maybe she needed to get out, a break, hell he didn't know what he as thinking when he sent that text, he just wanted to see her, like a damn fool. She was a suspect, and she had daggers for him. Text probably didn't go through anyway.

He just needed information, that was it, he assured himself. He'd get it another way.

His inner monologue cursed him. *You're being a dick because you're on your ass Luke, and you can't handle it, hoping with everything in you there is no case.*

He grunted his thoughts back and shook James's hand. "I'm on my way out. Have a safe night."

Star threw her arms around James giggling. "Funny, he's on his way in."

Wow.

Luke forced a smile and grabbed his coat turning right into Sam's shocked face.

"You're leaving?" She pulled her phone from her pocket and waved it confused.

"You came."

She shrugged. "You called."

Hold the knees deputy. "Uh, yea I just thought, maybe a-"

She slipped his jacket from his hand and threw it on the stool that once had James and Star in it, now empty. "Guess my drink, and I suppose you earn me staying for it."

He gave a half smile that showed that stupid dimple on the side and slid his hands in his back pockets, scanning the menu. "No pressure then huh?"

Sam leaned back on her hip. You're too tall deputy, but that dimple might just earn you a few minutes.

"Choose wisely Lucian." Or don't, she was fine with pulling an Irish goodbye at any moment.

Less than a minute later, and two glances back at her that had Sam raising a brow, he flagged John down.

"Tell me big guy." Luke met Sam's wary eyes and grinned. "You got fixings for a dirty martini?"

Shit.

Chapter 7

They sat at a corner table, slightly out of the very jolly locals creeping towards last call.

"Martini wasn't even on the menu Lucian." She pulled the olive from the toothpick and pointed it at him. "Neither was my number. Spill it."

"Luke, please." He spun his water bottle and shrugged. "You're simple in projection. Something told me your drink was classy, or at least maybe there was more to you. Blame the Ops training."

Danger Will Robinson, danger. "And my number?"

"Town listing Samantha. Not weird."

"Sam, please. Still weird." And invasive and risky and took huge balls, considering she's been a proper bitch to him. Intriguing.

Luke met her troubled expression and they both huffed an awkward laugh.

"Well at least something about me is classy."

She scowled at Brad's taunting 'you remember?' glare as he grabbed one of Charlotte's cashier's asses and pulled her into him. She was 28 and never drank, so Sam knew Angela was fine, but could stand to see Brad leave, or choke on something.

Luke caught the lines in her forehead, distracting him from removing his foot from his mouth, and glanced over. "Am I ever gonna learn that story?"

"Ask me that one a bit later." Sam slid the second martini in front of her and spun it with her finger.

He didn't break eye contact.

"Not worth telling Deputy. He's just a dick." Luke glanced again. "She's fine. Doesn't drink. They hook up regularly."

Star and James came out of the bathroom just then, fixing their clothes and parting ways.

"Do they?" He looked amused.

Sam shrugged. "Who doesn't bang Star that isn't married, or sometimes is. Surprised you didn't mark that immediately." Sam waved a hand like she was talking too much. "Ah hell, sorry. That was rude, to both of you. I'm a salty fish." She adjusted nervously and rolled over it.

"She's a damn good vet, big help to me. It's impressive she embraces herself so much. I would if I was built like that."

"You're built just fine Sam."

She paused at that.

Just fine? Luke you loaf. He should have just gone home. Every girl wanted to bed a Marine, let alone a trooper who wasn't carrying an extra fifty pounds, so he'd never really noticed he had no moves, until he wanted to make them, and he was failing. Sam stirred that dusty, forgotten part of him in a way that he did not appreciate, nor did he ignore it. In fact, it pulled at him mercilessly, something that made the cop in him very uneasy.

Taking a gulp of her martini, Luke watched a soft curl dangle to her collar bone. "Is that official police work, keeping tabs on who bones who?"

"Oh uh no..." Luke sat back. "So, how'd you get into bounty running?" Smooth moron.

She laughed. "Surprised you're still standing after that run."

Sam toyed with the paw charm across her collar bone. She'd painted her nails. Red. Why he noticed was beyond him.

"After I was removed- ah, stopped running the Iditarod, it seemed a good choice. It sucked money and time I didn't have anyway, after I lost my sponsor." Her eyes flicked to Brad and Luke caught it. "Trapping is not my favorite thing and doesn't pull much at times, with how the fur trade fluctuates, and I refuse to pull wolves. Too close to dogs. Call out my biased, but I own it."

Luke could not fathom how she could compare one of the most dangerous animals on the planet to domestic dogs outside of their four paws, but he didn't dare ask.

"There was a big cat by the school one day, I was passing by after taking my team to the vet. The concern was palatable, I guess it started on a kid before taking to climbing the backstop. I let my team rip and we chased it a few miles into the bush. Really fun, except I ruined my boots." She smiled. "Not exactly my plan for the day ya know? Anyway, the calls kept coming in after that. Sometimes they pay in cash, sometimes they pay in pot pie. It's a living."

"I have never heard of such a thing." Luke was stunned by how casual she spoke of chasing giant predators, like it was just a Tuesday. She was insane. Definitely not his type. He adjusted his pinching jeans.

"You never had to lose money coming upon many head of your herd taken by wolves either. Most people in Alaska can't afford that. It'll ruin them. We earn hand to mouth Luke, and we don't do fences. Kids play outside. Families have dogs. Predators don't deserve to die because climate change is mucking up their resources, so I run em back. Most bounties kill, I refuse, unless my dogs or I, am at risk of getting hurt, they don't need to die. I take jobs out of town best I can, James planes me in; I'll take the train if I must. Less so lately with Paw…" Her face saddened. "I don't like to leave him long."

Luke knew her grandfather was a delicate subject. Based on what Frank had told him, Kallik Shaw was about the only thing she'd ever had in her life that was consistent. Based on her face, he was also the only man that had loved her for exactly what she was, and never otherwise. He had her trust the way she doubted anyone ever had.

"Tell me about him."

"He's the only man I'll ever love, and that speaks enough I think." Sam plucked up another olive. "Tell me about you, I'm tired of talking. There is nothing else about me worth knowing anyway."

Again, he doubted that seriously.

"Uh, well. Small town. Dad in the pen, mom had her issues." He grunted down the anger before setting his jaw. "Joined the military for stability, found I was really good at taking orders and getting shit done, so being a cop after seemed logical. Seen about every climate you could short of this insanity." He waved a hand at the increasing weather. "So I came here when the opportunity presented itself. I like simplicity and take comfort in consistency. Figured a small island might give me that." And he was scared to death of himself, needing a safer routine to control the temper he fought not to lose every time some kid was affected by their parent's drug habit. The city burnt him out, damn near broke him. His pride left that part out.

"Folks still around?"

Luke took a long pull from his water bottle. "No." His tone said drop it, the muscle that ticked in his jaw, demanded it.

She could take a hint, maybe he'd return the favor. "Well, you picked one hell of a town for stability Officer. Nothing ever happens around here-short of a few tourist morons stirring the pot-until it does."

They held a long look that illuminated the elephant in the room, one they'd been ignoring since it started following them around the second he'd set foot on her property.

"Tell me I'm wrong." Sam whispered. "Tell me you didn't text me to-" She never should have come.

"Alright here's the deal." Sam lifted slightly in alarm at Luke's tone. "I don't know how to talk to you, and it's pissing me off."

Temper. Noted.

"Most people don't want to talk to me at all, who don't know me anyway." She leaned back inquisitively. "I prefer they don't, so you're off to a brave start."

He leaned his elbows to the table. "I want to find out what happened to Brad's dogs, need to, so it doesn't happen again."

"Congratulations officer. You found the *only* thing we have in common."

He doubted that. "It's my job Sam, but every time I think…" He cleared his throat clasping his hands angrily. "You perplex me. I can't figure out whether to interrogate you or-" He stopped himself. Barely.

"Is that why you're being nice to me? To get information?" She went to get up and he grabbed her hand. "I don't need charity."

"Sam no. Please wait." His brown eyes were bolder than a casual conversation would necessitate.

Neither of them moved. The heat that pulsed through that first touch was mind numbing for both of them. Luke's throat bobbed and Sam leaned back a beat in alarm. That torched touch had just taken a battering ram to his bunker walls and an ice pick to her glacial ones.

Neither of them knew exactly what to make of it, so they just stood there.

Luke knew he had one shot to not screw up whatever it was he was doing. He had no idea what he was doing, besides risking his suspect and the case. The fact that those things crossed his mind first before his reckless intrigue with her, had him recovering quickly and letting go of her hand.

He was a solid oak; a dead one she didn't need nor want to try to climb. His face melted into the law, and he went rigid.

Sam did not fail to notice.

"Goodnight Officer Rose." She gulped the last of her martini and shifted around him.

A foreign panic rifled through him. "I needed to be honest before we spoke any longer. So you didn't assume…"

Sam spun around, swaying slightly. "And now you have, and I didn't assume *anything*."

That stung, and a buried part of him unearthed itself suddenly. Her security system had activated, just locked him out. The cop in him didn't budge, the soldier in him didn't blink, but Lucian Rose, the man, caved like an old mine shaft.

"The Officer didn't ask you here, the man did." And he didn't know why, either. "I'm glad you came."

She stopped, immediately cursing herself for the slight.

Walk away Sammy. This is bad news and you're just one hormonal mistake away from jail time. This man only felt safe because he didn't know you, and once he does, he'll disappear. That's if he doesn't put you through the hell of trying to change you first. You know that clear as you know your face. He'll notch his belt and get ideas, discover what you've done, what you do, and book you for it. He'll walk you in like Frank walked in your mother, and then just keep walking. Don't be a dumb female, too many who can't speak for themselves depend on you. They will always accept you. Walk away Sam.

She set her fingers on the table to steady herself, rubbing her temple before she walked away.

"Thanks for the drink." She didn't look back.

She knew better than to think anyone in this town had intentions other than to pick her apart, and she would keep telling herself that to keep herself safe, whole, until she was old and grey.

James was eyeballing the scene while keeping his conversation with Tig by the dart board. Sam didn't look right, and would probably need a ride home, one thing he wasn't about to let that overgrown doof do. How he'd got her here was irritating enough, but Sam can hold her booze. Two martinis wouldn't glass her eyes like that, flush her like that. If anyone was going to benefit from Samantha Shaw being a wanting woman, it sure as hell wasn't going to be some ass from the Outside who didn't know her. He threw cash on the counter and slapped Tig on the back. Time to go.

"Fine Char really, just a little tired. I'll drive safe." Sam gave her a quick hug, slung her coat over her arm and slipped out, James on her heels.

"Strike out buddy!" Brad rapped his knuckles on the table as he passed Luke. "Don't take it personal, she hates everybody."

Luke's eyes slitted. He decided Bradley Oliver was someone who deserved what he got. Those dogs of his though, did not. So Luke would have to put extra effort into keeping the two facts separate while he figured it out.

He sat awhile longer, the conversation rolling in his head. He'd never been so incapsulated by a woman before. Guess he wouldn't have to worry about it after that shit show. He rubbed his jaw frustrated. Something about the way she'd swayed didn't sit right. She was small, but built like a tank and in the shape she was, two martinis wouldn't-

Luke snapped up and made long strides to the door as John hollered out last call.

"That's not a good idea James, I'm fine, really." Sam steadied herself on her Bronco. "Fuck!" She should not be this dizzy.

James turned her back against it, pressing his body against her, clasping her face. "You're not fine, and you're not driving. Let me take you home. We'll get your car in the morning." He dipped his head to her ear and whispered something.

Whatever James just said had Sam shaking her head and pushing him back off her. Luke approached from behind slowly.

She was laughing nervously, and clearly uncomfortable, but in a way that showed her friendship with him held weight and cast her thoughts in doubt. Luke did not miss how unsettling it was to see a woman with no filter on her mouth, and a fearless demeanor, weaken herself against someone she cared for, as if she was already guilty. Luke's cop brain didn't stand a chance against the moral man riling to the surface.

Sam shook her head. She knew she shouldn't drive, but letting James take her home was bad news, given their history. He was relentless sometimes and ending up alone with him in this state would take them back so many good steps she'd taken back from him. He was a good friend, but his motives…

She was so dizzy. She could just call Frank. Damn her need to turn her head off. Maybe two Xanax was too much. Sam shook her head again.

"You feeling alright Miss Shaw?"

James stepped back from Sam with a start and turned to eyeball Luke. "She's good, little tipsy is all." James caught the glint of Luke's badge clipped to his hip, his shirt tucked intentionally behind it as he approached. "No worries. Gonna get her home safe, Deputy."

"Miss Shaw?" No sooner had the words escaped, did Luke lunge forward and grab her elbow, stopping her from falling. He pulled her into him. "Sam?"

"Xanax." She whispered. "I'm just wanted to turn it all off for one day, I didn't know…" She was so embarrassed.

"I will see to it Miss Shaw gets home safe." Luke said militantly.

Her Bronco was a clear sign they hadn't come together, and the fact that James had her pressed up against it and she was rebuking the affection didn't sit well either. You could add that he'd just had his dick in something not an hour ago to it, and he was willing to bet the lack of respect James had for Sam in his drunk state, was something she didn't see. Perhaps when he got to know him better, he'd give him the benefit of the doubt, but at this moment, he had a vulnerable woman that was not getting in the car with him.

Luke could have never spoken to Sam in his life and he still wouldn't leave her like this, friend or not. The snow began its dance as he took Sam's pulse, her grip hadn't released his arms since he'd caught her.

Please be smarter than me please, she internally pleaded. She had no reason to trust the man, but his honesty about wanting to question her about Brad's dogs, the clarity he offered, his intuition popping out here like this, told her she didn't have to trust the man yet, she needed to trust the cop, and get home. She'd never been like this, and she was scared.

"Weather is getting a little nuts Luke." James was clearly agitated. "I know these roads like the back of my hand, and her dog won't let you in the door. I'll get her tucked in."

Sam dug her fingers into Luke's arm. "Luke." Her timid voice was a plea.

James opened his door and reached for her. "She knows me."

"I don't." Luke bit. "And this woman is vulnerable. I will escort her home."

James puffed up like a bull and stepped into him. "You accusing me of something Deputy? Because we've already been there, many times, and I ain't after that right now. I don't trust you for shit."

"Key word; Deputy. And from what I saw, she already told you no. Back.Up.Porter."

"You pulling your badge on me officer?"

"Do I need to?"

Sam put her palm on James's chest and shook her head. James held her pleading stare for a long while. He couldn't. He wouldn't. He could ruin everything. He'd made her a promise, they were a team, best friends. He had to stand down, and keep his ass off Luke's radar.

James glared up at Luke, who had a good few inches on him. "Things get out in a small town. Watch your step."

Luke started.

"Still shooting your shot Deputy?" Brad leaned against his sparkling truck as the snow flurried around them.

James and Luke broke their stare down to pulse in into the rich asshole who needed to leave, and now.

"Maybe you should whisper some sweet nothing's Lucian, makes her buckle like a fawn before she brays like a mule."

Sam felt Luke's entire body shift to rock hard with a jolt. James slowly moved his head back to meet the deputy's fury, matching it, a silent question, and they both held. Luke finally gave him a firm nod of affirmation, before turning to walk Sam to his patrol truck.

As they pulled off, Sam slid her eyes to the rearview mirror, catching James crashing his fist across Brad's jaw, sending him tumbling violently to the snow.

Luke's jaw was tense, his knuckles white on the steering wheel, every muscle in his body veined out and bulging.

"What the hell was that?" Sam whispered.

Luke pulled his shirt over the badge on his hip. "I don't know what you're talking about."

~

Damn it'd been one hell of a night. First his plans hadn't been able to unfold. He'd seen Sam pull up at the bar and knew he couldn't do what he needed to. Still, he was able to observe and take some notes. Do a quick recon on the dogs, and shift gears. He didn't want to risk more than he already had in recent weeks, and knew some of this would hurt her, but in the end, it was to redeem her.

Sam had been through so much more than anyone should, plenty of it he caused. Now she risked herself even more to do the only good she thought she was worth, and it plagued him. He had his own crimes against her to make up for, and he'd have to commit more to fix them. He begrudgingly pulled into his drive, far later than he'd planned thanks to the accident on Pine Rd and sat for a moment. Surely the only peace he'd have for a few days.

That mess outside the bar would be more to deal with once everyone crawled out from under this storm. There would be noise about it tomorrow, but who Sam had left with made him even more uneasy. Surely Lucian Rose was not meant to be more than a new recruit, though he was proving to be a threat if he got too close too quick, and one he hadn't anticipated upon meeting him.

Chapter 8

"I know he's a friend, Sam, and he didn't mean harm, in theory. You don't need to explain anything. You wanted a ride, you're getting one." Luke was crawling at the pace of an eighty-year-old blind woman and doing his best to pretend he wasn't about to piss himself. "I'd do the same for any woman in there. It's cool. You can still be mad at me in the morning."

He surely looked foolish hunched over the steering wheel. He'd seen some snow, Idaho got some gnarly whippers, but this was not the same, and it had been quite a while since he'd had to traverse such weather.

Sam had her head back against the rest and her jacket pulled up to her chin, staring out the window. She looked like a little girl scared of the dark, but he knew better.

He considered striking up a more casual conversation but didn't think she wanted anything to do with him at this point. Nor was her state one to take advantage of. The silence lingered for some time.

"He hurt me."

The car jerked when Luke's foot slipped, steadying it quickly. "I'm sorry?"

Sam shifted slightly, keeping her face turned away. "Brad. You asked for the story." Her voice was strained, a rock tumbling in the cliff of her throat. "Might ease that death grip you got going on there, Deputy."

Luke flushed and turned down the roar of the heater. "I'll listen if you want to tell it, but I think you wouldn't want to if you weren't loopy." He selfishly wished he wasn't so noble.

"Or maybe… maybe I only can tell it, because I *am* loopy." Luke opened his mouth. "Just shut up Rose."

He smirked over the shock of her insufferable audacity. "I think I like you." He murmured.

The roller coaster she sent him on as the story unfolded, made it far more difficult to keep his truck from flying off the road into the bush. She had only looked at him once, right before she turned away and mentioned the worst part, and it wasn't what he'd thought he was about to hear, it was worse.

The entirety of her last four years here, had been worse than the assumptions he had. Her friends, the exchanges he'd witnessed, had been something earned over a long, lonely road. When she'd come back from leaving the Anchorage troopers, she had anything but a warm welcome. Something she'd kept well hidden from Kallik Shaw, to not worry him, and Luke wasn't certain if she'd ever mentioned that to anyone else.

The rumors of her actions while badged were thick and had spread back home. Dog thief, crooked cop, abuse of power, assault. While the suspicions were being investigated, the town remained uneasy with her presence. Even the women she grew up with had given her the cautious shoulder, being extra kind when Kallik was at her side, the respect for him among the locals was fierce.

James had gone to help her many times in Anchorage on what she simply called 'rough nights', details Luke was certain involved answers to many suspicions that had been raised about her, but she didn't offer any. James had been the only one who'd come to see her, spend time with her, but for many months wouldn't address her comfortably in public, something she could not explain her forgiveness for.

Luke was beginning to pick up on a pattern of her making excuses for people, out of survival or lack of self-worth, maybe just to convince herself it hadn't hurt her. Perhaps all, he didn't know. Either way, he didn't like it.

Then Bradley Oliver's house on the coast was finished being built, and he saw Sam for the first time.

"He didn't care. About any of it." She shook her head. "None of it. He didn't even ask for details. Just asked about me. He was so attentive, different from anyone I'd ever met. Walked around town with me like I was a trophy, shamelessly. He spoiled me. Took me to dinner. Bought me clothes to help me feel better, showed off my body. They didn't suit me, but he loved me in them. Bought me things I'd never dreamed of owning." She rubbed the pendant on her neck. "Meaningful things."

Luke didn't need to say it. When someone was in such a lonely state. Town snubbing you, the man who raised you deteriorating, no parents to go to, gave up a job you loved... even if she was the cause of that resignation... her childhood alone... most wouldn't see the red flags in Brad at first, when finally feeling good was such a foreign concept. Jesus, she was only twenty-six then...

Luke grunted down his itching tongue. No. He didn't need to say it, the tone of her voice permeated the knowing, painfully.

Then it got darker. Her meeting his sled team. How well they responded to her, how well she groomed the new pups, how they ran better after she came around. He had always come in second in the Iditarod, filled her head with glory if she helped him.

'Race with me Sam. Help me train my team. Who cares who wins? We'll share it together. Don't you want this? I love you Sammy..'

"I gave myself to him so fully. My body was no stranger to it, but my heart was, and I let him have all of me. He told me he would keep me forever. Take me away from all of it. He won my first year back, he was so beautiful in his joy. Said I would always be his greatest prize."

The air stilled and the snow began to fall hard and steady. Luke made the turn onto her private road and began the arduous climb, the words she spoke churning in his ears, boiling his spine.

That summer, Kallik had worsened, and Sam had to focus more on his care. Brad got demanding. Claimed she didn't love him, or care about their dreams.

His dreams, Luke thought.

She had outright exhausted herself trying to care for two men she loved and prepare their teams. She'd noticed the dogs struggling. Exhausted. Injuries going ignored. Brad had been driving them too hard, determined to win again.

When race day came, Sam begged him not to run Sully.

She was exhausted and had refused food. Brad promised he'd watch her carefully and take good care of them, and they pushed off, separating by what had to be miles, based on how long they'd been apart before she came upon Brad bedding down for the night. He was not pleased to see her at first, asking why she had run them so slowly, turning it to demanding why she was on his heels, stealing his show.

So many red flags.

Sully was stumbling and shaking, bile coming up from her. Sam gave her a settling mixture and wrapped her in straw. An argument ensued, Sam pleading they take her in to the vet instead of finish, Brad insisting he could win without her, to leave her.

"Sully was my baby. Roy's the first dog I've ever loved so much since her." Luke stole a glance at her, the cabin coming up ahead. "He softened suddenly, charmed me with warm whiskey and his smooth tongue... Promised, as he took my body, that he'd do what was right for Sully, to sleep, everything was ok. He was sorry. We were more important... the dogs were more imp-" She sucked in a deep breath.

Luke threw the patrol truck in park and didn't dare move, his face pinned on the stalking dog that had just slipped out of the large flap in the door.

"When I woke up, I was so groggy, it was well past sunrise." Sam's head listed to the window. "Sully was dead, my sled rail was broken, and my lead dog missing. She might have gone in her sleep, but I-" She choked. "But I can't say for sure. I broke. Sent up a flair, and waited, devastated. The rescue team came and got us out. I went home. He won 3 days later."

She turned her head to meet Luke's eyes. They were in a state of chaos.

"I was packing the things I kept at his house, I was done, when he pulled up. He was so calm I knew it was going to be bad, still I hoped.... 'You weren't there for me' he said… 'You owe me'…'" She turned away again. "I could have fought him off, but I loved him, thought I did… I was shell shocked. He took what he wanted, as he cried heaving sobs over me, telling me he loved me. That he couldn't live without me. That I needed to understand that Sully was already dying, that he did what he did so I wouldn't watch her die."

"Jesus Christ Samantha."

"It's not like I don't enjoy it rough sometimes." Her damp laugh spoke of that level of intimacy being something sacred and not meant for the evening in question or wanted. "When he was done, he put my things in the car and told me he couldn't have me holding him back from his goals. That'd I'd used him. That he should have known better given the rumors… He was always hot and cold. I put it away for Paw. James helped me cope, but not in the way he should have, we both acknowledged that eventually, and don't sleep together anymore, haven't for a while."

A dark sound came from Luke's depths.

"Don't blame him too much. James gets a little suggestive at times, but he and I have history, we dated in high school."

"Pushy is still BS, Sam." Luke spoke slowly to mute his concern for her self-worth. "History or not you said you were done."

"It is what it is. I'm an adult. In a way I thought being intimate with James would help drown out the feeling of Brad's hands on my body the way they had been, but nothing ever has. I can still feel it sometimes."

"Samantha, why didn't you press charges?" Luke snapped his head to her. "Jesus why didn't you press charges!?"

"I complied and Brad knew it… I never said it was right." She cut off Luke's protest. "Shortly after it all, my record was deemed hearsay, closed. The town suddenly began to relax, my track record must not have been as bad as they heard. No doubt James had let slip of Brad's foul nature. I'm sure Frank helped a bit there."

He wanted to ask her about that track record but didn't dare. Not right now. "Does Frank know?"

"Yes and no. He knows enough. He stood stand by when I went to get the rest of my things from Brad. What he risked helping me in Anchorage… I didn't deserve more of him. Besides, Brad and I had been a tight item for a long time, he got rough, he hurt me, but it wasn't the first time. I had some growing to do, I don't have much relationship experience, but now I know what I don't want."

"You didn't deserve any of this, or *that*. I've never been in love, but I know that's not what love is." Luke wasn't sure if he was helping but didn't know what help he could be. "Frank cares more about you than you realize, from what I can tell."

Sam unbuckled and pulled down her hair, rubbing her head for a moment so the spinning would stop. "My life seemed to balance out a bit with everyone accepting me, even got a few apologies... it was easier just to pretend, let it go." She shrugged coldly, like a paper bag in the water accepting it was going to soak up and sink. "Doesn't matter. I don't need anyone. Just Paw."

Damn this woman had built a fortress around herself, not of cold indifference, but one of desperation, to save herself from feeling *any of it*. She felt, and so much deeper than anyone else he'd come across, but she didn't want to. He didn't need to know her, to feel that burning like a buried volcano from her depths.

She was passionate about everything, broken down to cage it all. She loved hard, hurt harder, deciding to no longer do either.

"Brad came by after about a month. Dropped to his knees and begged forgiveness. Said he'd taken too many pain pills and mixed with the alcohol... that it wasn't him. That I had to forgive him, remember everything he'd done for me. That we looked so good together."

"He tried to make you what he wanted. He didn't do shit for you."

Luke watched her shrug again. With how much strength she pulsed out, he never thought he'd ever see this woman hang her head the way she was in that passenger seat.

"He'd never truly hurt me before that, a part of me believes him, nobody is perfect, but I was done. James drug him down the driveway only because Paw couldn't. I trained hard and exposed his battered dogs at the end of the next race. Officials chalked it up to normal wear on race dogs. Part of that is true, racing is hard, and Brad loves his dogs, but we know money talks, and he does push them too hard, or maybe I'm just too sensitive to dogs because they are the only thing that doesn't hurt me. I'm rambling." She waved a hand, dismissing the vulnerable statement. "I was warned to back off. So I busted his nose last year and was banned from running. I only did it to spite him anyway, and Paw needed so much more from me... So, I just... went back to what I'm good at."

"I am not fond him..." She sucked in a sob. "I hate him."

Luke gently turned her head to face his, a tear rolling down the side of her cheek. "Let's get you inside."

~

Roy was angry for about two seconds before he realized the strange man was holding up his mom, and ran over licking her weak arms, giving the deputy and wary once over with his nose. Luke scanned the layout and determined the stairs led to her room and shifted to help her up them. They were both wet and shivering.

"Paw." She whispered sleepily, pointing to the living room.

Luke lowered her to sit on the bottom step. "I'll check on him, stay here."

The old man was asleep, his breathing seemed steady. Luke loaded a few logs into the wood stove before turning to flick off the light, Roy plopping down at Kallik's feet.

"Good boy. I got your mom buddy." Luke patted his head, surprised he still had his hand attached when he pulled it back. Not really a dog person.

When Luke got back to the steps she was gone. Not wanting to go into her room and not wanting her to hurt herself, the worry of the latter won, and he jogged silently up the steps.

A light coming from the cracked bathroom door to his left, illuminated the trail of a woman who had stumbled out of her clothes messily. Her room was painted with a gold metallic paint that would grab any light the season had to offer from the large window across from him. He found her lying on the large bed beneath that window, the final remnants of her disrobing on the bench at the foot of it.

Thank God she was dressed. Sort of. A large t-shirt and underwear were better than nothing. Her hair was a wild mess of curls sprawled across the pillows, and her breathing was heavy. He crossed the room with careful steps and put a few logs on the smoldering embers simmering in the corner wood stove.

He touched two fingers to the pulse point on her neck and counted. She'd be fine. He didn't feel right leaving the house unlocked, but figured Roy had that covered and would rip apart anyone who would risk this storm. He moved to the window, the snow a blanket of warning, causing a heavy exhale to leave him. He was not looking forward to the hazardous drive down.

The woman passed out safely in her bed was worth it. Every woman was, and any man worth his weight in morality would have done the same. He pulled a blanket over her and turned to leave.

"Stay." Her hand brushed close to a place it should not be.

He ached with masculine need, desire. She would use him to ignore all that had come tumbling out of her, amend it with blurred lines, to not walk the harsh ones she drew in her sobriety.

It'd be easy. A lesser man would. Nothing about the silky skin splayed on that bed made him want to deny the request, but everything about the storm raging inside it, did.

Luke turned his head over his shoulder. "I think in the morning, you will wish I hadn't."

He wanted to hold her, with a small hope to make her feel safe, but something about the way she iced over everything, kept everyone at arm's length, even those who tried to care for her, concerned him. The morning would have her finding a reason to hate him, push him out before he had a chance to hurt her, because she'd find a way he would before he could.

He didn't blame her for it, but nothing would quench that fire until she stopped carrying the tragic steps of her life as if she'd scripted them alone. He stood a better chance just pretending she hadn't unloaded what she had and being a good deputy that offered a casual nod as they passed in the street.

His body wanted otherwise, to sink deeply inside her warmth and hear her cry out, but who's wouldn't?

Still, he had nothing that could mend her, a caged man himself, running from everything he didn't want to be, controlling everything so he didn't lose himself to the trashed legacy of his parents. Even if she thought a night of distraction would numb it, it would only add him to her list of criminals, and he still did not know if she was one.

"Is it because I'm broken?"

God, she made his chest cave. "Sam, Jesus fuck no." He hipped his hands and hung his head, his dick cursing him as he remained steadfast. "Listen, if you ever ask me that again, with a clear head, I'll stay." He began to pull the door closed. "You aren't broken."

"Deputy Rose?... Luke?" He paused. "Thank you. You're a good man."

Her tone spoke more volume than the words. The innocence in her voice at that moment, the grateful, broken little girl, safe in her bed, safe from herself, safe from everyone she wouldn't let near, punched a hole right through him. He managed a nod before forcing himself to walk away.

"I have had dreams."

Luke jumped in the hallway, started by the old man's rasp. "Sir?"

Kallik waited until Luke broke the entry to where he rested. "I dream often. The same dream since she was born. It visits me like the seasons. Lucian Rose, is it?"

"Yes Sir." Luke straightened, trying to look as official as he could, given his soaked hair and civilian attire. "I just brought Sam home. The roads are a mess is all. I'll leave you now."

"You think I don't know how well she can manage these roads son? Or a man? Do not insult my intelligence."

"I ask that you do not insult my integrity, Sir." Luke's voice came out sharper than he intended, immediately grunting down his flaring temper.

Kallik rose his head weakly and looked at him. "I hold hostage a temper as well my boy, so I will not call you what I wish to in response to your assumption, as I believe we are all the children of Creator."

Something told Luke he'd just been spared a slur far worse than Moose-looker or Outside.

"I'm thanking you. I know my granddaughter, and the decisions she makes. You are a good man, Deputy." Kallik lowered his head. "Some closer to her do not hold such honorable reserve as you have shown her this night."

Kallik Shaw was far more observant than his condition would have one believe. Both impressive and threatening, in a fatherly way.

"My apologies Sir. It is what any man should have done. I'll be on my way. I'll have Forest and Willow return her Bronco once the storm clears."

"My dream was not one of fiction it seems."

Luke sighed at the shifting topic, the old man's mind was slipping, and he needed to get gone before the roads worsened.

"You should get some sleep Mr. Shaw. I look forward to meeting you properly at a better time."

"We have met before; your current form simply does not recognize me in the current state of mine." Luke curiously brought himself into Kallik's line of sight, though his eyes remained closed, idly tapping Roy's head. "Bears you see. Always the same two. A young bear, only changed by the years but eyes remaining the same, though they have hardened over time."

The shadows on the wall seemed to dance with the fire, forming shapes to mirror the story as it unfolded on the lips on the old man beside him.

Luke rubbed his eyes.

The snow whipped mercilessly through the dense wilderness. Tall trees dancing as the fire spit. A small black bear wanders, braying for her mother, her father, food, that which a lost cub might wail for. A tattered and worn old grizzly, nudged the furry loaf, guided it firmly, but kind. The little bear stumbled, receiving no hand from the old grizzly, just direction, encouragement.

"Over time, the little bear has grown, still wailing for something, but growing claws, feeding herself, needing the old bear less and less. Wandering in solitude, stopping occasionally to play with a fallen leaf or stray wolf. Still the old bear watches her as he weakens. Strong little bear."

Ah. Sam, himself. Luke put it together. Kallik's concern for her, and now his coming death had manifested into these dreams.

Luke crossed his arms, resting back on his hip to wait out the senile babbling, not wanting to be rude to a respected elder. That would not be a good move, especially from a pale country boy. He felt sorry for him. None of this could be easy, but he had no doubt Sam could take care of herself.

"Save your pity for the weak." Kallik grunted, before a slight cough left him. "These dreams have come since her birth, and do not waver in their tale."

Luke lowered his head in apology, even though the old man's lids remined closed.

The same two bears repeated the dance, over and over on the logged walls. Luke squinted as a form shifted among the bushes that had formed out by the crackling light of the stove. Always watching, never part of the journey. Fumbling through its own but always part of the image as it faded in flickering shadows of antlers and framed photos, to billow back out and repeat the story again.

Luke blinked repeatedly. He was far more fatigued than he'd originally thought. One time in the desert he thought he saw a white wolf standing on a ridge. It had vanished when he'd approached it, but the water well his unit had been searching for was in its place. Fatigue will do strange things to your mind.

"The same dream always, the only change that of the little bear's strength, and the old one's crumbling. Until a few nights ago. The quiet bear finally emerging. Strange fur from the bush. Odd looking. Sticking out amongst the species, seeming to stumble in its environment, but steadfast on its direction you see. Slowly it sniffs upon the trail of little bear's paws in the snow, following them tentatively."

The fire flared and the shadows became larger than life, reaching out on the walls to suck you into their seductive dance. Pull you in to their relentless course.

Luke's arms dropped at his side. One beer and a stressful drive does not make you hallucinate.

The strange new bear slowly closed the distance between itself and the little bear. The old grizzly trailed behind, the gap between the other two widening with every crack and pop of the embers. The strange beast paused only at the swipes and lunges the little bear offered to him, returning to its footsteps after she put some ground between them.

She stumbled and slid, roared angrily at the rugged terrain of the hill she fought to scale. Varying branches and rocks beckoning her to slide down with them. The strange new bear turned his head behind him, the Grizzly raising to his haunches to loose a mighty roar Luke swore he actually heard, before lowering its head to the odd one, and a swooshing shadow of snow taking the grizzly with it.

Then the storm died out completely and the air warmed. Luke physically responded, as he watched the strange bear scale the mountain. It did not lead little bear, it did not trail her, it simple walked beside her, slow and steady, until the wall was nothing more than trophies from hunting trips and grainy photos of ice fishing.

Luke held his stunned expression on a photo of what he assumed was a young Sam, cotton ball of frizz on her head, atop a younger, fit Kallik's shoulders, holding up a fish bigger than her.

Roy whimpered and trotted off, the sound of his weighted paws disappearing up the stairs.

"I don't even know her." Luke said involuntarily.

"Oh…" Kallik smiled, as he scratched his forearm, revealing a faded inked bear paw on it. "But you wish to."

Luke paled. "Sir…" He shook his head and determined he needed to get some sleep, immediately, they both did. "Is there anything I can get you before I leave?"

Kallik began a lazy rock. "You already have."

"Goodnight Mr. Shaw."

Luke jogged up the steps to check on Sam before his exit. Prompted by the whine and move Roy had exhibited, of course, not Luke wanting to see her one more second where she wasn't spitting fire at him.

She was sprawled on her belly, Roy's large paws and head pulling the shirt down from her shoulders where his head rested. Something dark, like a birthmark peeking out from under the collar, called to him.

He shouldn't, but curiosity had brought him to Alaska, so… He lightly moved her shirt down, and Sam nudged her lips across his knuckles, sinking deeper into sleep. A low whine escaped the large dog watching over her, as Luke snapped his hand back and, like the special forces trained man he was, silently ran from the house.

Covered in snow and his mind a pile of slush he could not logically explain, Luke stumbled into the station. It had been a sharp learning curve trudging that plow on his truck, but after many reverses and a tire dig out that had him cursing and kicking himself for not dressing better, he'd made it in by 2am. Tomorrow was going to hurt, and he hadn't drunk enough to warrant it.

He dropped his jacket and leaned over his bathroom sink, brushing his teeth. After splashing warm water on his face, he stood there dripping into the sink, taking deep breaths.

"Hokey pokey bullshit." He squeezed his eyes. "Stability. No chaos. No Storms." Luke pulled his shirt off his chiseled body and stared at himself.

The bear paw tattoo over his heart burned into his defenses. The same tattoo that had been on Kallik's arm.

And Samantha Shaw's left shoulder.

Chapter 9

The storm raged for three days. Not the overnight dropping they'd been told it'd be.

Luke was left to manage the station. No need for Darleen and Anita to come man the phones, when the only calls coming in were reports of outages, a local who got stuck out in the shit on his snow mobile, and an angry tourist who thought the hotel not having milk reserves for his morning cereal was a lack of preparation on Shavila's part. He swore he'd never come back, Luke assured him nobody would care.

His mood had been shot for days.

Sam hadn't answered his text when he'd thought to check on her. He'd like to think it was lack of cell service, but he knew it was more than likely her pride against what she'd spilled a few nights ago, sending his playing piece back to start.

Do not pass go. Do not collect two hundred dollars. All for the best, Luke told himself.

When the storm had lightened, he'd gone out to remove the ropes he'd been told were put out so folks could guide themselves along the walkways. Why anyone would be out walking in that mess was beyond him, but it seemed a normal excursion for many, especially when Big John was offering take home brews.

He shoveled out the patrol truck, and out of sheer need to burn off going stir crazy in that tiny apartment and the high caloric pastries he kept picking at that Darleen had left, he dug out Sam's Bronco, and any other mode of transportation that had been left on the main street, including Denali's bike.

Despite being named after a fierce mountain, that was one teen who'd lose his head if it wasn't attached. Even in the week he'd been here, he'd seen Denali run back into the general store for his house key, and slide into the station to declare his backpack was stolen, while it was on his back. That last one earned him one of Anita's cinnamon rolls and a pinched cheek.

He pounded through each vehicle like a maniac. Throwing snow was good for him, and even though his muscles screamed, and his lungs burned, he was a masochist for physical punishment. It kept him in top shape and kept him in control. Trying to drown out his punishing mind, he ran old drill cadences through his head. It didn't work.

Luke had been too young to remember his father beating his mother, until he wasn't. Until he pegged the old man as often as possible to turn the blows on him. Logan Rose had been a short man with an inferiority complex, and no neck. He was built like a bulldozer, and didn't pull his punches, regardless of who he threw them at. He beat Luke's mother for her drug problem, only to take them and tie off his own arm as she begged for some.

He resented how tall Luke was getting, and beat his ass regularly, dragging him in to the workout room later to insist he get bigger. Luke did, but when he'd lost his last fight against his father, he'd called it in; he had to stop his mother's screams and wasn't strong enough to do it.

Alexis blamed her son for their financial predicament. No doubt Logan knew how to manage his drunk problem and his job well. She used more heavily, and Luke did his best to keep her out of the gutter while finishing school. He graduated by the skin of his teeth, and no doubt pity from teachers who knew his situation, but none of them did a damn thing about it. Guess the passing grade helped them sleep at night.

He'd been scrubbing the head with a toothbrush in the training barracks, reprimand service for fighting again, when his commander coldly handed him the message of his mother's passing. Overdose.

Luke graduated at the top of his class, part of a small handful of other misfits who did not have a loving family member walk up to release them from formation. Luke's commander hand simply put his hand on his shoulder to order 'at ease', and he'd walked off the field, through proud parents and crying girlfriends.

He spent his two-week leave shoveling through a storage unit for the remnants of his life, a few books he loved and some old t-shirts, his father's motorcycle, before heading to the military offices to ask to be sent out, immediately. They'd obliged.

He'd had brothers and watched them die. He'd done what no one else would because he had no one to miss him, and had been immediately sworn into the Idaho State police department upon his application, without so much as a single day in the academy; his glowing marks on his online classes and phenomenal military record requiring nothing more than the penal code test and a slap on the back. He was a good cop, but every time drugs were involved, his temper flared.

That outrageous temper the only thing his father left him besides an inability to trust people, connect. He'd been screamed at by his Chief, many times, wondering why his fugitive was bleeding when he came in, and why that kid had been taken to get ice cream before he was turned over to social services. The amount of drugs Luke hauled off the streets were the only thing that kept his badge on his chest, his record beyond impressive.

It'd also been the only thing that drove Luke to finally disappear into the tiny town of Shavila.

Holding an infant and watching it die in your arms after pulling a needle out of its mother's arm -before helping her through labor in the back of your squad car- would break anybody, no matter how much brain matter had been splattered across your face in war.

He was done. He needed to control his mornings and control his temper. He couldn't see what could possibly set him off here. Moose were easy enough to swerve around and locals were easy enough to oblige. Most of them.

He rubbed his tattoo as he shuffled his tired body into Frank's office. The snow had stopped, and the sun was out, he could hear the plow going and a few voices mingling abut outside. The general store would be open and hopping soon he bet, but school had been set to resume Wednesday. He'd sent out the bulletin himself, much to the joy of many parents who had no desire to haul their kids in on snow mobiles this late in March.

It was looking like Spring would come a bit earlier and warmer than normal this year, according to the 'ever dependable weather man', said every local humorously. Something he wouldn't mind after the bite he'd felt arriving here.

He imagined he'd prefer a better dwelling for the long winter. He'd look into it on his day off, as his mind was so fogged up, he didn't think he could get it up to save his life, even if he did pull a bar bunny in Anchorage.

He lifted his left hand. "You'll be working overtime buddy, nothing new."

The door pinged and he lifted his eyes to see a heavily haired teenager clonking messily in the door.

"The pole by the vet's office, Denali." Luke smiled into the hall. "Imagine the chain is good a frozen still."

Denali flopped his arms and rubbed his head. "Awe man thanks Chief, shit my mom was so pissed. 'Can't afford a new bike' and all that."

"How do you steer that thing on the slick roads man?"

Denali grinned wide. "Pure talent." He turned to go. "And snow tires."

Luke gave an impressive shrug and started the coffee pot. The rumble of an old truck pulled him to the door, much needed coffee forgotten.

Sam tapped her hood like a good dog, before giving Tig a hug and what looked like a big thank you. She shook her head at Denali kicking ice off his bike lock, sending him into a guilty laugh, before she glanced at the station.

Luke involuntarily locked up. Even from across the street he could see those wild green eyes raise arms for battle.

Suddenly she was in nothing but a t-shirt and panties, sprawled on the bed, her hand moving suggestively up his thigh as it had before he'd left her.

His body quickly confirmed that he could, indeed, still perform quite well if he wanted to. He rose a shaky hand to wave.

She reached in and pulled her key out, before heading to the Vet's office, not so much as a smile coming from her.

Maybe it was the glare of the window, and she didn't see him. Still, his body did not give a damn, and his uniformed slacks became tighter by the second.

She messed him up without even liking the bastard. He tried to shift his belt around in futility.

Luke finally glanced at the clock defeated. Nobody would be in for another hour or so.

"Just get it out of your system bud. Get it over with."

He locked the station door and stomped up the steps to his apartment, all but kicking the door in. He couldn't work like this.

The craze of adjusting to this place had made it days since he'd handle himself, and somebody was liable to pay dearly if he didn't check it. For someone only five years from forty, his drive was still animalistic. He chalked that up to his obsessive fitness level, and his body count being rather low, considering, leaving him pent up often.

He had walls up many women couldn't handle, diving deep and quick into women who bailed before the condom hit the trash can, to keep any of them from trying to climb them. There was nothing but rage and fear on the other side anyway.

He ripped his shirt off and started the shower.

He should have just bent Star over a toilet like she'd wanted, anything would have been better than his body surging for a woman who'd rather mop the floor with him, less return a wave. She was nothing like he'd ever come across, and he suddenly realized why Frank had been so taken with her mother. Wild women were a drug, and he didn't touch drugs.

He palmed himself and the wall, trying to push Sam out of his mind with the sight of Star's huge breasts plunging in his face. He'd seen enough of them at the bar to make this work for him. His body responded, blandly, but enough.

He focused on the bar emptying, laying her face down on the bar top, and pulling her dress up. The strap of that tight dress slipped down her shoulder, a bear paw tattoo revealing itself.

Luke's eyes shot open as his erection hardened.

"Ah hell."

He snapped his eyes shut and that dress had become an oversized t-shirt licked with wild black curls raining down her back. She rolled around to face him, and Sam's green eyes shot into his soul as she pulled him into her, her head falling back as she cried out.

His fingers dug into the shower tile as his hand punished his arousal furiously.

His fisted her curls, she said his name, sending him to his knees on the shower floor, buckling under the explosion that had just left him. The water rained on him as he fought to fill his lungs, the image dissipating with the mist.

It had never been that easy, or that intense. Luke punched the wall to pay for his lack of control, his knuckles bleeding. He could not be broken by a woman he may have to cuff.

His body responded to the thought of her in cuffs, on his bed…

"You are pathetic." Luke gritted. "Absolutely pathetic."

~

The little licks were so cute Sam could hardly contain herself as she rolled around the little fluff balls to examine their frostbitten paw pads.

"Poor little things. How long were you out there?"

The barn was a ruckus of curious yips, even though the team was pretty wiped out. It'd been a long time since they'd made the ice-highway haul, but it had to be done, and they did it well last night.

The puppies were a bit too skinny and lacking proper fur for their breed and age, but Chinooks were strong, and she knew they'd be ok, now that she had them.

It'd been one hell of a ride out, cold as sin, snow thick as shit, and they went through a few pairs of doggy booties that'd be pricey to replace. Regardless, she'd known her dogs could handle it, and they'd gotten her and the litter back across the ice in record time this morning.

She'd have to go get them some fresh fish as a reward. Money was tight, but they deserved it, Sam decided, as she put balm on the puppy's feet and administered the shots she'd picked up from the Vet, along with her truck.

Damn she was tired.

With the warm spring coming, break up would be earlier this year, and Sam imagined they'd needed a good straight rip before the summer hit anyway. Her fatigue was worth her dogs doing what they loved best, as was getting these pups out of the hell they'd been in.

"Nothing like some babies in need to rile you all up aye?" The barn sounded off in more a demand than celebration. "Alright alright hold your tails."

Snow White growled slightly at the strange loafs before circling them and plopping down to warm them.

Sam gave Snow a crooked glance as she hauled the steaming food bucket through the kennels.

"Yea we'll see how long that lasts, crabby ol husky." Sam ladled hot dog food and broth into the bowls as she past each team member. "Just give me a warning before you get sick of em and boot em Snow, I'll do my best to move them quick."

Many families were looking to adopt in Spring, big time for new pups. Green grass and kids playing outside with the new addition to the family. Ideal time to train them before they have to run the trap lines, behave inside, or be large enough to endure an outdoor doghouse.

Still, they had to get well first, and she had to rehome quietly. Didn't need anyone sniffing around as to where she got them, not that what she'd done was a crime, where'd they'd come from was the crime. Pigs.

She looked at the skylight and smiled. Lid should be blowing of that shit show in about an hour if it hadn't already. Her smile faded.

Certainly didn't need a law-happy new deputy catching wind of it, fine as he was. And he was-

"Grumpy! Stop lunging for Dopey's food! You got the name for a reason you dick!" Sam laughed and flapped her hands to shove Grumpy off his ego. "Big ol bastard." She ruffled his scruff lovingly and reminded him where his own bowl was, locking his kennel door. "He gets extra cuz He and Doc run the bounties. You would too if you didn't insist on running off you putz."

She walked to the back office in the barn and viewed the peg board across from the couch, made a mark on her map.

"One less to worry about." She sighed. "For now."

Rubbing her sore neck, she flipped through the pages of families she'd printed out. They'd all lost dogs in the last year, a few she had hacked from the humane society's data base.

She plugged her burner phone into the solar battery pack on the table and headed in to make Paw lunch and let him she'd be back in a few hours, potato chips in hand. She loved the man, so if he wanted chips, then back to town she would go.

~

The twins had just left to divide and conquer clearing the out-of-school kids wreaking havoc on the dock, when a ruckus billowed from the front of the station. It was enough to pull anyone out of their funk, sending Luke dumping the case file on the Iditarod dog slayings on his desk, before throwing himself into the main lobby.

Darleen was plugging her ear, fighting to hear a call, as Frank was trying to get James to concede to go down the cell hall, in cuffs.

"James come on now son, we gotta take it as it was. It's a serious charge."

Frank was a hand shorter than James and decades more worn, but he held the pissed of pilot steadfast.

"A nap in the cell ain't gonna kill ya until I take down the report and figure what's what."

"This is bullshit Frank!" James jerked. "Idiot face planted drunk and ain't nobody saw me do shit!"

"Well, I can't very well do nothin' about it, so knock it off before resisting arrest will be enough!"

James gave Luke a glare as he yielded to the walk down the cell hall.

Bradley Oliver sat swollen faced and indignant in the row of chairs in the waiting area, murdering Luke with his eyes.

It was going to be a long day.

"You eat baby?" Anita offered Luke some scones. "You look like you got snowplowed honey."

"Or snow plowed *somebody*." Brad hissed.

Luke's face reddened but he kept his cool, ignoring the asshat out for blood. "No thanks Anita. Appreciate it." She lifted a brow. "I ate, promise. Just a little wiped out from the storm."

Brad sucked his teeth. "Or fucking one."

Luke was inches from Brad's face before the man could stand up.

"I *know* you little spit fuck." Luke's voice was low and just for Brad, who had suddenly gone pale. "So, while others may kiss your ass because you have gold in your veins, it will never make up for the mud it mingles with."

Brad scowled as Frank walked in, catching the tail end.

"My office, both of you."

Frank dropped the file on his desk, as Willow jogged in, handed him a paper and another file, and ran back out to his charge.

Frank eyeballed the paper, briskly tucked it in the file it'd come with, and sat back. It was the same file Luke had left on his desk.

He opened his mouth to inquire when Brad threw photos of mutilated dog kennels and the busted front end of his truck, on the desk in front of Frank.

"I got four puppies missing, a busted vehicle and a busted face, all on the same night." Frank flipped through the photos as Brad barked. "You know Sam has a history of taking dogs Frank, and that hairy gorilla you have in that cell, has a history of taking *her*."

Luke bit his cheeks, his crossed arms strained to busting. The way Brad spoke of her, any woman really, was deplorable and Luke had had about all he could handle.

"She was at the bar that night, was she not?" Frank seemed almost, bored.

It didn't escape Luke.

"Yea so? Doesn't mean they didn't pull it off before they came, busting my face for good measure. If it wasn't for the storm, I would have reported it sooner. James and Sam showed up together."

"False." Luke stated. "They came in separate vehicles, you were already inside, far too busy with your hand up Angela's shirt to notice. The timing cannot be proved nor verified." Brad's mouth dropped in shock. "Small town Mr.Oliver. I'm a quick study."

"Regardless, there is more than enough probable cause to look into it, and you know it, Frank. As for that idiot James," Brad tugged his coat and sat down. "I want to proceed with charges. Your sparkling new deputy saw James bust my head in."

"Deputy Rose?"

Luke casually lifted a shoulder to his ear. "Brad spit a little vinegar his way, nothing too serious, it simmered out."

Actually, it had infuriated Luke to the point of wanting to pummel Brad's face until it disintegrated, but that was irrelevant.

"I was leaving when they parted ways."

"Bullshit!" Brad spit, stepping up to Luke. "You saw and did nothing! You practically allowed it to happen! Encouraged him! Crooked ass cop!"

"You're gonna want to step back from me civilian," Luke was stone-faced, "before a single slip of your finger catches you a bigger charge, one I have no problem filing."

"Badge pushing Moose-looker."

Frank laughed and sat back. "Brad, boy, you are LA money on Alaskan coastline. Shut your mouth and sit the hell down."

Brad remained standing but backed up rather quickly from a very pissed of police officer.

"Didn't see huh? Tell him why Deputy Rose."

Frank folded his hands on his belly, intrigued.

"Miss Shaw found herself in a compromised position and required a ride home." Frank's eyes slitted. "I dropped her off and returned to the station, as I would have done for any woman in a vulnerable state."

"Certainly." Frank steepled his hands. "Well, that lines up with what I took down from James as well Brad. Since no one else was outside, and you had been drinking last night, I have no way of knowing if your face was a result of James, or *you* smashing the front end of your truck, driving when you shouldn't have. Perhaps you should have let Deputy Rose give you a ride home as well."

"This is such horseshit." Brad balked.

"What's horseshit is you driving under the influence and trying to peg it on a man who is friends with a woman who left you." The vein in Frank's forehead was bulging and he began to shake.

Luke lifted from his lean.

"What's more," Frank slapped at the file of the Iditarod incident. "Is nobody saw these two dogs after the start line, and you've showed up without team members before."

"No, but that-"

"Shut up!" Frank stood. "No tire tracks but your own at your home the night they were hung, not even the many town hussies you pull up there. So, who should I be investigating Bradley Oliver!? A man who has a witnessed history of mistreating his sled team," He slammed his hand on the table, "or the girl who has unwitnessed *rumors* of mistreating the men who hurt them!"

Luke thought Frank would burst into flames at any second. It was a part of himself Frank had kept well hidden.

"Perhaps I should take my concerns to the Anchorage department Bradley hmm? Something isn't adding up with you."

Luke had never perceived Frank capable of such an unprofessional outburst, not that he himself had not just had one, he had just whispered through it. Still, this was a bit of a reach. Or was it?

Maybe Luke was looking in the wrong direction, and his focus should be expanded to a more suspicious suspect… and stop looking at Samantha Shaw like one.

Bradly fumbled over his swollen lip. "No I… I run em hard Frank I do, but I don't hurt my dogs I swear! I love my dogs. I just know when it's time to let go is all. Sure they get injuries and all but… no no… Sam and I fell in love over dogs!" He looked panicked. "You know I would never hurt my dogs, Frank!"

"You fell in love with what Sam *could do*… for your dogs," Frank corrected, easing his tired body into his chair. "And you know damn well Sam is incapable of hurting them as well."

Brad nodded faintly. "Ok, listen I- … I'm angry. The rest I'll figure out, forget it ok? Maybe they just wrestled their way out ya know?" He flicked his eyes to Luke nervously. "But missing pups aside, James assaulted me Frank, I have to get my tooth replaced." He pulled his lip back.

"Your word against his Brad. Nothing I can do." Brad fumbled up his photos and turned to leave. "And kid?" Brad turned. "If you cannot act like a man, you had best get used to fighting like one."

The silence hung, after Brad left, like a spouse had just walked in on their lover in bed with another, and it unsettled Luke.

He grabbed some coffee to do something with his hands.

Finally, Frank rapped his knuckles on the Iditarod file. "You seem pretty focused on this case Deputy. Focused enough to take a woman to bed for information?"

It was not a case question. It was a personal demand for an explanation.

Luke's duty belt creaked as he sat and kneed his elbows, giving his boss a hard look that drew a line in the sand.

"With all due respect Chief, what I do with my dick is no concern of yours, unless I use it with my badge on." Frank's lip twitched angrily. "Out of respect for you; Yes, I took her home. No, I did not sleep with her, nor have I attempted it."

Luke sipped his coffee trying to keep his cool. He wasn't sure if what Sam did to his insides, showed on his outsides.

"However, if for some reason it does happen, Chief Frank Brown, it is none of your god damn business."

"This ain't the city kid. We're a community. It *is* my business if you're going to use the girl like that to get information, especially that one."

"I have no doubt in my mind Sam didn't hurt those dogs." Luke rose and set his coffee cup on the table. "But I have heard of enough men in this town hurting one woman, to not put myself in the position to become one of them. Good afternoon." Luke slipped up the file with intention and marched out before Frank could counter.

"Hey honey you want a-"

"Not now Anita!" Luke snapped, slamming out the door of the station.

"Jesus Frank what'd you spit at that boy?" Darleen balked. "He's mad as hornets!"

Frank scratched his beard and shook his head. "Not mad." He grabbed a scone and bit into it. "He's on a drug I haven't seen in many, many years. And the poor idiot doesn't even know it yet."

Chapter 10

Main street was beginning to come alive with activity. A few folks shuffling in to retrieve their cars, a good number of tourists excited the bar was open early. Something Luke told himself he was out here to keep an eye on, and not sitting in his patrol truck brooding.

He flipped through the file again, narrowing his eyes on the report Willow had taken down.

Known dog breeder's kennels destroyed outside Anchorage.
4 puppies missing, 5 found dead.
Outside kennel destroyed.
Possible connection to Iditarod dog incident.
Further combing of the property underway.

Date of occurrence was yesterday. Willow had noted the department had called and asked them to see if Brad had any enemies or knew of anyone who'd shown this kind of behavior before.

Luke clapped the file shut and ran his hands through his hair in frustration. What the hell was going on?

Nobody had seen or heard from much of anyone during the few days the storm raged, all assumed to be at home waiting it out. The train wasn't running, and nobody could fly in that. Frank had read Willow's note before his outburst against Brad. If they were connected, there was no way Brad could have gotten there and back, so Frank's accusations were simply to throw Brad off his mark, off Sam's mark. He'd threatened him, in a roundabout way.

Then again, a good team of sled dogs could have made the ice highway and back in that time. It would have been a suicide run, but it could be done. The weather had lightened the last day. It was more than doable for an Iditarod runner... or a previous one. Brad could have.

Still, Sam hadn't answered his text, and neither of them could be accounted for. The report didn't say if the other puppies were killed or simply already dead when the others were taken. Unlicensed breeders weren't exactly known for humane conditions.

People had plenty to say about both of them, but Brad was the only one who claimed she could have hurt those dogs.

The way Luke saw her protect them on the bounty, the way she was with Roy, and every damn person who truly knew her speaking so highly of her love for dogs, Luke refused to believe she had anything to do with either incident.

It had to be Brad. Playing up some sick game for attention, or revenge on Sam, trying to take her down? Why so long after the fact? They'd been apart for years. Well, that punch was last season...

Sam's accusations in the force had been tossed, but they were all connected to dog theft and assault against dog abusers. It didn't look good, but she wouldn't lynch dogs she helped train, dogs she loved, especially how devastated she was about Sully.

Sam seemed more broken than angry with Brad.

No, Luke decided. Either they both were Brad, or they weren't connected, and another person was slinking by their eyes. Sam could have made that run yesterday. Or they had some maniac on their hands that none of them knew? Maybe more than one?

Luke banged his head against the seat repeatedly. Everything spun around her like a tornado, yet nothing landed.

A rap on his window jolted him from his thoughts.

"Thanks for the jail brake copper." James shook Luke's hand and lit a smoke. "Might dislike you a little less now."

"Yea well, just doing my duty." Luke glanced in his rear-view mirror.

Sam was walking out of the vet with Star, bags of potato chips in her hands.

"Guess they waited long enough to haul you in huh?" Luke played cool. "Storm was pretty good."

James took a long pull and zipped up his coat. "Ya, Frank gave me a ring to come talk to him yesterday morning, Brad blowing up his phone, but I had to finish helping Kallik. Didn't know I'd be arrested when I was done!"

Luke leaned up to watch his face. "He alright?"

"Oh yea just sleeps a lot. Sam just doesn't like leaving him alone too lo-." He stopped suddenly, took a long drag. "She needed help shoveling out the dogs and juggling the old man's meds." James tapped the door. "Thanks again. See ya round."

God damn it.

Luke truly felt Sam didn't hurt the dogs, but did she take Brad's puppies? Manage to take the other's near Anchorage too? In the span of three days and a storm? She'd have to be superwoman to pull that off. Maybe there was two working together…

Sam threw a couple of brown bags into her car and gave Star a hug. The seductive vet pulled her fingers across her mouth in a zipped-motion and waved her off.

Luke straightened as Sam drove by, her eyes jerking away from his as she peeled out towards her house.

He was about to trail her, when his radio squawked. "Go ahead Darleen."

"Anita this time Deputy, I'm older but I'll make it worth your while."

"Gross." Forest's voice radioed in teasing.

Luke huffed a laugh and jiggled the mouthpiece. "No doubt you would Vixen. What ya got for me?"

"OH! Vixen I like that!"

Luke had his knuckle over his mouth chuckling when a snowball hit his window and some kids ran back giggling to their face-palming parents. Luke waved off their apologetic hand signals.

Frank was right in more ways than one. Small towns were a whole lot different than the city, but this, this Luke could definitely get used to. Steady. Comfortable. Safe. That was it.

Shavila felt like security, a warm home, a dinner table. He'd never had it, and it was sinking into his skin more every day. A woman would never get past those barriers, but Alaska, Shavila… Well, Shavila just might, if he could make sense of this damn dog issue.

"Got some moose-lookers causing hell at the bar." That didn't take long. "Angela called, it's her first day waitressing and she's a bit rattled. Afraid Big John will make a head roll if you don't go put that stove on simmer."

"I'm on it Anita, don't fall sleep till I get back."

"Deputy Rose you dog!"

Luke laughed and lifted his height out of the cab, fixing his hat and belt before heading across the street to the bar.

He walked in and it didn't take him long to spot the issue.

The two men in Big John's face, or rather, John was in theirs, had snow jackets on that had yet to see a single winter. Angela was over by the tap, looking a far cry from the spicey energy she was giving out when he'd seen he on Brad's lap last week. She looked rattled.

"I said get out of my bar." John scowled, damn near twice his size, like that was even possible.

"Listen pal, you get a hot piece in here like that and you expect us not to look?"

The guy looked like he should be skiing in Aspen at his private resort, not in Shavila.

Great, Luke thought. Another Brad-type.

Funny how quickly the vibe of this town had already gotten under his skin, and into his heart. He wanted to protect it. Protect a lot of things... *her.*

Two men might be a handful if it got messy, even if Luke was a big man in his own right, and nobody could wrangle Big John alone, no matter how big you were. He quietly radioed for Willow and Forest, before narrowing his focus and engaging.

"Looking is free, touching costs you teeth pal." John clapped the man up by his arm.

"Hands off Big John." Luke squared up between them. "What's going on buddy?"

John shoved the guy back and tugged his half apron back around straight on his large frame. "Rolex-Ralph over here thinks he can slap a waitress's ass when she walks by and not get thrown out."

Aspen's friend threw his head back. "So *she* says. We were just thanking her for the excellent service. We tip well."

You've got to be kidding. Luke glanced at Angela who looked like she was about to cry as she shakily placed a drink on the counter.

"An ass slap wouldn't rattle her that much." Luke slitted his eyes. "Stay put."

After assuring Angela she was fine, and he'd keep her safe, he got her to spill it, sending her to the back before he returned, Willow and Forest flanking the door.

"Telling a girl you'll both be waiting for her when she gets off work after she repeatedly told you she wasn't interested, is a threat, not a thank you." Look twirled his finger in the air. "Clear out. Do not come back to this street or I'll arrest you for harassment."

The two men began to scoff and laugh. Luke zeroed in on their eyes; pupils the size of olives.

They were cracked out of their heads.

No. Luke's blood began to boil. Not here.

"Awe you rural folk are so touchy; we'd take good care of her." Aspen boy slapped his hand on Luke's shoulder and paid dearly for it.

Luke clipped the tourist's foot and shoved him, sending him to his ass while simultaneously grabbing Aspen's arm and twisting it behind his back, pinning his belly to the bar.

Willow and Forest had immediately engaged, hauling the side kick up and holding him firm.

Luke wanted to break this puke's arm. He could write a book on how many native women go missing every year and nobody cared. Visions of them forcing that shit into Angela's veins was sending him into a war-level fury he'd wish didn't live in him. Control Marine. Steady Deputy.

95

Sam was suddenly glad she'd taken Big John up on that truce beer. A good show like this? Hell, everybody needed a little fantasy fuel now and then, and Deputy Lucian Rose was good for it.

"You can't do this man, I ain't done shit! Fucking assault!"

"Stop struggling." Luke bit. "You got anything on you I should know about?"

"Hey boss?"

Luke whipped his head to Forest, holding up a balled-up piece of tin foil from his current charge, kicking a dirty spoon that'd hit the ground, presumably when Luke had dropped him.

Luke pulled out his cuffs and ratcheted them on his catch.

"Guess that answers my question." He pulled him back and spun him around. "You are being detained. You have the right to remain silent."

"I just met him! I don't do that stuff!"

"You bought it Tom!" The side kick struggled as Willow cuffed him and spread him for the search.

Mirandas were read and more paraphernalia was pulled and bagged by Luke's truck at the station. Forest and Willow hauled them in to call for transport to Anchorage and start the paperwork.

Luke sprayed his hands down with alcohol and was shaking them off when a snowball hit his chest again.

"Okay, the timing is not the best right now kids-" His tongue turned to lead as Sam stood there, tossing a snowball in the air, plotting her second shot. "Thought you went home?"

She shrugged and bent down to pack more snow onto the ball.

"Nobody turns down a beer offered from a guy who's teeth ya knocked out." She planted that snowball square in his chest. "Thought you could use a cool down after that hot take, Deputy."

He brushed the snow off himself and hooked his thumbs in his duty belt. "Caught that huh?"

"I did. Might need a cool down myself actually." She adorably scrunched her face and winked.

Luke had no idea how to handle her like this. At all.

"Unless you'll let me make you to dinner first, Deputy?"

Her eyes were dangerous. Tantalizing emeralds that could render a man weaponless regardless of how much clothing covered her body.

Luke cleared his throat. "I'm sorry?"

"I didn't stutter Deputy, and if I did, well, I guess you heard me twice." She headed towards him.

He instinctively took a sidestep back, a brace move that happened automatically whenever someone approached him unexpectedly. His heel hit his tire.

He had nowhere to go.

"Doesn't the man pay for dinner?" Smooth Luke. Real smooth. Nobody would every believe you'd talked your way into saving lives in hostage situations.

"I said make, not buy. I'm guessing you don't cook."

"Ah, no."

"Me either. I bake but." Her lips formed a teasing curve. "Guess we'll see if we live through it."

He answered with that damned half smile, creating that stupid dimple of his. She hadn't seen it in a hot minute. He was so odd. Like a caged animal stalking back at forth. Begging to be released but taking comfort in the bars. She had a thing for strays...

His face twisted a slight angle of doubt. "Why the change Ms. Shaw?"

She got close and craned her neck to look up at him.

"Drugs took my mother. A man took what he wanted from me. Any man who doesn't hesitate to take down those who do either, and gives compromised assholes like me a ride home in a storm, has more than earned himself a dinner." She flicked her gaze to his lips and back to his bewildered expression. "So, Sunday?"

~

The rest of the week kept Luke rather busy, helping his mind stay off what he'd agreed to in an arrest haze earlier in the week. He'd been too busy to fine tooth comb the file, and Frank hadn't mentioned it. He was starting to think maybe he was overthinking it.

He could also be trying to convince himself of that due to a pair of green eyes that'd had eaten him alive on Monday.

Luke wasn't Chief yet, and if the chief of police wasn't pushing the subject, maybe he didn't need to either. Luke was struggling to figure out how something that happened on the mainland had anything to do with Brad all the way over here anyway. Seemed a personal isolated incident, or self-inflicted, and they had no leads.

Frank had been rather distracted lately, but it'd been picking up around town amongst tourists. He'd even overheard the twins mumbling about the Mercado twins 'locking their panties' till they got some 'quality time', as they had been so busy.

Brad had been quiet and demure, a good boy, and James had been enjoying the bar or MIA all week. At the very least, he needed to get to know this town better, pay attention, before he could make any assumptions.

The last time he'd assumed, it was about a certain icy female, and she'd just knocked him off his horse and made him agree to dinner.

According to Vanessa, she never agreed to anything, and he'd gotten her out to the bar last weekend.

Luke:1 Sam:1.

He'd managed to find time to text Sam a 'hi' once, after he'd noticed she hadn't been in town for a few days and got a middle finger emoji back. The fork emoji that followed, he hoped, was a dinner reminder and not meant for his eye.

The days were getting longer, tourists were filing in, but the snow had made for a paper pushing week of traffic reports and one giant moose that had to be dispatched. The meat was apparently processed by a local family and handed out to those in need, something that had Luke falling more in love with this little rock.

He'd had to peel Denali off some teen-tourist for making fun of his bike and sent them both in separate directions.

Exhausted, but not in the soul sucking way, Sunday evening had come, and he headed to pick up some wine at the general store.

~

Sam fed and medicated the puppies.

Star had run some tests on the blood Sam had brought in earlier in the week, no parvo. Thank Creator for small favors. They had done good the past few days, but they had kept her locked to the house and busier than normal. It was good.

She'd run one bounty, but had spent a lot more time with Paw, and that was something she was soaking up. Even if most of it was just talking, sharing memories and reading to him. The photo album had brought here to tears, but she'd needed it. Her life had been hard, but she was so lucky to have Paw see her through it.

She had a few other things she needed to accomplish, but Paw needed her, and he would be number one until...

Roy snarled and backed into her. He was miffed as hell with the pups and curled his lip at them anytime they got near him.

"Awe come on buddy," Sam patted her leg, and they left the barn. "You're still my number one guy. Always you and me pal. I'll never replace you. You know that."

She showered and diffused her curls, deciding not to pick apart why she took the time to do so and not just let them air dry like usual. Black leggings and a loose white tank top over a sports bra would have to be enough. Black liner and simple black studs.

She didn't know how to dress for this crap anyway.

Her reflection was showing a bit more tone as of late. She could stand to eat better, but the stress was killing her appetite. She flipped the standing mirror away from herself and jogged downstairs.

She'd assumed he had next to nothing in his apartment, so she loaded a box with supplies and pots and muscled it into her Bronco. Roy jumped into the cab.

"Not this time pal, I need you to watch Paw, I won't be long."

"A date then?" Kallik took the book she'd been reading to him in exchange for his half-eaten dinner plate.

"No Paw, just a dinner with a friend. The new deputy. He got some drugs out of the town today and-"

"That meant a lot to you."

Sam snickered. "Or revved my engine a bit."

"Gross Samantha."

"I'm kidding I'm kidding." She put the phone by his chair and pulled his blanket up, kissing his forehead. "I won't be long. I'll be back in time for your 11:30 dose, okay?" She went to go and stopped in the doorway. "I love you Paw."

"And I you, my little bear."

Sam bounced to her coat, locked the door and jogged from the house.

"Kidding, my Alaskan-ass, kid." Kallik Shaw smiled wider than he had in months and turned off his phone.

~

"Never paid so much for wine in my entire life." Luke mumbled.

Charlotte clicked her tongue. "Neither have I Deputy, but suppliers catch wind of a dry town turning on the tap, and they hike up their prices. It's bullshit."

"I agree."

She scanned the crackers, cheese.

"Flowers?" She dropped the blooms and elbowed the tiny table to get close to him. "Spill it. Who is she? I won't tell."

"Like hell you won't." Luke rolled.

She eyeballed his face interrogatively, causing it to redden steadily. Finally, she glanced over the purchases again as he dug out his wallet.

"Dog treats? Why do you-" She sucked in a breath and slapped her hand to her gaping mouth.

"Don't do it." Luke blushed. "God damn it Charlotte, shut your hole."

He regularly went into the general store and had quite a rousing relationship with Tig and Charlotte. He really liked them both, and they stocked good protein bars.

Dumping the pockets of the occasional thief and dragging him out by the ear to their parents did wonders for their friendship too. Booking a local kid just didn't work well here but having them come mop the floors after school for a week seemed to do the trick. Ruining a rich kid's vacation doing the same thing had been far more satisfying. He liked that so much better, seemed to have the desired effect too. Hadn't nabbed the same kid twice. Not yet. It'd been an eventful week.

Charlotte flapped her hands. "Oh my god Oh my god Oh my god."

Luke pulled his trooper hat down and lowered his head. "Charlotte, I'll arrest you for disturbing the peace." He was so red. "I swear to hell I will."

"Like spit Deputy." She put her hands up before scrambling to bag the items with theatric calm. "Okay okay, I'll be quiet for twenty-four hours. That's it."

"Nice of you." He took back his debit card and grabbed his bags.

"I'll be prying her for details, Rose!"

Luke turned and walked backwards out the door. "Your funeral Charlotte!"

"It'll be a good death!" She laughed boisterously and began scanning Vanessa's purchases.

"I've never had to work so hard to bite my tongue." Vanessa whispered.

Charlotte winked. "You and me both girl. Creator help him."

Vanessa sighed. "He seems like a decent guy. It could be good for her, ya know?"

"Or very bad. Here's hoping."

The town was planning a local baseball game after the big break up, and Luke had walked in on the battle of the bulge in the station. It went on for far longer than he'd expected and was still raging after he'd dropped his bags into his flat, his presence fiercely demanded by all present.

After Frank and the twins went toe to toe with Big John and Tig, it was decided that all deputies needed to be on the same team. 'For morale' Forest had demanded, sending Tig into a snow kicking fit and swearing they should draw names from hats next year. Luke made it clear he'd never played ball of any kind, and Big John had called him an outright idiot for not playing basketball.

"With those broad shoulders?" Anita fanned herself. "He should have been a linebacker!"

"Give it a rest Anita." Frank drawled.

"Awe no." Luke winked at her. "She knows she's got me."

Anita feigned a faint and Darleen started waving her arms in a dramatic show of revival, before finally proclaiming that was quite enough nonsense and shoving them all out the door.

"Try ladies against the gents this year boys." She challenged. "I got $50 on the ladies."

The men stood silent for a moment, contemplating the idea.

Some paperwork was finished, trash cans emptied, and Luke made a quick stop at the bar to grab a last-minute thought while the sun dimmed its glow slowly.

"Sure you don't want to come to dinner son?" Frank zipped his coat as Luke jogged back into the station. "Calls are going to my cell so you can enjoy your night off, maybe sleep in tomorrow. I may have to leave, but Darleen makes a mean lasagna."

"Thanks Frank. I better get some sleep."

Frank's eyes drifted to the narrow stairwell that led up to Luke's flat. "Be good to her."

Luke jerked a nod and locked the station, killing the lights. Was he wearing a sign? 'Be good to her'? She's a grown ass...

Her. Shit.

He hadn't asked Sam where, what time, nothing. He shouldn't just show up at her house without calling. That certainly hadn't gone well last time, and he kinda liked didn't-want-him-dead Sam. He jogged up the stairs. "You're such an idiot Lu-".

Sam leapt around with a start to Luke slamming through the door, sending a spoon with sauce sputtering to the floor.

She had bare feet poking out of her leggings, which seemed out of place with how cold it was, her hair was a wind whipped willow tree of swirls encased with darkness, teasing to tantalize you or wrap around you and drag you to a watery grave.

It wouldn't be the first time Luke had considered allowing both.

She cursed at the mess on the floor, and something was starting to boil in his sorry excuse for a kitchen.

Slab with a burner really. Who was he kidding, it was hideous, and she was standing in it barefoot. He loved and hated it all at once. He'd never had a woman in his kitchen before. Come to think of it, he'd never had a kitchen.

"How did you get in here?" He rasped, the shock of her, doing what it always did to him.

"Uh, the door?"

"Where... where did you park?"

"You gonna interrogate me Deputy, or make me a martini?"

Luke noted the bottles in his hand and shook his head. "Shit sorry I uh, need a shower. I wasn't sure when we were going to do the dinner thing. Guess I should have..."

She walked over to him and took a bottle from his hand. "I'm not taking you to bed tonight cop, so you can skip the shower and-" The timer pinged. "Does now work for you?"

~

Sam was in his apartment. He couldn't believe it. Was she out of her mind? She never agreed to any outing, and she'd taken him up on two now. This guy was a simple replacement, right? Somebody to come in, clueless, and take over the department. Not get close to the one he himself was trying to… it didn't matter.

She couldn't stay from Kallik long, so while he couldn't accomplish much tonight, less risk running into her on her way home, he could take comfort that not much could happen in an hour or two. He'd make the next move when the time was right. Patience had never been his strong suit, but she was worth it. This was all worth it.

Justice needed to be served, and the badges in this town had already proven they don't do that very well. Not in this case anyway. Sam would never have agreed to dinner if she thought she'd be interrogated, so he didn't have to worry about the deputy finding too much tonight. He was Bold, but stupid. Ass hat couldn't see what was playing out right under his blind, smitten nose. Now that he thought about it, Luke was a good distraction for her right now.

Chapter 11

Luke did shower, after he'd loaded the small woodstove in the living room, if only to use it as an excuse to gather himself. Sam was just easy like Sunday morning in his space, as if it wasn't weird, she'd just let herself in.

He'd taken plenty of women to bed, but just a need to be filled and he'd never, *ever*, been fed by one. At least not in a way that looked… so unnervingly normal, easy, as if it'd always been. There was nothing normal about that honey badger in his kitchen, but the first thing he did was make sure her feet weren't cold, as she laughed at him for worrying about it…

He'd never had more than bare walls and a bed after he'd left home, let alone a kitchen for a woman to giggle at him in. After the military, being a cop consumed his life, and he'd only needed a place to crash, nothing more. He usually showered at the gym and certainly never took the time to date.

He never wanted to. It would just be a distraction from work, and he never wanted to risk losing his temper. It scared the shit out of him and figured it would be worse if he loved someone. His Dad always claimed it was.

Maturity knew better, his fear didn't.

He watched his mother hurt so much at the hands of a man, and was hurt by her frequently, deeply… He'd seen atrocities done in the military few would ever admit, only to take those traumas with them to a self-inflicted grave.

Luke rubbed his face with soap. Human beings were dangerous, and he'd rather just deal with the ones he knew needed to be caged.

It just had never been worth it.

He wanted to be in control of how he felt, and not let anyone have that. Yet some angry green-eyed dragon with a personality he'd never encountered before, makes it clear he can pound sand, and he suddenly wants to frolic in it. He gets ready to let the tide come in, wash his fantasies away before he did something stupid, and she offers to cook him dinner.

This is why being a cop appealed to him. Laws, protocol, sleep, repeat. Dependable, stable, calculated risks.

He palmed the wall grumbling.

Guess that's why she intrigued him so much. She didn't make any sense. She kicked him back and reeled him in. Or he was making that up and had lost control, while she'd been merely existing in a way that seemed to cripple him just thinking about it.

Nothing about Samantha Shaw made him feel in control. It should send him running, but here he was, showering so he could balance his head and make sure she *didn't* run. The plan had backfired slightly, considering the woman he'd fantasized about in this very shower a few days ago, blowing his desires out like a cannon, was stirring something that smelled so good he might lose his load again.

His sex threatened to oblige him.

"Don't you dare, help me out here man."

He slammed the water off and was rubbing his hair dry when he found her with a martini in one hand and balancing two stacked bowls in the other.

"I have bowls?"

She set them next to the boiling pot before turning to him. "No. But I do."

Sam brushed the curls hanging in her eyes back and stared a moment.

He was rubbing that dark brown hair with a hand towel, those chocolate eyes darting around like landing them on her would activate a hundred-year-old curse. White V neck and black sweatpants that showed off, what she already knew he was packing, when she'd made that towel drop in a start last week. She'd had a hell of a time ignoring it, and that disciplined build he hid under that uniform.

Could have been a testosterone driven, strategy move on his part, but something told her he didn't have much laundry, and wouldn't bother to do it until his last pair of boxers demanded. She shared the sentiment anyway. She'd rather shovel shit than do laundry.

He tossed the towel towards the bathroom and leaned across the counter, spinning the wine he'd bought to read the label.

"You curious what I made?" Sam said over the rim of a glass, that she also brought.

"The smell tells me I won't care." Luke stood up and frowned at the bottle. "Curious how I'm going to open this bottle though. Didn't think about it."

Sam flipped her pocketknife out of her sports bra and had the bottle open, before he had a chance to worry about cork bits floating in the ferment.

"Impressive."

"I aim to please." She poured Jambalaya into the bowls and turned to face him. "Where do we sit?"

Luke blushed and looked around. "I uh, didn't really think about that either."

He frowned again at the dirty love seat and coffee table that had just received a phone call from the 70's telling it to come home.

Sam bumped him with her hip and headed towards it. "Couch it is."

His planned chivalry was in serious trouble. He'd heard stories. Military men talking about their wives, girlfriends… recent lays. Women were not so easily pleased, he'd learned.

Yet she didn't even bat an eye at the arrangements. He'd seen her place. It was modest but it was nice, clean, and she spent her winters beyond comfortable. It was clear she loved to read and had a knack for plants. How does anyone keep plants alive in this climate? Kallik had really gone all out building that house. Luke had never seen such gorgeous floors and the bed…

Her bed looked like it had been hijacked from an ancient elf colony. Sleeping on trees was suddenly appealing.

She plopped down without even a glance at the dust lurking there; Her lack of disgust proving she clearly had no designs on him outside of filling his gut as a drug-bust thank you. Hell, Darleen brought him a plate of leftovers twice, simply for scrubbing the station's head.

He decided to ignore his disappointment and put reality in check. Problem was, he didn't want to, and by the way she rose her brow at his hesitation, he really wanted reality to take a hike.

They sat quiet for a few minutes, his legs wide, elbows to knees as he ate. His broad body and long legs took up most of the couch, and she looked so small sitting cross legged next to him. He smiled internally.

Samantha Shaw was anything but small, and he'd put money on her in a fight any day, but it tickled him in a weird way, a foreign way he had no experience with, how feminine and soft she looked against his bulky frame. He liked it.

He noticed things about this woman he wasn't even looking for, had never looked for, and it stirred in his belly like a deep thirst even the desert hadn't shown him.

Time was an illusion, and she'd slithered into his cells like the first hit of heroin and taken root. She was a drug, and she didn't even have to try. The silence suddenly got too loud, even for a minimal talker like Luke.

"I thought you said you couldn't cook?"

His full mouth made her laugh, spilling some on her white tank. "Well, I clearly can't eat." She rubbed a paper towel on it. "That's never coming out."

Luke chuckled and kept shoveling his face. "This is really good thank you. What's in it?"

"When I hear the spoon scrape the bottom, I'll tell you."

He froze. "It's not dog, is it?" She slowly drug slitted eyes to him.

He thought he was about to lose his grill to her knuckles, until he saw the corner of her mouth twitch.

"Sorry Sam, that was-"

"Funny. Risky play, but funny."

"Yea well, I'm not the smoothest man on Wall Street." He sat back and marveled his full stomach. "Okay chef, give."

She poured them more wine. "Squirrel."

"No shit?" He put his hands behind his head. "Squirrel Jambalaya. First for everything."

Sam curled her feet under her and rested her head on her hand. "If you're not hugging the toilet later, we'll know they didn't have parasites."

Luke scowled. "That wasn't funny."

"It was a little."

"You have a sick sense of humor Samantha." And a stunning mouth when you smirk.

"I'm just sick period."

"No, you're not." Luke reached for his wine and took a big gulp. "Bit of a wild card maybe, but you aren't sick."

"Careful deputy, I might actually start to like you."

"Shame." Luke turned to face her and got comfortable. "I was kind of hoping you already did."

"Ask me that a bit later." She waved her empty glass. "Filling this would help your cause."

They stayed on that couch for hours, stopping once for Sam to use the restroom, only to come out teasing about he possibly used such a small toilet. The conversation flowed easier than either of them expected, more words than they'd spoken to anyone in weeks, possibly years.

She asked about his childhood, his life before he came here, and he told her. Even the ugly parts in the military that he wasn't proud of, that haunted him. Stories no one else had ever heard.

He asked why she wanted to be a trooper, her youth, and she told him. He wiped a tear when she talked about Paw, and he welcomed her comforting hand on his arm, something he never allowed, when they opened up about how drugs had ruined their mothers.

They lightened the mood going over the insane bounty they'd run together.

"Not gonna lie, thought I might die after." Luke rubbed his sharp jaw. "My drill instructors never ran me that hard."

Sam shrugged. "Good for your heart, wild cat."

Luke flushed a little. "Yea I guess it was." Or maybe she was about to eat him alive.

The topic neither dared mention seemed to temp an entry, and Luke's silence grew.

Sam knew the risk, but she could not deny that he'd been pulling her in since he was bold enough to come to her property, meeting her spewed acid with humor, that ended up with him following her on a bounty. Text her to come have a drink with him, been honest about his concerns with the case, not letting her drown after she took the oars and left in a huff over it.

He'd been a source of turmoil for her for a while, but not in the way she knew of turmoil, a more enjoyable type of torture. Maybe she was an idiot, maybe she was a flesh and blood woman who was done lying to herself.

She had very little energy left in her broken soul to study the matter, and very little left he could find that wasn't already in pieces. Pieces she herself had given up trying to repair years ago, letting them be buried deeper in the snow with every season.

Lost, was better than found and unwanted... still...

"Tell you what." Sam set her wine down and moved to center of the room, confusion washing over Luke's face. "I know its lingering. You pin me, and I'll answer any questions you have."

"That's the wine talking." Luke put his hands up in surrender. "No way."

"Afraid I'll take you down, Rose?"

He stood slowly, exaggerating his staggering stature and broad shoulders, waving his hands up and down his muscular frame, then to hers.

"Really right now?"

She hipped her hands. "Sexist much?"

No. Maybe.

"Never judge a book by its cover, *officer.*"

Ooo she was spicy, and it fired Luke up immediately.

"With you, definitely not." He pushed the coffee table against the couch. "Alright Shaw. Rules?"

She spun and buckled his knees to the floor with a hooked foot, pulling his neck back with her laced arms before planting his back to the ground.

"Rules are tedious." She got up and cracked her neck.

He grunted as he stood. "Indeed."

He reached one hand over his head and pulled his shirt off, discarding it down the hall, before bracing.

"Trying to distract me, Deputy?"

He was. "Is it working?"

Yes. "In your dreams."

He smiled. "I've had a couple."

He lunged and she dropped, crawling between his legs, flipping to her back to shove him across the room with her thigh strength.

"Dreams or fantasies?"

Luke gained his footing and whipped around surprised. "Squats?"

She slapped her thighs. "Bounty running honey." She ripped her tank off and lofted it over her head in a very mean way. "Dynamite in a small package."

"Indeed." He rolled his shoulders.

Her heaving chest rippled the lines on her stomach. Maybe it was the wine, but Luke wanted nothing more than to fall to his knees and run his tongue across the parking spaces on her belly, the soft curve below her waistband hinting at a slight feminine curve she had never tried to harden. Perfect size to slid into his hand and pull against his body.

If they were going to sit here and pretend neither of them were attracted to each other, Luke was going to have a hard time keeping this wrestling match PG rated.

"This little dance might fall into the 'fantasy' category, if you're not careful, Samantha."

They began to circle.

"You're simply earning your interrogation cop." She lowered, he lunged. She dodged.

"There is more than one way to interrogate a woman." God he was going insane.

A thrumming filled her ears, sending a vibration straight to her core. No ignoring that, and she was tired of trying. She had to watch herself but didn't see what a good roll in the hay would do to compromise her secrets, other than quench a need he brought out of her simply by being in her space.

Still, she resisted.

"You're too tall for me. We wouldn't fit anyway. Guess you'll just have to win the match to get your information."

He lunged again. She went to drop, but he was ready, wrapping his arm around her waist and flipping her up so her legs were over his shoulders. He could smell her arousal and it made him pause, one deadly second. She locked her ankles and squeezed his head like a grape, twisting him to the ground. She ignored the rug burn and was about to declare victory, when his brutally strong hands pried her ankles to unlock.

"Shit!" She grunted.

He flipped her to her back, threw her legs apart and pulled them around his kneed position, pinning her arms beside her head, her hair splayed across the carpet like a splatter of black paint.

"Pinned. You're done." His chest was above her face, slick and heaving, hers rising and falling in rapid response.

Sam craned her neck far back to stare at the underside of stubble on his sharp jaw.

"See. Too tall."

He snickered wickedly. "Miss Shaw…" He slowly bent his back to a sharp curve like a black cat, causing her breath to hitch when he met her nose to nose. "Don't judge a book by its cover." He angled his hips down and his arousal met the warmth of hers, sending her into a sharp inhale. "I win."

The fireplace flared sharply as their breath mingled, dark shadows of beasts and windstorms performing a show neither of them would look away from each other to see.

He ran the tip of his nose down the bridge of hers and tightened the grip on her wrists when she struggled against him.

"Don't do that." He growled, his lips brushing hers. "Or this interrogation is going to get very, *very* unprofessional."

"Then you better start asking Deputy Rose." Or don't.

He squeezed his eyes a moment as they panted, afraid of what he might hear. The trooper facing off with the man. The man who was hooked on something they didn't have rehab for.

"Did you take Brad's pups? Bust those kennels up?"

"Ever the cop." She loosed a heavy breath, flexing her hands in his grip. "I do not go anywhere near the hell I ran from."

He searched her eyes, not wanting to ask the rest. "The rumors. When you were a trooper."

She knew it was coming, but it still strangled her with a force she had not anticipated. Why did she care so much what he thought? Why was he different? And why the hell couldn't she lie to him?

A tear raced to her ear. "True." She did not blink away from him. "All of them."

Luke pulled his head to the side and squeezed her wrists, his jaw clenched. "God damn it Sam."

"Tell me how the world is worse having dogs taken from torment and given to love." Her voice quivered. "Tell me Luke…"

"It is not my job to answer that." He bit his words. "It is my job to enforce the law. You stole-."

"I took abused animals out of hell, don't think I didn't try to do it the right way first."

"You tied a man up and left him to the dogs, on duty!"

"And what law protects the beaten dogs?" He dropped his head shaking it with frustration. "The ones who say the shelter is full? The ones that leave them out in the snow for weeks because a speeding ticket or noise ordinance is more important, more money? The same ones who just send them to a kill shelter because they want to get off in time for happy hour?" She swallowed and fought to catch her breath. "I regret nothing."

He put his forehead to hers. "Tell me you're done. Tell me…"

"Tell me you regret beating that soldier to the point of hospitalization after he brutalized and raped that local woman?"

"Sam." His voice was deep with anger.

She didn't budge, and it scared the shit out of him.

"You knew they would cover for him, so you served it up yourself. Tell me you didn't know James was going to beat Brad down that night."

"You're not being fair."

"Neither are you."

He gritted his teeth and his body bulged. She didn't waver from him, raising her lips to his ear.

"I own my choices, and do not judge you for yours. Law or not, you did what you felt was right, what had to be done because no one else could, or would. The cop may not feel that way, but the man does." She pressed her whispering lips to his ear. "All I'm looking at is the man. What do you see when you look at me Lucian?"

Luke's arms began to shake. She was causing him to lose control, simply for calling him out on the times he'd done it on his own. Without a second thought he'd put that man down in the desert. Without a shred of connection to Sam, he'd turned his back on his badge, his duty, and let James use violence against a man who'd simply spoken in a way he did not like. At the time he had not known their story, and still, he compromised the law, a civilian's safety, to wallow in the shallow harbor of his morally grey justice, over words.

Excused it, rationalized it, while having the balls to be disenchanted with her own missteps. He was a coward.

This woman owned her walls, her damage, her actions, her demons… with a fortitude he had always run from, disguised under a flag of virtue signaling in more than one uniform. Unable to face his weaknesses, his fears, hiding them so he didn't have to look at them. Enforcing the law so he didn't have to own what was corrupt inside him, what he found unworthy, what he feared he'd become.

Sam faced all of it, every day. Making him claim his, with a few daring words from this smoldering inferno beneath him, had stripped him bare, and left him yearning, a song of promise on her lips to fulfill it.

He angled his head to face her, defeated. "I see a woman who loves dogs, and serves up a stiff warning to those who don't…" He swallowed the rock in his throat, nudging her lips. "And a broken heart, who's shards of strength… could either fix the fishers in my foundation or leave me crumbling."

Her voice came out faint, afraid. "What kind of man gives a woman he barely knows, the upper hand like that?" She trembled slightly.

"One who no longer cares if she has it."

He pulled her arms above her head and claimed her mouth. Gently exploring her lips before her faint plea had him devouring her with a dangerous hunger.

She opened for him with needy abandon, her name rumbling from him as he searched for salvation on her tongue. He released her wrists and drove his hands down her body, pressing her lower back up and grinding into her, as her own found his hair and pulled him down harder, the kiss becoming almost violent as it overtook them.

He broke free gasping and nibbled her neck, shoving her charm necklace out of his way, his back muscles flexing erotically against her palms while she clutched him.

She cried out when his mouth found her breast, the warmth seeping through her thin sports bra and sending her body into waves that had him swelling firmly against her need.

"Let me take you." He breathed, his fingertips digging into her flesh, a young boy afraid his new catch would slip back into the watery depths.

She ached deeply. Her body no stranger to it, but her soul trembled in fear as she felt his weight on her. The stress was melting away, even as the risks his closeness teetered her on the edge of destruction, holding a match to her gasoline. She thought of nothing but the smell of his ivory soap and the heat from his body. She was clear headed and still a wanting puddle beneath him.

She'd had others listen to her, but they had never offered themselves up the way he had. Met her honesty tip for tap, as he met her energy, met her bouts of silence, met the fire she'd spewed trying to singe him back. Their minds and bodies had been a wave of ebb and flow all night, effortlessly traversing terrain they'd always walked alone. They were both iron boxes sealed from the world, both burning hot enough to melt each other. Only time would tell if the forge exploded, or the metal fused together to create a shield no one could dare break through, or ever break apart.

She lowered her eyes to the bear paw tattoo on his chest. It'd been the 'what if' in her mind since she'd pulled that shower curtain back, the white rabbit that led to wonderland, or madness. She was terrified.

Luke felt her hesitation and clasped her face, breathing hard.

"Me too. Fuck." He drug his tongue across her bottom lip before pulling it into his mouth and letting it slip away slowly. "I don't know how to do this." His huge hand squeezed her hip, shaking. "I don't want to hurt you."

"That's not always a bad thing." She did that adorable face crunch thing again.

"God damn it Sam" He laughed into her collar bone. "Killing me." He searched her flushed face for answers, his own expression pained. "Too soon. This is reckless. All of this. Time-"

"Time is all we have," She quivered as everything she'd ever been sure of, went up in smoke. "And don't have."

His kiss was gentle, soft, a caressing of understanding, his body cursing his tenderness.

Luke had never had intimacy, emotional connection, let alone a relationship. Just empty sex. He'd told her as much over the hours they'd spent talking. She herself had never had the passion she gave returned and had resigned herself long ago that it'd always be that way. It had been the only awkward moment they'd shared that evening. Both of them stood on the edge of the cliff, too afraid to jump.

She watched his chest heave, witnessing him war with pure primal need and the question of what the hell was happening. Seeking a label, an outcome, an order, some sort of logical explanation. A promise that it would not destroy him. She couldn't give him any of that, while she herself longed for it.

"You will hurt me." She brushed his hair off his forehead. "It's just part of it."

Luke buried his face in her neck. "What are we doing? Is it just this? Or-" He sunk onto her. "God I want all of you. It's been driving me mad."

She kissed his lips with a long gentle pressure that Luke had never felt in his life. It said more than either of them needed too, but still she offered his turmoil a place to rest for the night.

"We'll figure it out as we go." She glanced at the clock. "Shit."

"Kallik." Luke nodded and backed off her, resting back on his heels. "I'm sorry."

She crawled to him and straddled across his lap, pulling his face to hers. "Let's start with one thing at least. Don't say I'm sorry."

He gripped her rear and pulled her in tight, biting her lip. "Then you need to get your sweet ass off my dick or I'm going to have to say it to you *and* Kallik, a *lot*."

She threw her head back laughing, subsequently gutting whatever sanity was left inside him. He'd overthink it plenty. Dissect it. Scold it. Find a way to debunk it. But right now, he could stand to watch her do that for many more nights. Maybe even longer.

He pulled Sam's tank top over her head and imagined a night when he wouldn't have to. He made her leave the dirty dishes, claiming them as collateral to see her again, which she found adorable, and packed the rest of the things she'd brought as she slid into her boots and zipped her coat.

"I'll walk you out."

"No." She touched his tattoo. "I want to take this shirtless image with me." He blushed as she ran her thumb over the bear paw. "Why did you get that?"

"Strength. Courage. I needed it." He cleared his throat. "Why'd you get it?"

"The only man who truly loves me had it. Got it for the same reasons you did, said he saw them in me the moment I was born. He calls me little bear." She shrugged. "It symbolizes many things, but I got it for what I need."

"Which is?"

"Love. Bears are a symbol of love when given."

Luke shoved his hand in his pockets. "I don't think I even know what that is."

"I thought I did once, but…" Sam's eyes got damp. "Maybe we'll figure it out one day."

Luke slipped his hand under the box so she wouldn't drop it, and the other clasped her neck and jaw, pulling her in to kiss her slowly.

"Goodnight Samantha."

She only smiled and turned to head down the stairs, digging her keys out as the back door clicked to self-lock behind her.

"You screwing the new Chief now?"

Sam damn near dropped the box, her keys tumbling to the snow. "Jesus shit you asshole! What the hell are you doing here!?"

James stepped out around the front of her truck into the light and blew out a long drag into the icy air.

"Frank needed me to sign off on the final report. Came to slip it in the slot. Saw your truck." He looked up at the light coming from the small second story apartment window. "Was worried they sniffed you out and hauled you in." He picked up her keys and glanced in the box. "Guess I misunderstood."

Sam swallowed hard and grabbed her keys before pushing him back a step. "You do that a lot, J."

Her heart was pounding out of her chest. She wasn't afraid of him, but him scorned… well he could ruin her, and suddenly, for new reasons she didn't want to tarnish so quickly after they'd formed, she didn't want her life ruined.

"Thank you for caring, but I'm good." She focused on loading the box in her car to avoid his penetrating stare.

"I had my hands on you less than two weeks ago. You came on command Sam."

"Over a year of me telling you our boot knocking days were over." She threw her head back. "God damn it James you know that was a mistake. I was pent up and I'm a human being." She turned to face him,

113

and sighed. "We have never been a thing. I have always been honest with you. I have never lied to you about how I feel and you always knew where we stood. Accepted it. You literally pegged Star in the bathroom last Friday and you're giving me shit for dinner?" She rubbed her temples. "I don't want to do this. I don't have to do this. You're a good friend to me James, but what I do in my free time is none of your business."

"You're right." James got close to her face. "But some things you do in the dead of night… are." He gave her hood two solid taps and sauntered off. "Drive safe Sammy!"

Luke held his back against the door a moment. That had escalated far quicker than he could have made up in his head, and still, he couldn't muster the strength to pick it apart in his usual fashion.

He walked to the kitchen to shelve the martini makings and sink the dishes. A worn, black hair band sat on the backsplash by the dish soap. Dish soap he didn't own. Damn she was something. He licked his lips chuckling, the taste of her still lingering, and slipped the hair band on his wrist.

No. He wasn't going to count the days he'd been here on his fingers. He wasn't going to find a reason why she reminded him of all the things that scared him. Wasn't going to draft up the what ifs, the hows, the risks, pack up his mental bug-out bag and run. No, tonight he was going to just let himself be smitten.

Smitten and frustratingly turned on.

He leaned on the sink and shook his head grinning widely. "Smitten… you fucking pussy, marine."

The faint rapping of a car hood slid him towards the window. He hoped Sam wasn't having car trouble. She'd be worried as hell about getting to Kallik. He'd get her there.

Luke peered out the window and narrowed his eyes. James was disappearing into the lot, Sam hastily getting into her truck before peeling out. He needed to look a little closer at James Porter. Sam may think he's alright, but that wound on his hand the other day… A power surge hit Luke's receptors. Sam had not answered him when asked if her vigilante days were over. They might be working together.

"Ah hell."

Chapter 12

Frank put the checks on the counter and gave Raine Buckowski an apologetic look. The stout bank owner nudged his glasses up and scooted in his chair to pull them closer.

"Darleen having you run around today mate?" He squinted at his computer to pull up Frank's account.

"She always does. I had a call late last night and it kept me out a good deal longer than she approves of. Been a bit more frequent than she tolerates." Frank heaved his belt higher. "Not like I can control the folks of Shavila."

Raine looked over the brim of his glasses. "Been quite a bit more activity lately, not lessened since that new deputy came in. Sure you made a good choice?"

Frank leaned on the counter and blew air out his cheeks. "He's handles himself pretty well, given the adjustment he faces. Still... hell I don't know Raine."

The banker pulled off his specs. "Heard he's got his eye on Samantha. You uneasy Frank?"

"Unfortunately, the whole town has heard, and its only nine AM." Frank rolled his sore ankle, sending Raine to peer over the counter.

"You falling apart already old friend?"

"Nah, just had a good stumble the other night." Frank shifted gears. "You met Lucian. What do you think of him?"

Raine shrugged. "Sam's a big girl, she can take care of herself. Don't know either well enough to make that call, but my bet is Sam will lay him out flat if he can't walk the line."

Frank frowned. "Yea but he's moving a bit fast for the new kid in town don't you think? A real Johnny-come-lately. He doesn't even know her."

Frank was looking for some justification for his wary heart and was reaching hard.

Raine rocked his lenses by the bridge on his finger. "You set your sights on Elizabeth the second Liam Shaw brought her on this rock, the one he put on her finger the only thing that stopped you from stealing her, Frank." He leaned back. "Had Kallik not kept you off his property with a shot gun for a while, you wouldah had her on her back before Liam's body was cold. Even then it didn't take you long to sink into her." He slipped his glasses on and returned to his computer clicking. "Can you really clock the boy's blue line to blue line?"

"Hey who's side are you on?"

Raine shrugged and tapped the checks straight. "Right now, whoever keeps me in business. Quite a few this time."

"Yea sorry about the checks. Can't get Darleen out of the stone age."

"No sweat off my back." He began to rapidly enter numbers. "After the paperwork I had to process this morning, this is a vacation."

"Big account?"

"I'd say. Ol Blue-blood-Bradley took out a multi-million-dollar policy on that house of his." He waved his hand. "Gotta protect that big money I guess."

"Convenient."

"What's that?

"Oh nothing." Frank shrugged. "Just interesting." He turned at the scoff delivered behind him, not surprised. "Come on James, we don't have to like him for him to cover his assets. You would if you had em."

James rolled his eyes. "Pretty boy can kiss my ass, I hope his house burns."

Raine Bukowski shook his head and kept tapping. "Always the aggressor J."

"You hate him too Frank." James grumbled.

"Yea well, anybody who knows Sam, does." Frank noted the wince on James's face. "I know son. We can't protect her from everything."

"Certainly not the new Deputy. You shouldah given that badge to Sam, Frank."

"Yea well, sounds like she's managed to get one anyway." Frank rapped his knuckles on the counter. "Thanks Raine. Send the receipt over whenever you can. I'll see ya."

~

The general store was a flurry of activity that did not suit a Monday morning. The weatherman had been right, shockingly. An early warm Spring was upon them, seemingly overnight, and the quickly melting snow had the townspeople slipping and sliding through there celebratory moods.

Underneath all that excitement, reserved mainly for the younger crowd, many along the river were loading sandbags and had pulled their animals to the public kennels behind the vet's office.

If the break-up was rushed, the possibility of flooding was high, and the talk of global warming coupled with lending hands to the elderly to move them to higher ground, was giving the town a roller coaster of energy that offered a slight relief from the ongoing concern that tourist season would be ramping up soon. It brought in good money, but it also brought in a layer of disrespect to the land that many in Shavila could live without.

Sam herself, spent most of Spring running predators out so some idiot wouldn't get mauled trying to take a picture with a 'cute fuzzy baby bear'.

Tamar Richards and Tig were having a jovial conversation as they loaded sandbags, outside the general store, that Big John planned to haul out to the river-riders when he got back from fixing Sal's car.

Denali was learning how to drive and had seriously underestimated the slush on his way to school, landing his mother's beater in the curb, and Sal with a flat tire she couldn't afford to replace. Luke had taken the call, subsequently handing John the cash to replace the tire, unable to handle the woman's sheer despair at the expense. It was way outside of protocol, but he had never known anyone on a call he'd answered before, and it hit him differently.

John had promptly handed half the money back and they shook to split it, Denali giving them both a huge hug that neither man knew how to digest. Sal swore she'd pay them back as Luke got in his patrol truck and told her to spend it on Denali's car insurance instead. Lord knew he'd need it.

Luke had accepted John was a damn good man outside his piss-poor moods, when he pulled up to the general store, starving.

He hadn't slept much the night before, his mind anxious over the endless possible case leads, his body restless with the scent of Sam all over it. She smelled like lavender, all.the.time. He had never liked the scent until it mingled with her own. Now he found himself not showering that morning just to catch a faint hint of it when his body temperature rose, which happened involuntarily every time he thought of her.

So did his concerns with her activity. He was due for a day off, and planned to spend it figuring out whether his conflict was going to make him sink or swim. Unless she wanted to see him, then he'd happily drown. Shit he was tired. A good breakfast burrito and energy drink ought to help him survive the day.

Judging by the looks on the men loading sandbags, as he got out of the truck, he'd need more than that to make it through the store alive.

Luke flopped his arms on the door and top of his truck, nudging his hat up. "She didn't."

Tig and Tamar both erupted in laughter.

117

"Damn it, Charlotte." Luke slammed the door of his truck and walked over, grabbing a bag and tossing it onto the flatbed. "No offense Tig, but I may have to kick your wife's ass."

"Only if I get to watch." Tig grunted, slamming a bag down. "Because I would have given anything to watch you survive Samantha, so you owe me a show."

Tamar wiped his forehead. "You're a sick man Tig."

"Horny man, and there is nothing sexier than a woman wrestling." Luke flushed horribly.

"You mother fucker." Tamar danced around and offered a fist bump, which Luke reluctantly met.

"Shouldn't you be teaching Tamar?" And letting me bask in peace.

"Highschool assembly. Sam is reminding the kids about predator safety and the risks Spring brings. Hungry hibernators and all that. Have to help with this break up risk, it's a town affair." He slapped Tig's chest. "She *was* in an awfully good mood today."

"Just dinner." Luke put his hands up. "And she didn't knock my teeth out." He flashed them, before jerking his head towards the general store. "So how bad is it in there?"

Tig wiped his hands and leaned far back to peer through the doors. He grimaced.

"Burrito and a liquid fuel my man?"

Luke tipped his hat. "You're a good man Tig."

And Luke would be sure Tig got his fair share of warnings instead of tickets if he ever had to pull him over for something. It was the least he could do for Tig saving him the heat of walking into a grocery store full of woman salivating at whatever Charlotte had managed to spew out in the last two hours.

"How's the little Tamar?"

"Oh ya know, screaming for daddy with mommy, screaming for mommy with daddy. Sleeping all day for the sitter and keeping us fumbling through the dark all night." He smiled warmly. "She looks like her mama. I can't ever be mad at her. She's gonna ruin me Luke."

"Women got a way."

"Yea well." Tamar threw the last bag on the flatbed. "Some men need ruining, they come out better in the end."

Luke stood silent for a moment, looking towards the turn that took you towards the school.

"She's under your skin man." Tamar hopped up to sit on the tail, twisting the cap off a water bottle. "It happens fast brother."

Luke didn't pull his eyes off the turn. "How long did it take you?"

Tamar chuckled into the water bottle. "Three days."

Luke turned around then. "Like 72 hours?"

"Yup." He looked up like the sky was a blue diamond, telling him the future. "First day in town, got me some food for the hotel. That little, tiny thing came in all bubbly and sweet and shit. Obviously a teacher, because she could tell I looked lost." He shook his head at the water bottle he was now crushing. "Showed me where the toothpaste was and said she'd be happy to show me the school early so I didn't feel lost on my first day teaching. I was only planning on staying for one school year man, just until they found someone more permanent, but," He lofted the bottle into the recycling bin by the door. "I asked her out to dinner on day two, and had her in my arms on day three. Never let her go."

Tamar chuckled and leaned back. "Ya know, the thought of my daughter ever letting a man close that early scares the shit outta me, men are pigs. But then I think how much I worship Vanessa, how much I'd cut off my balls for that woman, and I think maybe…" He listed his head to meet Luke, hanging on his every word. "If she trusts herself, she'll get a guy like me, who will love her just as much as I love her mom, ya know?"

Luke was floored. He'd never heard of such a thing.

"Funny too." Tamar hopped up and grabbed his coat off the side. "Cuz I hate the fucking snow."

"I think…" Luke was surprised as the words formed. "I think that's the bravest shit I've ever heard." His throat went dry. "You really just said fuck it and jumped, didn't you?"

Tamar slipped on his coat and reached out for Luke's hand to shake it. "My mom always said, you might fall, but hell kid, what if you fly?" He pulled the door open to go inside. "And I'm flying brother."

~

James paced the barn as Sam dumped the steaming food in the dog bowls. He'd came to apologize for his mouth, and Sam had asked why he'd bothered to get it so close to her fist.

"Sam come on. You can't expect me to just not care I wasn't good enough."

"Gaslighting. Smooth. Play victim next and we'll have gone full circle. Then you can leave."

She walked to return the bucket to the feed room and check her burner phone for any responses to her rehoming inquiries. She had to scoot these pups. They were a handful and Snow White was already sick of them.

James leaned on the door jamb. "Sammy."

"Shut it." She slammed the phone down, more aggravated she had no takers, than at him. "I *never* fronted with you. We enjoyed a safe physical space occasionally. One you didn't hesitate to jump on after I'd been hurt, and badly."

His mouth began to form acknowledgment that she shut down with her palm. "I own my adult decision to allow it, I never held that against you. But I never let you sleep over, I never played house with you, I never got mushy. I was clear. Jesus even in high school I was clear. You said it was 'great, best of life without the bullshit'. You remember that J!? You not owning that is on you."

He nodded and dug his hands deeper in his pockets.

"You coming at me like that, threatening what you know as leverage, when I had *dinner* with someone? Fuck right off. Friends don't do that to each other. Someone who wants something, that was never offered to him, does. You lied to me, when you told me you had no issue with our arrangement."

She felt a shred of guilt. "James you're a good man, and I'm sorry your feelings got involved, but I never led you on, and I cut it off last year because it was the right choice. Fuck buddies don't last forever."

"I'm cool Sam. My ego just got bruised a bit is all. He's fucking huge, and Outside, and fuck I just never imagined it."

"*Dinner*, J." She caved to the obvious and dropped her sarcasm, sighing. "I never imagined it either, but don't overthink it. I'm trying not to. I don't want to. I like him."

He shrugged. "You don't know someone for fifteen years and not see their eyes change Sammy." She schooled her face neutral, something he also saw through. "It's cool. We're cool. Just my ego. It's a guy thing."

"Must be." She rolled her eyes. "Because I was never, and will never, be the tall voluptuous breathtaking blonde Star is, but I was just stoked for you. Her name is Star for shit's sake, when you shorten my name, it's a boy's. I have about as much tits as one too. She's a walking Jessica rabbit, I'm a backwoods rambler, and I just wanted to give you a high five man!!" She winced a little. "Although she is kinda easy."

"Asshole."

"Dick."

James looked at the map of her targets and back at her. "We good kid?"

Sam took a deep breath and narrowed her eyes. "Yea, but I may swing on you when you ain't looking, knuckles are still itchy."

He gave a 'fair enough' smirk, wouldn't be the first time.

"Just don't wap me too good, gotta fly a rescheduled ticket soon, Darleen had me rush her into Anchorage yesterday and I'm tired as hell."

"I hope you suffered the whole flight." She turned to face the map. "I'm not getting any takers on these pups, and I gotta move em. I know Denali has been wanting one."

"That's a little too close Sam, how you going to explain it?"

Sam rubbed her neck and grimaced in pain. "I don't know. I haven't had much time to think about it. Paw needs help with showering, medicine. These pups are nuts. Bounties are going to pick up soon. I'm so tired." She wrung her hands in front of her. "We can't save them all."

"Hey hey." He pulled her in for a hug. "We always knew that. It's getting a little hot anyway. One more and we're done. We'll find another way."

Sam pulled back and clocked him in the jaw, but gently. "Jesus Christ Samantha!" He laughed, shoving her.

"Told you."

"Yea you did." James pointed to two spots on the map, surrounded by a bunch of crossed off locations, as well as circled ones. "Which one is gonna be the last ride sugar?"

She pressed her lips into a thin line. "I think, even though we hate to admit it, this one has already been proven to be ok, not ideal, but not as bad as we thought." She pointed. "Even though we'd like nothing more than to have a reason to ruin his life." She glanced at her watch. "I gotta get back to the school, second assembly."

James watched her run out, Roy on her heels with false hope of going with her. He grabbed a red marker off the desk and leaned to the map.

"Guess a coin toss would have been better odds for everybody." James crossed off one location and drew a circle around the other one.

Bradley Oliver's house.

~

Detective Harley Scott grabbed her minimal suitcase and stepped off the train. She narrowly escaped being run down by an excited child and clicked her tongue. While she loved Alaska, small towns made her insides want to revolt, if only to cover the residents in her bile to make them more appealing.

Shavila was a hot tourist spot, and was known for its lovely hotel lodge and adorable shops, but small-town locals were all the same, and she could already smell the fish guts they dwelled in. She jerked her suit jacket down and ignored the shiver threatening to make her look weak.

She would clean this up quick and be back in the big city busting pieces of shit before the air of this town stuck to her clothing. This case had too much circumstantial evidence for Chief Frank Brown to have not come up with probable cause to make an arrest, which only added to why she was here, and clearly Deputy Lucian Rose had proved to be no sharper a tool. No matter, she had some new goodies to slap on Brown's desk, when the time came to knock him on his ass. Patience. A few more pieces.

121

Detective Scott scoffed at the car that had been reserved for her and got in. If one good thing would come from this resentful trip to this rock, it would be a good ride on that dull tool Luke, before she hauled the one she knew was behind all of this, to Anchorage, in cuffs.

Chapter 13

Darleen was full of piss and vinegar when Luke walked in. Pissing and moaning about how an old man doesn't need to be running out so late and not telling her about some injury he'd gotten last week that was still giving him hell. 'I can't hold out much longer' She'd muttered into a scone, Anita rubbing her back like she was carrying the world upon it. Darleen did look a bit paler than usual.

Luke figured he'd take his chances stealing Frank's office to devour his burrito, before he hung around in the lobby where he was sure to meet his death at the hands of an angry wife that wasn't even his.

The Iditarod/Bradley Oliver case file was left open on his Frank's desk, so Luke flipped through it, almost choking on the last bite of his burrito.

A pile of ash labeled with Brad's name and last night's date, made the food in his mouth taste of the photos appearance. If it hadn't been for the sparce paw and bone, he never would have known that pile was once puppies. Luke spit the rest of his burrito in the trash and swished his mouth out with water. God who could be so sick and twisted?

He shoved the file over slightly to look away, a faded, beaten letter peeking out from under it. Luke shouldn't, but he did, thinking it was more information about the case, even as its yellow twinge and torn corners proved its age.

He froze, a rapid realization taunting the breakfast he'd just eaten to cover the desk in an array of his shocked insides, as he read.

No. No way...

He heard Frank's voice holler something at Darleen outside the door and quickly covered the letter, schooling his face neutral.

"You ain't chief yet son." Frank looked exhausted. "Get outta my chair."

"Sorry boss. Just dodging the viper out there."

"She never did get used to me being a cop. Sit."

Luke kneed his elbows as Willow and Forest came in. They didn't look much better.

"Your night off last night was an act of luck son." Frank grumbled, tapping the horrifying photo. "Brad's missing pups were returned, and he put in a call to the big dogs, no pun intended."

"Jesus Frank." Willow covered his mouth.

"Give me a break kid I ain't slept. Brad isn't waiting for us to figure this out, and I guess…" Frank's eyes went distant for a moment. "I guess I pushed this too far. They got a detective coming in today. Brad wants answers and we don't have them."

Luke leaned forward. "Talk straight Frank, what are we looking at?"

Frank looked out the window and nervously tapped his fingers on the arm of his chair. After a moment he rubbed his mouth, pawing at his beard like he was about to cry.

"Frank for fuck's sake." Forest snapped. "We know everyone around here. What the hell is going on!? We're a family! This is our town!"

"This is my town too!" Frank barked. "And I have done everything I can to protect it, and everyone in it longer than you've been a sperm Forest, so watch your damn tone deputy!"

Luke stood up. "Is it Sa-"

Sam burst in and did a ta-dah motion, instantly curling into herself. "Oh god, I… guess I should have knocked." She nudged the twins aside after returning Luke's worried face with a nervous grin. "Frank, you alright. You look awful." She cared regardless, she always had, and felt his forehead.

He moved to grab her hand. "I'm ok Sammy, really. You got what I asked for?"

"Yes of course, but I gotta run, I have another assembly soon."

She dropped a train stub and flight log copy on his desk, and Luke felt his legs go to jelly.

He locked in and tried to hide his relief. He knew, God he knew she didn't have anything to do with hanging Brad's dogs, or with the photo she slowly picked up, her eyes welling. But the relief he felt the moment that alibi hit the table, had him wanting to throw out every other thought in his head and show every inch of her that he regretted his doubt. That it would haunt him brutally.

"Frank…" The look on her face ripped through Luke like a killing blow.

By the way Forest and Willow were looking at her, the same fate had met them as well.

"Don't look at it, honey." Frank grabbed her hand, crushing the photo and pulling her forehead to his. "I'll fix it. Everything happens for a reason. Don't you let that light go out. I'll fix everything."

Sam nodded and sniffed, hugging the man tightly before rushing out the door, wiping her nose.

Luke pivoted. "Frank I-"

"Go."

Luke shifted towards the door.

"Luke?" He turned to face Frank. "I told you it wasn't her."

Luke barreled out the front of the station.

Sam was kicking her tire, wiping her face ferociously when he snatched her up by her elbow and spun her to face him. She hauled back to clock his jaw, instantly crumbling against his badge.

"Easy. I know."

"I'm so angry." She clawed his arms and took a deep breath. "I have to find this dirt bag."

Luke pulled her face up. "You need to take care of Paw, and you. We'll get him."

Sam nudged his hat up and touched his face.

She had become a tower of control and calm in a silent instant. Luke could not fathom the fortitude this woman had.

Sam could not decipher why he made her feel so safe.

"Luke, James could never do that. I… I saw his name on the suspect list. I always knew I was one but… He couldn't. He's a reckless idiot Lucian, but he couldn't. There's no way." She shook her head. "I used to think… god no Brad couldn't."

"We can't account for James or Brad during those times, nor a few others. We'll narrow it down, but you need to steer clear, because-"

"I know why." She went to pull back angrily, and he locked her against his chest.

"Because I'm not done with you." He slid his hand across her neck and jaw and took her mouth in his.

She rose instantly to meet him, her body surging with the desire sparking from him. Whatever she may be doing, wasn't enough to keep him out of her storm any longer. He pushed her against her Bronco, clasping her face with a desperation only a starving man could rival, every flick of his tongue and brush of his thumb a tiny tear in the fabric of her being. Her hands sought his backside and a grumble of frustration left her when they hit his duty belt.

"That's gotta stay on right now, princess." He nipped her lip and was rewarded with a whimper. "Mmm. Do that again for me later." He suddenly dropped his head against her shoulder. "Fuck. I'm working a twelve. I'm not off until ten pm."

Sam didn't give a damn. She may have had a conscience last night, but what the hell for? She was done playing cautious and resigned herself that if it was going to hurt, she was going to make damn sure it felt good first.

She licked his Adams apple. "You got a bedtime Deputy?"

He pulled her head back and looked down at her. "Don't fall asleep. Tomorrow is my day off." He barley managed to keep his voice steady, his need ricocheting inside him like a pin ball machine.

Sam only maintained her footing because she was a born and bred Alaskan, or she'd have been buckling out of delightful fear and blind anticipation. His lips brushed hers again, beckoning she let him in, and she obliged. They fused together so easily, that Luke had lost all sense of his surroundings.

A shrill whistle flew from across the street.

They broke free and saw Tig pantomiming a bat. "Swing-it-Sammy!!"

Luke backed off her sheepishly, adjusting his hat and fixing his belt, biting his smile back.

"I'll see you later." He pinched her chin and turned to head back in, stopping when she swatted his tight ass.

Luke hipped his hands, keeping his back to her. "Sam." He was so irritated.

She giggled. "You'll get used to it big boy."

He didn't think so, but he didn't care either. He all but skipped back into the station.

Luke's cloud nine turned black and burst into a thunderstorm when he breezed into Frank's office to find Detective Harley Scott stirring a paper cup of coffee like it was the most disgusting thing she'd ever seen.

Frank was white as a ghost, and the twins were both cross armed and looked like they'd just been scolded by their mother.

"Ah, the talk of the town returns." She flicked the stir stick and missed the trashcan, not bothering to pick it up. "I was told you'd be in shortly. Nice of no one to leave me parking in front." She looked Luke up and down before putting a suggestive curve to her lips. "Good to see you again, Deputy Rose."

Luke ran his thumb on the side of his mouth and squared his shoulders. "Detective Scott."

"You've met?" Frank's brow flickered.

"Yes." The detective spoke over Luke. "In Anchorage. I had inquired if he would keep an eye on the evolving case here over…" She turned villainous eyes toward Luke. "Drinks, was it?"

"And has he?" Frank was doing his best not to leap across the desk and strangle him, and Luke knew it.

Still, Luke didn't have to lie. Sam had an alibi, and the rest, well whatever she kept under her thumb, had nothing to do with this whoever was killing Brad's dogs, and was none of Detective Scott's concern. He'd would handle it if it was meant to be handled. A part of him he didn't recognize, was still praying he'd never have to.

She dared Luke to respond, and he shrugged casually. "Nothing to report other than some nervous locals and more dead dogs. I have my suspicions, but nothing concrete enough to move on."

The edge left Frank's shoulders slightly, his mind dancing over Luke's actions with a fine-tooth comb of curiosity.

"Oh bullshit." Harley spat. Forest dropped his arms, Willow's hand meeting one in a silent plea. "Keep your cool baby face." She sneered at the twins. "Or I'll have your badges for a coaster set before you can tell your mother you're moving back in."

Every vein in Luke's neck bulged, their only challengers the ones forming in Franks own.

"You have a right to do your job Detective." Frank fought to keep his voice steady. "But you will refrain from threatening my team or insulting them."

"I will do," she flicked her eyes to Luke, "whatever the hell I want, and need, to get this case handled and make an arrest before my digestion is disrupted by the peasant food you serve here." She tossed her coffee in the can, brown tar sloshing up the wall. "I have a report drafted, one which none of you shine in, and my suspects." She pointed a finger at Frank. "You have been dragging you ass when you have enough circumstantial to move. I'm here to gather the solid matter you have been overlooking and be back in anchorage with the perpetrator in less than 72 hours."

She smoothed the side of her gorilla glued bun. "I expect the report sent to the hotel within the hour, and none of you to interfere with my investigation or you will be charged with harboring." She made her way to the door.

"Chief Brown, you more than most, know that being important to someone, doesn't mean they get to break the law. This town and its people may mean something to you, but it is a sore on the ass of Alaska and the foul puss it has been oozing will be expelled. Bet on it." She paused and glance back at Luke. "I'm sure you will not have a problem finding my room number Deputy, should you have… anything you'd like to add to my stay during this…" She glanced around in disdain. "Charming stay in Shavila."

"Start talking Luke." Willow's fists were clenched and ready to throw blows as soon as the door clicked.

"You're wearing a badge Willow, simmer down." Frank's face said he'd like an explanation as well.

Willow did not break his glare, unhooking his badge and chucking it to the desk. "I'm waiting, Outside."

"Easy brother. Luke?" Forest palmed his own badge. "So help me I'm not above it my man."

Lucian squared up and briefed them on the ninety-minute past he had with the badged insult that just left the room. He was shameless in his explanation, making it clear if it wasn't him it would have been a random bar-benny she'd scrounge up, and that 90 minutes included the drive, one drink, and her jerking his dick out before he thought to argue.

He owned it and emphasized with great seriousness that he had no loyalties to that woman, outside of the law he's sworn to uphold. He was far more shocked than they were that Detective Harley Scott was now slithering around Shavila, and after the twins eased off and apologized—in the only way men usually could—they all agreed the last thing this town needed right now was another reason to worry. But it was here, in a tailored suit and bitchy blue eyes that were out for blood.

Willow may have grumbled he'd like to ring Brad's neck as he headed out the door.

"She's like a sister to us Luke." Forest's voice held concern that had poked holes in his cup of anger. "We were only a few years younger than her ya know? She covered our asses a couple times when big brother Tig was about to knock our heads together for being stupid. Her side arm Charlotte, batting those eyes to get him to lay off. Sammy stuffed a plant a time or two in her pocket that may have made it so we couldn't be wearing these badges today. She knew we were just bored and dumb, not trouble."

Luke felt Sam understood that about a lot of people. Shavila, as a whole, seemed to humanize folks in the way the law often neglected. It was uncomfortable for him, but he saw the good it could do.

Big John had done some time sleeping off booze in an unlocked cell when the town had been dry, but he always made sure everybody was safe and got home in one piece from his bar, and cut people off, when he'd doubted they would. And from what he'd just heard, Sam had slapped them upside the head and hid the twins weed exploration, the result being two good young men were now two damn good cops.

They kept the kids in this town stimulated and using their heads, in a way he doubted he or Frank could pull off. They didn't tow cars, they shoveled them out for each other and rung a reminder. They didn't toss roadkill in the woods, they fed the people with it.

It seemed backwards in a way, the bending of the protocol, but so undeniably right in the end. If the world could expand that mentality and the efforts to practice it, Luke realized, so many good people would not be losing their jobs because they couldn't afford to get their car out of impound to get to work. Parents would be in rehab instead of jail and their kids stood a chance of having them. The world might be better.

Shavila was better.

"I'm not playing her Forest." Luke sterned his face. "That much I can tell you."

Forest strained a smile. "Sam means a lot to a lot of people, she's just too scared to let us. Hope your tenacity is stronger than ours. She deserves it."

Luke felt Frank's permeating hatred as the room closed around the two of them with the efficiency of a vacuum sealer.

"We need to look into other suspects Frank, and keep Scott away from Sa-"

"Get out." Frank was lost out the window, the last shred of peace he had thought he could save, turned into an apple peeler and was fed to the pigs, the moment that detective hit his rock.

"Excuse me, Sir?"

"You heard me. I told you to stay away from her, not fuck her and her head up so you could be certain, of what you already knew, for your little raise that you clearly fucked out of that detective."

Clearly the detective had popped out more than she needed to, but the raise was offered by the Anchorage Chief, not her. Luke supposed that didn't matter to Frank. It didn't need to. Luke had more things to be concerned about at current. If he wanted to call out dirty pasts, then Luke was ready to tee up.

"She means more to me than you understand, she doesn't need your bullshit." He shifted his gaze to Luke. "Get out of my office."

Luke's brain waves cracked and popped, seeing red. The temper he had held so deeply inside him since a drill sergeant spit in his face, give or take a few moments, came bubbling up in his throat ready to blister the man who held his job in his hand. Luke slammed his hands on the table to regurgitate everything forming inside him like an exorcism, when the wind of his palmed table assault made Sam's photo slip into view.

It quelled him the way nothing ever had, and he paused. The expression molding to his Chief's face was one of slight regret, and painful realization.

Luke rose slowly, exhaling carefully. It was time to poke the bull, see if it would kick. He would not be made into something he wasn't from a man who hid his own demons.

"What she needed was the father figure you made her believe you'd be, not one trip to anchorage to stir the soup, one you only made to make-up for forcing her to traverse the unwanted feeling she carried when you left a kid to be an adult."

Frank started.

"She could have gotten out of that on her own, she threw her badge down to save yours, and you let her do it. A theatrical show that raised more eyebrows, all because you needed to make yourself feel better for leaving Kallik to hold a girl who lost her mother and father figure in one shot. And it backfired."

Frank stood forcefully.

"And I would have had her in cuffs the minute she told me what she'd done with that badge on, if I wanted to." Franks face hollowed.

"Oh yea, we talked Frank, I didn't fuck Samantha." Luke fixed his trooper hat and looked over his shoulder. "But I can promise, I'm going to, but unlike you, I won't be leaving her to clean the mess up when I'm done."

"Drop your badge, Lucian."

Luke smiled to the ceiling. "You know what's odd Chief? Nobody knows where the hell you were during those dog slayings either." He gave Frank a minute to panic. "And I'm willing to bet, what Brad did to her and your need to drown the guilt you carry, could prove to be quite a motive. You never did hesitate to hurt her to make things work for you. Your little dance in Anchorage got her back here quick enough." He turned and took two casual fingers, sliding the file off the letter. "If she meant as much to you as you say, you wouldn't have abandoned her because your wife couldn't handle what her mother had meant to you."

Frank bared his teeth and threw the papers off his desk. "Are you threatening me!?"

"Maybe you should just be careful how you judge others." Luke opened the door and tipped his hat. "And I think I'll keep the badge, *Deputy*."

Frank picked up the letter as the blood drained from his body. The letter from Elizabeth Shaw, the one he'd read and cried over at least a hundred times, more so lately. Telling him she was pregnant, and that it was Liam's. He'd secretly held her many nights when Liam would go fishing to bring in a paycheck, the days too long for her to manage alone on the island he'd brought her too.

How he loved her. She'd broken it off then, and it had destroyed him. He'd always thought she'd leave Liam someday and make love to him under the northern lights until they were too old to screw. Nobody made fiery love like Elizabeth Shaw. She had ensnared his whole being just by breathing.

Luke was headed down the same path of destruction, and it could destroy both him and Sam. He couldn't have it. Frank had no idea what Luke could be calculating in that over jacked head of his; he could still be playing Sam for his own gain, despite what he said. He was wrong. The letter however, was enough to fill Luke's head with problematic assumptions.

That overgrown shit smear, who was to bring him to an easy retirement, had just threatened his very being, and to take the one he held so dear.

Frank had hurt Sam, he knew it, but there was still time to make up for it. That was all he ever tried to do. Frank struck a match and lit the letter on fire, tossing it out the back window to the wet ground below.

Chapter 14

Sam stalled slightly as she spoke. The tall, well-dressed woman, having not taken her hard face off of her since she'd walked in to the gymnasium, sent a wave of notable observation up her spine. Who the hell was that? She reeked of bureaucracy and well-placed ass-sticks.

A merciful teenager made a fart noise in Sam's silence, pulling her back in.

"Good tactic Harper. Yea I know it was you." The teen flipped his hood up, sinking low to the floor. "Blowing your breakfast out your ass just might throw a predator off your scent when hiking." The kids laughed as Sam flipped a trap up in her hand.

Detective Scott curled her lip in disgust.

"But you'll want to be more wary of *these* babies when mucking off out there. We're the deadliest predator there is, and when we try to catch them, we use some serious digs."

The detective gave a wry grin, thinking joyfully. Indeed, we do Samantha Shaw, and in a few days, I'll have enough to light this fire, so enjoy your little performance, because mine will be so much better. Her smile suddenly flattened.

Unfortunately, Sam will suffer greatly, whether she deserved it or not. That, the detective could be sure of. No matter how hard hearted a cop she was, Harley's personal disgust to Sam's rough edges aside, no human being wished for someone to get the life altering earthquake that was heading for the woman before her. Harley quickly swallowed the compassion, there was no room for it. What needed to get done, was to be done, and Sam was the center of it.

"Trappers occasionally miss a few when wrapping up the season, so pay attention. Catching your foot in one of these bad boys will mean the bush gets one more foot, and you get to snowboard with a stump."

A round of 'Ooos' and 'Ouches' seeped from the small crowd of kids that, while already aware of it, the reminder was enough to make their tendons ache. A great excuse to writhe on the floor receiving a few good finger snaps from Ms. Eska.

Vanessa quickly turned to offer Sam an annoyed look.

Sam looked at the clock. "Alright nose miners, I'm going to leave these on the table for the next few days."

"Uh, Sam..." Vanessa lifted a worried finger.

"They've all been disengaged and can't be tripped." Vanessa blushed like she should know better, loosening her shoulders. "And you can mess around with em until the bell rings. No swinging them around, Denali..."

The kids bum rushed the table and Sam threw her hands up to wiggle out of the fray.

"Holy children of the corn Vanessa, I don't know how you do this every day." Sam threw on her jacket and grabbed her backpack.

"I dunno." She shrugged. "Keeps me young I guess."

"Well, it's great birth control for me."

Vanessa shook her head. "You were never one to long for kids."

"And you were so ready you were peeing on a stick after only 2 months."

"Shhh jesus Sam we don't need these kids thinking that's a good idea." She raised her voice slightly. "Because it certainly isn't! Patience is key kids."

None of them gave a damn or were paying any attention to the two friends, too busy pretending to be bears and writhing to their deaths on the gym floor.

Strong birth control. Very strong.

Sam covered her mouth and blushed. "Sorry. But I think it worked out for you just fine Vanessa."

"Yea, I'm really happy." She discreetly nudged her head to the frigid female in the corner, who promptly turned and made her exit. "Who the hell is that?"

"I don't know." Sam made her lips into a thin line. "Judging by the looks I was getting, I'm about to find out. I'll see you later."

"Swing-it Sam."

Sam turned and walked backwards. "Don't worry V, I got it."

"I know Sammy, you always did." Vanessa tightened her cardigan and rubbed her arms in a whisper. "I just hope someday, somebody has you, so you don't have to, anymore." She turned as the bell rung and roars of celebration erupted. "Any jackets left in my classroom I'm adding to my closet! Don't run!"

Sam was already amped to break her nose when the overdressed rubbernecker thought it was a good idea to lean on her Bronco. She steeled her nerves and walked straight into her.

"You always touch people's shit or are you just a stickler for thinking your badge don't stink?"

Detective Scott quickly covered the insult on her face and put out her hand. "So you know? Seems fitting as you used to wear one."

Sam eyed her hand and smiled sarcastically. "Mine are full. You mind?"

Harley waited a beat too long to move off Sam's driver side door, just enough to make a point, before tilting her head. "Of course. Detective Harley Scott. I was-"

"Samantha Shaw, and don't care." She threw her bag in the cab. "I've been questioned six ways from Sunday, and I'm not making my old man wait for his dinner to be a broken record."

"Married?"

"Grandfather. Not like it's your business." She smiled sweetly in a way that told the detective she was being called a cee-u-next-Tuesday. "Hits the sack early. Oh, make sure the tape recorder is in your outside pocket or it won't catch the irritation in my tone." Sam took great pleasure in the grind she heard come from the detective's pearly whites.

"Let me try again. I need to speak with you abo-"

"Am I being detained?" Sam started her truck, revved it.

"I'm sor- *what?*"

"Am.I.Being.Deeee taaaained?" Sam hollered over the obnoxious revving, that was totally unnecessary, but damn fun watching the exhaust annoy the tight wad. "You know the word, ya detective?"

"No, I- Yes I do. No you are not being detained, at the moment." She was doing her best to intimidate and Sam was eating it up like a chainsaw to bar oil. "There's a matter most urg-"

"Then get your hand off my truck and go talk to Frank sweetheart, because I got shit to do, and not a damn thing is tying me to your case except that I'd like it over too." Sam peeled off with a wink. "Good luck!"

"Careful what you wish for girl." Scott coughed and waved her hand in front of her face. "I'll throw some extra sucker punches in for free for ya."

Sam caught Luke's patrol truck in her rear-view mirror, starting to pull out from behind the school dumpster. She scrunched her face and did a little wiggle.

"Thanks for looking out for me, you big ape." Her body heated.

Damn she couldn't wait for later. She wasn't even sure if she'd let him hit the door jamb before she ripped his clothes off. Oh Sam had plenty to worry about. Paw was fading, and she had one last hoorah to pull before she threw in the towel, but as long as that arrogant detective kept her head on the dog slaying case, she'd be fine. She had nothing to do with that, and what she was doing, well they hadn't caught her yet, and she was done after that last red mark on the map.

James had known why. He saw it in her face. She wasn't afraid of getting caught. No. She was clinging to the chance to have a man who made her feel like she never had before, stay maybe just a little longer. It made no sense, but it didn't have to. Nothing in her life did, so why did this? Maybe because she was afraid if Luke went in the barn, he'd choose the badge over her, and she wouldn't blame him if he did.

The way he made her feel, no matter how new and scary, was more than any man had ever done, pulled things from her no one had; Sam wanted the chance, however fleeting. She'd find a way to do the good work, keep saving dogs. Just needed to find one that didn't risk her doing time in the pin, or ruining the first time she'd thought about letting someone in that had less than four legs.

"And doesn't drool." She laughed out loud. "Oh my god but what if he does?"

~

Damn this is fun to watch. Luke rubbed his lips and felt Sam on them, sending him checking the clock that hadn't moved since the last time he'd warned it to hurry up. She tasted like winter water, fresh, invigorating and just the right amount of pain when you swallowed it, and he was in desperate need of a cold plunge.

The ever-confident Detective Harley Scott being cut down to size by a spit fire who stood half hers, had made his uniform unbearably tight under the belt. He watched that woman stumble over Sam's wit like a kid fresh out of the academy. Tall, polished and prepared, swallowed by a barbaric snow bunny who hadn't even washed her hair that morning. The scene was making the countdown till his shift ended, all the more painful.

Luke adjusted his pants begrudgingly, and pulled out from his hiding spot, slamming his truck to a stop, halting the detectives own exit.

"Thanks for the assist, Deputy." Detective Scott flapped her hand out her side window.

Luke tipped his hat up to feel the sun. "We don't make a habit of harassing the locals when they aren't doing anything."

She leaned out her window further, scowling. "She's a suspect in a case Rose, might be connected, and you'd do well to remember that, when you don't have your tongue down her throat."

Ah, so she'd seen that. Alright. Guess she was a little sore he didn't take her up on the offer to ruffle her hotel sheets. Good.

"It's a good throat Detective, and my tongue wouldn't be down it if I thought she was connected."

"Her history says she is, and now you're in conflict with the investigation." She narrowed her eyes. "So unless you want to change my mind on the matter, I suggest you watch your step if you enjoy being employed."

Luke pulled up so he was in her face. "Oh sweetheart, she isn't a saint, but just because you slammed your Sahara Desert down on my underwhelmed dick, heaving like a cat hacking up a hairball, doesn't mean your sandstorm scares me." His face washed over in amusement when her jaw hit the floor. "It clearly didn't scare Sam. Good luck."

"I'm ripping this town apart Lucian! I'll finish it!"

Detective Scott slammed the steering wheel watching Luke pull away. "They both called me sweetheart. Fucking small towners."

~

Sam was staring at the photos on the wall as she waited for Paw to take his meds. Fishing had been the biggest part of their lives before Paw slowed down. Her father Liam had been one of the best-known fisherman on the island. Boat, river, ice, didn't matter. If it was water, Liam Shaw could, and would, haul fish out of it. Paw had always said he used to whisper to them. Seduce the fish up with promises to join them some day if they fed his family that day.

Sam's panning fell on the picture taken the day her father died, sighing, tapping Paw's hand before stepping to it.

He was a tall lean machine, decked out for a day of ice fishing. Sam was only a few weeks old when it was taken, and as he'd stood there making a funny face, pointing off camera at, Sam never knew what, he had no idea he wouldn't be coming home that day. Liam was always safe, an ice master, yet it fell beneath him and his promise to the fish had been fulfilled.

"Not a person in town hadn't seen your newborn face by the time that was taken." Sam reached down to grab Paw's hand, Roy deciding his nose needed to be in there as well. "Your mom was fussing about the cold, but he paraded you in and out of every open door. He was so in love with you."

"I wish I knew him Paw."

He tapped her hand. "You did little bear, long before you were born." Sam glanced at the clock. "You look at it again, it will stop counting for you child."

Sam hushed a laugh and pulled Paw's blanket up. "I'm having company later, so don't be startled." She gave him a stern look. "And don't you dare hesitate if you need anything. You are my number one guy, Paw." Roy whimpered. "You too pal." She gave Kallik a kiss and trotted upstairs.

Paw patted Roy's head and closed his eyes. "It is high time neither of us were, old boy."

An hour later, Sam flipped her long curls back and clicked off the diffuser in a start. After a beat of silence, a truck door slammed, no fuss from Roy. Sam threw on a loose V-neck sweater that hit her knees and, forgetting her leggings, hastily ran down the stairs grumbling.

135

Roy would be barking if it wasn't a familiar, and she had no time for interruptions at nine PM.

"Swear to shit James I said we'd do it tomorrow night." She grabbed the knob and ripped the door open. "Why are you so stubbo-"

Luke poked out behind flowers that had probably cost him a small fortune this time of year. "I got off a bit early." Roy ran a circle around him and licked his boots, Luke's eyes raking over Sam. "I don't get to take your pants off?"

"Smart ass." She yanked the flowers over her shoulder and leapt on him.

"Hey those cost more than my-" Sam leapt and locked her legs around his waist, biting his lip, her hands pulling at his hair. "Ok, shit whoa!" He stumbled through the door as she moved her tongue seductively down his neck. "Spider monkey, shit hold on." He dropped his bag and tripped back against the door, fumbled to find the lock, finally throwing it and grabbing her ass.

"Where?" He growled.

"Upstairs." She begged, claiming his ear and digging her nails in his shoulders.

She inhaled deeply, the smell of him sending her senses into anarchy, heat pooling between her legs. The lustful sigh she released liquified his legs.

Luke clunked the first step and caught himself on the wall, loudly.

"Shhh! Paw." She giggled and plunged her tongue in his ear.

"Fuck woman." Luke hiked her up before he climbed the steps, his knees already wanting to buckle as she tortured him. "You're not helping..." He gritted, stumbling blind towards the flickering glow coming from her room, her needy sounds assaulting his ears. "At all."

He tapped the delicate skin exposed from her panties and she chirped, the pleading sound barely audible over him fumbling to peel his jacket off from under her and close the door as she clutched him.

Luke pulled her legs out from behind him and fell back on the bench by the foot of the bed. She winced as her knees hit the wood on either side of his open thighs.

"I'm sorr-" He couldn't get a word out.

Her lips demanding every ounce of breath left in his lungs, promising to consume him before he'd even come to terms with his imminent death.

Luke was rock hard and ready, his denim becoming a painful prison, as the asylum on top of him lobotomized his brain. The cage that safely kept his heart in place, was crumbling against the slams ramming against hit, pills of sweat already forming on his brow. He had never been so turned on in his thirty-five years, a woman so desperate for him she could not maintain her own pace.

He'd never desired to conquer a woman so intently either. Still, a hesitation rose from an awakened cavern that had gone undiscovered until he'd tasted her.

She was fast and hard, and clearly accustomed to passion being delivered that way, but his passion was new, a greedy miner that had been buried until her gems had revealed themselves with a siren's song, beckoning from the darkest places he'd never ventured. He wanted more. *Her.* He'd pound her into oblivion without thinking twice, any man would, but he wanted the woman she buried inside first.

To discover, to unfold the map that was her body, explore the whispers of wilderness that flowed in her veins, hear them raise in voice and cry out in freedom. He wanted to conquer her, yes, but he did not pine for glory, he hungered for her to feast with him, watch her embrace her own as he did. Cut her teeth on all the things that he was seeking to claim, knowing that they shared them, that she was not being robbed; she was rich with him. And he no longer gave a shit why, it just had to be.

"Hey, HEY!" He jerked her back slightly, sending her eyes wide in shock, the grip on her waist firm.

Sam's face melted as if she'd done something wrong, a shame threatening to drape her in a shadowy place she dwelled too often. He drug his thumb across her damp bottom lip.

"Don't do that. We won't be doing any of that beautiful..." His hand journeyed across her collar bone, sliding the oversized sweater to expose her shoulder. "Just slow down a minute... I want to enjoy you."

Sam did not know what burst inside her, but he'd done it weaponless. Slowing her hands to trace his jaw line, illuminated in a new light, he was breathtaking.

He licked his lips watching her collar bone flex under her deep breaths, her curls cascading across her arms, hugging her elbows. He traced the delicate lines of the dip in her throat with his finger. Her breast seductively fell free and his foot jerked out from under him.

"Jesus those are perfect." He rubbed his lip on her shoulder, feathering kisses on a trail to her neck as the firelight danced across them. "You're perfect."

Sam's hands trembled on his thighs as she leaned back slightly to let him seek his fill. Her knees joined the quake when his hand slid further to cup her seat, his strong fingers cruelly moving under her panties, kneading her cheek gently, kneading in ownership. He moved slowly, marking each inch he passed with soft kisses and swirls of his tongue. She could feel him readied beneath her, so much so she did not know how he could stand it, herself about to explode.

137

Still his pace remained, slow and steady, peeling away the outer layers of her invisible protection. Disintegrating her fortitude with every breath he exhaled on her pebbling skin.

Fear rose inside her, no part of his demeanor familiar, no move he made expected. She hardly knew this man, and yet every part of her body said she did, thrummed with an ache and ease that simultaneously sent her head back in surrender, her shoulders back in offering, as every soldier that stood watch inside her, threw down their weapons and dropped to their knees.

"There she is." He whispered. "Stunning."

Her body curled into him when he found her breast, brushing his fingers lightly across her nipple before twirling it between them, sending her hands to his face, her gasp stealing the life force from his throat. Their tongues mingled and explored one another in an unspoked demand. His muscles bulging beneath her shaking hands. She needed his skin.

They broke free long enough for her to peel his shirt over his head, slamming back together, the distance too much. Her pleasure began to soak her, his muscled thighs flexing under her to kick off his boots.

She let out a needy plea. "Touch me."

"Let me see you."

She rose her arms and he made short work getting that sweater off, her curls a wild curtain to her softness, a bead of sweat trailing down the center of her.

"Look at you." His throat made a guttural sound as he lunged forward and licked the bead from her body, clasping to her neck and biting.

She gasped and her body offered itself on its own, his mouth claiming her breast, vibrating under his delicious moan.

"On my god." She cried. "Lucian... please."

She was begging and it shattered his reserve. He lunged up and carried her to the bed.

"I'm fucking done." He bit, trailing his tongue down her body, claiming her burning need through the fabric that imprisoned it.

The heat of his mouth sent her back to mountain, the sheets not enough to anchor her hands as she clung to them. He sneered at her panties as he ripped them down her legs, a personal assault to his need. Staring into her eyes, he pulled her legs apart slowly, deliberately telling in his primal intention.

"Holy hell." A deep rumble came from him.

Sam trembled beneath his firm grip, as his hands slid up her thighs and he claimed her mouth, plunging two fingers in.

"So soft." He smiled watching her whimper, her pleasure slicking between her thighs as he worked her deeply. He gave passionate attention to her breasts before burying his face between her legs, her hand clutching his hair as he feasted on her lust.

"Oh my... I... Luke!" Her body rolled and her mind began to spin, her skin a flame, her senses ensnared.

He short circuited in that moment, the scent of her too much, his name on her lips. Honey and heat tingling his tongue the way a poisonous plant would lure you in before it destroyed you. Her writhing against his stubbled jaw begged him to share his torment, her ocean crashing a warning of the coming storm.

He would have her, no other would ever taste the fruits she grew so tenderly while he walked this earth.

Lucian Rose was officially snared.

He pulled her closer and dug in deeper, declaring war on her resistance. She was fighting, a trepidation unable to allow her to let go. He felt it, and slid his hand up to lace in hers, beckoning her to him, anchoring her to rage on.

Sam flew; an outcry of vulnerable release that blinded her. A snowstorm flurried in her eyes as she rode violently where he'd taken her, clutching him between her thighs as he slowly consumed what he'd demanded of her.

He reluctantly pulled from her to remove his pants, running his eyes over the lines of her spent body, her arms stretching up like a pleased cat, purring at him to get scratched.

Sam watched him release himself and stopped breathing. She knew, but the dark look in his eyes made her knees meet, shaking like a new fawn before a hunter, and he was locked and loaded. She wanted all of him, and it made her eyes water, sending them clamping shut.

"None of that." He gently spread her knees and put his weight on her, his promise nudging her in warning as he nipped her lip. "Look at me." His muscles rippled under her hands as he tensed. "Samantha." His husky tone opened her eyes, the sea of desire penetrating her, willing her. He felt her hips relax and filled her to the hilt.

Her head arced back in his hands, her nails in his skin, the sound of her satisfaction bouncing off the walls as he moved inside her, deep and firm, his body rocking hers in a beautiful rhythm.

"I... oh my god." She fought to breathe as he retained her completely.

He was calculated and smooth at first, clasping her head and holding her eyes on his as he moved inside her. He pressed deeply and worked with intent, their bodies flowing in tandem with each other, accepting, surrendering, seeking.

"Look at us." He demanded with a low growl.

He supported her head, and she watched him glide in and out of her slowly, his abs flexing with terrifying control, his eyes committing her expressions to memory.

139

"Look at how beautiful that is." He ran his tongue over her lips and picked up his speed, greedily fisting her hair. "I see you baby."

Sam had never felt such intimacy before, and she allowed him to take his time, time a man had never taken with her, time she had never felt safe enough to give. He moved in fluid sweeps and hard slamming thrusts, licking her neck when her head shot back, kissing her eyes when they closed. Palming her breasts when she lifted, pulling her hips into him when she demanded.

She watched him smile at every sound she made, their bodies fusing together slick with a glue that threatened to never release its hold. Her sanity was lost, and as he claimed her mouth, she felt the shattering rise of her collapse begin its steady drum in her core with his steady pressure.

"I want to go with you Samantha." The words were weighted with more than she could hold, his eyes lined with silver… she was done.

A single tear slid down her cheek as she screamed his name, sobbing and writhing against him, his own roar hissing through his teeth as he pulled her into his chest and bucked into her. The fire hissed and cracked, distant shadows a haunting display around them as the warmth of their bodies clambered for the comfort of their icy chambers.

Sam could not find hers; it was melting as the heat of him filled her, a puddle of what she once was, a pool of what she had been. Destroyed. Ruined. Claimed.

He fell on her, supporting his weight on trembling arms, his breath assaulting her ear as he fought to pull in oxygen. His heat had burst from its kiln, shattering the safety it had promised. He was destroyed. Ruined. Claimed.

Her hand caressed his neck, and he let himself feel the tenderness he fought so cruelly. He had bed many women, but he had never *seen* them. He clenched his teeth, gripping her hair tightly.

"Sammy…" His eyes grew hot, words dying on his tongue.

"Stay." She whispered.

He nodded into her shoulder and buried himself there, unable to expose the dampness that had met his cheeks. The man who had been thrilled for hot sex, a passionate roll in the hay with a tantalizing minx, resigned in the probability of its short life, had just made love to her, and he was not strong enough to face her knowing it. He himself unable to face it. He was not strong enough to let the wind carry his caution. He held her close until he could gather himself, certain he would fail.

Sam felt the moisture gather in the crook of her neck. Felt his body tremble in a way that was not that of a man who had exhausted himself, but that of a man who had just lost himself. She swallowed down the rock building in her throat. She had never let a man in, the way she had just done. Letting him see her pine and want and only for him, let him claim every inch of her. She had been so ready for a rousing night that was sure to have a time limit, but now she laid there, his passion still resting inside her, and she knew she never wanted to see him walk away.

Sam pressed the back of her hand to her lips and squeezed back her tears. This was going to hurt so bad.

"Stay." He whispered.

Chapter 15

It wasn't ideal, but it'd do. There were a few people this could fall on, but as long as it wasn't him or Sam, that was all that mattered. A few dogs had to suffer, but you can't make an omelet without cracking a few eggs. It had kept the suspicion on Sam long enough to work undetected, kept her unaware, distracted. Now she had an alibi, so his time to end this was now, before it went up in smoke, no pun intended.

He loosed a sick laugh as he hid the gas cans in his truck. That fancy new policy on the house would make this look exactly as it should look, and the right people would suffer. He pulled his face away from his side mirror, unable to look at himself. Yes. It was the least he could do, after what he did to her… what he took from her, brutally that day.

~

Luke had watched the firelight dance over her naked body for quite some time before rising, her breathing a steady coaxing for him to join, finally adding logs to the woodstove before allowing himself to wrestle his mind to sleep. He should have been more exhausted, the best sex of his life having drained him exquisitely, yet he was restless. An uneasy cocktail of doubt would have been easier to swallow, more familiar, manageable, an expected journey of logic blistering the soles of his happy feet, turning him around to return to what he knew.

Instead, he'd wanted to stare at her, talk to her, make love to her over and over. He was not above simply wanting to pound her until she begged him to stop either, and he still couldn't stop imagining her lips wrapped around his need, neither of which was helping him to rest. Nor was it offering to drown out the distressing need to make her his, claim her, label her.

You could not collar a bear, he knew the moment he saw that fury in her eyes that she would not be caged, but it did not stop his heart from chanting with every beat, that he was going to try. Even if she simply promised to remember she was his, every time she pulled away.

Luke did not know how long he'd been asleep when he felt her leave the bed, no signs of morning showing through the window he was suddenly glad was in the middle of nowhere, or the whole town would have seen him ravage her. He secretly observed her stretching, oh so cruelly, in front of the amber glow, the tips of her curls cruising the delightful curve in her bare lower back, instantly making him ready for round two.

She cracked her neck, and threw on her sweater, jumping into some type of pants messily. He wasn't ready for her to run yet. Ever.

Luke abruptly sat up.

"Easy Deputy." She purred. "Just giving Paw his 12:30."

"You ok?" He didn't know why he asked, it just came out.

Sam smiled in the doorway. "If you're still naked in my bed when I get back, I will be. I'm not done with you."

Have mercy he was so doomed for her. Luke flopped back down and starfished dramatically, fighting against invisible restraints. The nerdery sending her to muffle her laugh as she disappeared down the hall.

Roy was curled up at Paw's feet, the flowers she'd discarded in a lustful impulse, mercifully not shred to pieces.

"Good boy." She whispered, before coaxing Paw to swallow the liquid medicine and tucking him in tighter.

"Little bear." He rasped. "I had a dream. You are ok… ok now."

"I'm always ok Paw, I have you. You need anything? Want me to read to you a bit?"

He smiled and patted her hand, his eyes hollow. "I love fishing. We should go fishing."

"I know Paw." She kissed his head. "We will." She put the old photo of her father fishing in his lap as he drifted back to sleep. "We'll go tomorrow, ok? I can't wait. I love you."

Sam fussed the flowers into the vase to calm her nerves. It had been a long and trying couple of years watching him decline.

Paw didn't know what was going on half the time anymore, and the other half he thought it was twenty years ago. Thankfully he still recognized her. It'd happened so quickly, even though it seemed her life had been consumed caring for him for so long. She didn't mind, even with the restrictions. The pain of losing him was always enough to keep her diligent and present, claiming every lucid moment he had.

Still, the man in her room was a wonderful release and… shit, everything. He was wonderful. She didn't want him to be, it'd be easier if he wasn't. But every time she blinked all she could see was him on her, holding her, that stupid half smile that irritated her. Could he just smile all the way!? He was so handsome… and strong. He'd caught and juggled every fire ball she'd thrown at him and then asked her to be around. He must be insane…

"Like me."

143

Ugh he'd boiled her pasta till tender, and she was cooked. She rolled her neck and padded up the stairs. Time to critique the chef.

~

Detective Harley Scott laced her fingers together with a frigid, forced calm. She was trying to be compassionate, something that rarely came naturally to her, but was needed here. This was hard for the woman, and she looked like a scared teenager, but what she confirmed tonight would set off one of the biggest arrests in her career, and rock the town of Shavila. It would make the papers, the news.

Alaska was a big place, but Shavila wasn't, and a small part of her, very small, hoped the town wouldn't be affected too deeply by a drop in tourism. The locals may not like it, but the money it brought in got them through the winter. PFD checks were pennies compared to the load a family had to carry.

Still, if the crying didn't stop soon, her militant reserve may turn into a table flipping tango.

"I know it's hard," Detective Scott repeated, "but I need you to look over these dates and times again and confirm if you knew the suspect's whereabouts or not and sign it." Scott grabbed a tissue and handed it to her informant. "Your information is invaluable, and we're grateful you called. We just need to verify a few things before we can move forward. Please."

"Why is this so hard?"

Scott grabbed her hand. "Doing the right thing sometimes is."

"It will ruin her."

Detective Scott watched her informant initial and sign the timeline. "It may Ma'am. Or you could very well be saving her, from others, and herself."

~

James slapped Star on the ass and grabbed his jacket off her office chair. A good after hours pounding in the Vet clinic, was not something you turned down. Star pulled her panties up and fixed her dress, smiling at him.

"You should come around more often." She grabbed his junk and pulled him back into her, pulling his beard to her lips. "You do me right James."

He grunted her onto the desk and grabbed her face. "I'm surprised you called actually. Not everyday something like you wants another bite outta me."

Her face got serious. "I like you James, a lot actually."

James backed up, cleared his throat. "I um. Well I'm good at what I do."

"I like *you* James, and not just because you're hung like a moose, although it's a lovely accessory to the rest of you."

"I can't get involved with anyone right now I-"

"I know what you and Sam are doing." She bit her words. "You think she could afford all that medicine she gets for your little rescue operation!? Or crime ring I should say? I donate that shit."

James grabbed her arm and hauled her up. "You got a wire in here or something!? What's your angle barbie!?"

She slapped his face. "Watch your hands unless they're inside me and simmer down. If I did, I'd go down for aiding and abetting you dolt. Clearly brains aren't part of your package." She tilted her head and sighed. "But I still meant what I said. I like you, James. I'd like to, I dunno, have dinner before we fuck. Try it again a few days later even."

James nodded, pocketing his hands nervously. "I'm sorry I'm a bit jumpy lately, I've had a lot of… things I've had to do… it's been…" He grunted back the words. "Sure, I'd like to try that Star, I would. I'd be humbled as pie to have you on my arm." He grabbed his hat to head out. "But I got one more thing I gotta do."

"You have to stop James. There are other ways for you two to make things right."

"After this, I'm done." He gave her a wink. "Maybe focus on something else for a while."

She filled her chest and let it roar out watching his truck fade down the street. "I hope so."

~

Sam had critiqued the chef, but not in the way she'd planned. The poor guy was passed out when she returned to the room. She covered her mouth to not wake him, her laugh almost hysterical. The sexiest man she'd ever seen, was still spread out like a star on her sheets, naked as a jay bird, hair a tousled mess and sheets everywhere, but his mouth was open, and he was completely gone. Out hard.

Under normal circumstances one would find this less than attractive after a first romp, but she was stunned to find, it made her adore him more. Luke must be really content to pass out so damn exposed like that, and the thought made her simultaneously swoon and slap herself.

A shower sounded fantastic, warm her bones to get some decent sleep before Paw's breakfast. So after looking her fill over the large man that seemed to dwarf her king size bed, and plotting what piece of him

145

she wanted next, she piled her curls on her head to keep them dry, and hopped in.

She had only been palming the wall in heavy lidded bliss, for a few moments, before his warm body pressed against her. He let his hands speak, and she felt no words were needed to answer. Their tongues wove together in between intimate washing and a hard glare from Sam when his ridiculous height curtained the water around her, leaving her shivering.

"I can fix that." He slid his hand around her neck and lifted her slightly, her moan of surrender vibrating his palm as he glided into her from behind. He held her, rocked her, worshipped her body until she unleashed the beast with one, breathy word.

"More."

Luke palmed her hands to the tile and pressed his lips to her ear. "You're going to kill me woman."

His thrusts became deep and territorial, animalistic grunts matching the tone of his fierce grip. He homed in on her sounds and gave her what she asked for, moving his hand to clutch her face, feeling her mouth move as she cried out in ecstasy.

He kissed her cheek as she came down. "The sounds you make when you let go." He squeezed her against him. "It does something to me."

He turned off the water and grabbed her a towel, drying himself as casually as you would if you'd done it a hundred times together.

She could, Sam thought, do this for a while. It wasn't hard. In fact, it was too easy. She wouldn't think about that now. She'd think about that tomorrow. Or not.

His stomach grumbled loudly, and she smirked. "Hungry big guy?"

"Yea but its 2am. I can wait. Unless you're hungry?"

He was still standing at attention, having reserved himself, and she suddenly was, very hungry.

Luke slammed his hands against the door jamb to brace as she snaked down his body and took him in her mouth. This woman really was going to kill him. She was a god damn animal. He undid her curls and ran his fingers along her jaw, feeling it strain around him with determination and laser focus.

He didn't know if it was her spread knees, the way she seemed to treasure every inch of him, or when she'd looked up at him begging, but he'd never come so fast in his life. And she had pulled him in to claim all of it like she'd perish without it.

He took a knee, unable to feel his legs. "You are something." He sighed, as she rose and ran to the bed.

She yelled 'BONZAI!' and flopped on the mattress before rolling herself up like an Alaskan burrito.

He grinned. "I'll be the adult in the relationship then."

"You better." She muffled under the covers. "I have no interest-" She yanked her eyes free and stared at him. "Did you just say the 'R' word?"

He yanked the blankets hard, sending her tumbling out of them in giggling protest. "Yes." He flipped the blanket up and dove under it before it fell on them both, pulling her to him as it tented around them like a secret fort. "It wasn't the 'M' word or the 'L' word, so shut up little spoon."

"Hey why am I the little spoon?"

He gestured to his height towering over her as he kneeled. "I don't make the rules toots."

"Hmmm." She shoved him down and monkeyed to his back. "Let's see."

There was a beat of silence.

"I feel ridiculous. Stop massaging my ass." She barked a laugh as he flipped on her, yanking her back to him and locking her legs down. "Little.damn.spoon."

She nuzzled into his arm pillow and sighed. "I'm letting this go out of fatigue alone. We will discuss it later."

He buried his face in her lavender scent and let his body wilt. "Later. I like that 'L' word."

Sam yawned contently. "Me to. Kinda confirms my consent of the 'R' word, without freaking me out."

"We are god damn children."

They both laughed and entwined themselves tightly, talking sleepily about everything and nothing, before drifting asleep, the paw on his chest, pressed against the paw on her shoulder.

Kallik clutched the photo of his son and smiled as the shadow of the grizzly bear stood stoically. He did not stand, he did not roar, the shadow on the wall simply bowed its head to the strange bear, watching him take his place beside little bear. They began their arduous climb as debris flew around them, the grizzly turning to take his final walk into the firelight.

"The top of the mountain little bear… you're almost there." He patted Roy's head. "Take care of your mom pal."

Chapter 16

"Day off he said." Sam flopped a mild tantrum on the bed as Luke snapped his gun into his duty belt.

He never went anywhere without his badge and gun but brought his uniform as a precaution and the forward thinking had proven valuable.

Willow had busted his foot taking the four-wheeler out in the shit, and Forest had to fly him into Anchorage to get him fixed up beyond the wrap job Doc provided while chastising him for four wheeling in the middle of the night.

"You keep throwing a fit like that and Daddy won't give you what you want later." He cringed and Sam laughed maniacally into a pillow. "Yea that didn't work for me either."

"We'll just have to keep trying, Deputy Rose."

Luke leaned across the bed and kissed her gently. "I'm holding you to that Miss Shaw." He grabbed his hat and fixed it to his head.

Damn it all to hell this man was good looking.

"I'll check on Paw so you can snooze a little longer."

"No." She swung her legs over and looked out the window. "He needs his morning meds and decaf anyway. I got it." She jumped into leggings and grabbed a book off her dresser. "We're on the last chapter of The Hobbit."

"Oooo when they-"

"Shoosh! I never read the books."

Luke bore his eyes into her from under his trooper hat. "That's it. We're breaking up."

"So, you have chosen death?"

"Glory glory…" He grabbed his bag and shot her a wink. "What a hell of a way to die."

The door clicked behind him as she hit the bottom step. "Alright Paw coffee coming. You up?"

Sam pushed the brew button on his mini maker and the caffeinated one beside it. Roy walked down the hallway and sat, staring at her motionless.

"Potty in a minute buddy, gotta mix Paw's stuff." She paused and turned to look at him again.

Roy didn't move, his eyes deep and sorrowful, guarding. Her hand began to shake, the medicine trembling in the cup. No. She was just tired. Over thinking.

"I have to get.. this." She swallowed shakily. "Al… Almost done." She began trembling violently, daring to look again.

Roy hadn't moved, just stared. She suddenly dropped the cup and ran to the living room, skidding to a terrified halt, afraid to go closer.

"Paw?" Sam wrung her hands in front of her, her toes clinging to the edge of the room. "Coffee is.. almost done Paw." She squeezed her eyes.

No. He was just tired. Sleeping in was… Roy leaned against her, nudging her forward, following her timid steps to the recliner. She reached a shaky hand to his face, the air leaving her lungs.

Sam fell to her knees beside Kallik, palming his cold cheek, silent tears streaming down her face. "Looks like Creator finally remembered you Paw."

~

Luke thought he had a situation on his hands until he heard the deep laughter rupture from Big John's insides.

The main door creaked to a close behind him, a large box of fresh baseball bats at his feet. He stood there observing two full grown men act like toddlers in his station. Darleen and Anita were rolling their eyes in unison at Tig and Big John flipping plain wooden baseball bats around like lightsabers, double fisting and circling like it was the greatest battle of their lives.

"You got first pick last time Big boy." Tig spun one in his left hand.

"On the contrary my good sir." Big John raised one to his brow. "You lie to dishonor me."

Hearing Big John's horrible, fake English accent and rather good use of words he often neglected, Luke felt compelled to let it play out, breakfast burrito and a free show. He had barley resigned to the idea before Darleen stood up in protest.

"Luke for god's sake this is a police station not a playground. Stop them before I waste a good pastry up the side of their heads." She sat down grumbling. "Knew I should have locked the front until-"

She snapped her head towards the stairs to Luke's station apartment then back at him wide eyed, prompted by Tig holding a bat like a huge phallic symbol and wiggling his eyebrows.

"Front door this morning I see." Darleen shook her head, a slight smile forming.

"Guess we're over." Anita winked.

"Yea." Luke flashed a guilty grin. "I hope we can still be friends sugar."

Anita waved him off with a laugh, under the shameless male eruption that exploded from Big John and Tig.

"And you lived!?" John hooted. "Atta way Lukey!"

Tig slapped Luke's badge. "You know pretty boy." He mocked a bad boy stance, Boston accent to go with it. "You mess with her you mess with me aye?" Luke rolled his eyes and nodded, playfully shoving him back.

Big John scoffed. "Sam can handle him."

"She did." Luke said. "And well, but that's as far as we're going with this conversation gentlemen." Tig and John both sunk their shoulders disappointed and drug their bats sulking, to the box holding the remainders. "You'll live." Luke grunted. "What's the dispute?" He took a chunk out of his burrito and leaned on the counter next to Darleen.

"Bats for the game." Darleen drawled.

"They're all fresh cuts, but you see," Big John flipped a bat and ran his finger along the neck, "grain is everything for a good show, and best show gets all the bats for firewood after the game." Luke raised his brows in question. "You'll see, just choose wisely Indiana, cuz it matters."

"What does the winning team get?" Luke was very curious how you could beat a good day's worth of firewood.

"Bragging rights my man." Tig jerked his head, confident in his bat choice, pointed the wood at Luke. "Last Sunday in April, bud. Get ready."

"Better be ready for more than that Deputy." Anita groaned and slithered from behind the desk. "Something smells like shit." She jerked her head towards the front before quickly making her escape.

Detective Scott was getting out of her rental car.

"Coward." Luke chuckled.

Detective Harley Scott came in tight lipped and frigid, giving Darleen a kind nod before turning to Luke, ignoring the two rugged men loitering to drink up the tea she may spill.

"Deputy Rose, the office if you please." She closed the door behind them, and her face changed, softer even. "I need to talk to you about Samantha Shaw."

"I figured you would eventually." Luke tossed his foil wrapper in the trash and crossed his arms. "What do you have Detective?"

She sighed heavily. "Certain information was being withheld to protect the Iditarod case, but this goes far beyond that, and it is why I'm here." She cleared her throat. "Given your assumed closeness with one of the suspects, I need to be quite frank with you, and bring you in on a few things about to happen." She gave him a stern look. "I am hoping you will still fulfill your duties and uphold the law, regardless."

"Get to the point Detective." Luke would figure out the rest on his own.

"Iditarod dogs or not, dead animals is a bit below my pay grade, as is missing ones. I was not called in for that." She had Luke's attention now. "While Sam's activities involving animals may be in question by some, we have a much bigger problem, Luke."

The use of his name on official business caught him off guard; this was bad.

She took a deep breath and said words he never wanted to hear.

Luke dropped his arms and took a step forward, impulsively wanting to demand where Detective Scott got off, keeping the woman he was falling in love with, and him, unaware of such a thing. The words turned to ash on his tongue and decomposed to liquid bile. A wave of realization mingling with his masculine need to defend Sam, kicked his breakfast up his windpipe.

Jesus… he was falling in love with Samantha, and the timing of this 'first time for everything', was seriously bad. He hadn't even felt it happening, yet here he was, more afraid for another human being than he'd ever been in his life, and he didn't even know what was about to follow from the badge across from him.

"Luke, listen, this is deep, but I can't go forward until you know what it entails. I have clearance from higher up to let you in on the details, but you must keep it to yourself, or you will destroy a case bigger than your balls, and we'll both go down for it." She stepped into him and whispered. "Luke you cannot tell Sam, or we won't stand a chance."

Luke ground his teeth as he listened to the Detective sketch a storyboard far beyond the one that had been in that file and fill in plot holes he didn't even know were there. He sunk deeper and deeper into himself as Scott said her name, said others, mentioned homicide, and laid out a timeline that surpassed him, punching tiny holes in his bubble gum dreams, her words all but destroying any chance he had to save Sam from the storm coming to swallow her, and rock Shavila to its knees.

"You need to continue to behave as you were Deputy, not a hair on your head misplaced, so that what needs to happen to secure this case, does." Harley put a hand on his shoulder. "Out of my hands Luke, and yours, but I will have no choice but to pursue your removal from service if you compromise this case." Luke pushed her hand off and clenched his fists. "Luke, this conversation was a courtesy to you, one I fought for. Don't make me regret it."

Luke went to speak when his phone pinged, Sam's text notification, the fact that he'd already personalized it, burning a hot skewer through his trembling heart.

He opened his screen and paled.

"Deputy Rose you need to-"

"Shut up." He hissed.

151

"Watch you tone Deputy, this is not my fau-"

"I said shut up."

He shoved his phone in his pocket and squared his shoulders, his militant face locking into place. The action sent Harley into a matching stance, one any ex-military knew very well. A standoff that could go one of two ways, usually badly.

"Her grandfather is dead."

"My condolences."

He leaned close to the harsh lines formed in her cheekbones. "You will do *nothing* until that man is in the ground you understand me? Nothing." Her face made it clear she didn't want to, but she waited. "Regardless of what you think is right or wrong, or what you feel needs to be done, *Detective*." He dug the word in deep. "None of it will, until she gives the only person that hasn't dicked her around, a proper goodbye. The crimes committed will not vanish by letting a woman who has just lost the only love of her life, have a few damn days to digest it." Luke looked away angrily. "She's about to lose so much more."

He headed towards the door. "You want to come for my badge later, then be my guest. But you will not light this fire until this town lays him to rest."

"Three days Luke, that's all I can give her. I risk too much even in that. I will do my job."

Luke nodded. "It's a small island Detective. I'm sure you can keep an eye on her."

"Get Frank in now." Luke spat at Darleen as he rushed by.

"He said he had something important to do, I can't-"

"Get him in NOW Darleen!" Luke grabbed his coat. "Kallik is dead."

Darleen's hand slammed to her mouth, Anita dropping down into her seat saddened.

Luke spun around and gave Darleen a warning glare. "Keep him busy, D."

Darleen gave a meek nod before Luke blasted out the front door, Tig and Big John leaping out of the way.

Tig opened his mouth to speak, but one look at Luke's energy and he swallowed them back down. "Awe no…"

Luke nodded and Big John sunk his shoulders. Tig gave his friend a squeeze before taking out his phone to the sound of Luke's tires peeling out.

"Char, hi honey. I gotta hit Doc's before I come help. No no I'm fine. It's Kallik."

Big John pulled his hat off and rose his head to the sky.

~

James shuffled through the barn and dumped hot food in the dog bowls as the hole in his chest widened.

Sam hadn't answered his phone calls and he had gotten worried. He never imagined he'd walk in to find her curled on the floor holding the hand of a dead man. He'd known Kallik since he'd known Sam, and seeing her shaking there, wrought with the loss, had been more than he'd bargained for this morning.

He'd kissed her forehead and asked what he could do. Unable to release Kallik's hand, she had just said, 'my dogs'. He wanted to hold his dear friend, but knew in times like this, you must help someone they way they *needed* to be helped, not the way you *wanted* to help them, and worrying about her dogs was the last thing Sam needed right now. He wanted to be a good friend, and would do whatever she needed, happily.

James was rounding the corner of the house to check on her when Luke slid sideways into the driveway.

"Try four wheel drive, numb nuts."

"What are you doing here?" Luke spit before thinking.

"Gonna chalk that tone up to concern and ignore it." James snarled. "I was taking care of her team and waiting for you." He lit a smoke and shifted his hat higher. "You think *she* text you, Deputy?"

Luke paused his run up the stairs.

"Yea you're welcome." He pulled his truck keys out of his pocket. "She needs you, even if she don't know it. I ain't never seen her face do what it does when your name is on it, ain't never seen her like she is right now either. S'posed they go together." He got in the truck and started it. "I'll be back to make the evening rounds for her. Ya call me with the shitty stuff and I'm here for it, ya got that?"

Luke nodded, his scowl turning into appreciation, and a massive humble slap in the face.

"Don't let her worry about them dogs Deputy, just..." He shook his head. "Get her to eat something will ya?"

Luke gave him a tight nod and calmly entered the house.

Roy lifted his head from her feet, Sam's remained on her knees, her hand clutching Kallik's hanging over the side of the chair. The fire had been well stoked by James, and her bare feet were curled together like a lost little girl's.

Luke hooked his trooper hat and took a knee beside her, touched her cheek, and waited. After what seemed an eternity, she met his eyes, and they widened.

"Thought I smelled bacon." She rasped. Luke offered a faint smile, and she shoved him away. "Leave."

153

He reached for her again and she deflected violently, thrashing her head from side to side. Luke whipped his duty belt off carelessly and grabbed both her wrists, jerking her to sanity.

"Sammy!" His voice became a lullaby. "Baby… let me be here."

She locked up and froze, grinding her teeth to avoid the frantic urgency bubbling inside her to cling to him, to need him.

She didn't need anyone. Especially some chiseled, lower forty-eight debutant who thought he could comfort her just because she'd freed herself so willingly in bed, talked to her for hours, given her the most content nights of her life. Told her secrets to, oh but not all. No.

This smooth operator would not be the thing to claim Samantha Shaw. She didn't need anyone, except the soul that had left his body behind beside her.

Old wounds formed into vicious shields as Sam locked her heels in and yanked her wrists in futility. "Don't you dare fabricate saving me. You don't know me."

"God damn it Sam." Luke grunted against her surprisingly powerful fight, causing him to shift his kneed position and growl. "I promise for the rest of your life, I'll let you go when you ask me too, but today is not that fucking day woman."

The weight of those words paralyzed her, the opportunity offered for Luke to pull her wrists to his chest, her face close to his. "I know you don't need me honey. I won't forget, but I'm here-"

Her face promptly crumpled into a hysterical cry, her fingers brushing his jaw as if confirming he was real. He pulled her into his lap, lacing his fingers in her hair and pressing her into him as she screamed.

And she screamed.

A gut-wrenching sound that Luke had heard before and knew. He'd never gotten over, hearing it from those crying over the ones who'd been lost to war, wives rocking over their husband's blow apart corpse, parents accepting the flags when both children didn't come home from what he'd somehow survived having no one waiting for him, and he would never recover hearing the echoes of it from Sam.

Her fingernails dug into his uniformed arms painfully, and he gritted silently through it. Her tears soaked through his shirt as she wailed louder. She curled into him, so angry, so small, he couldn't imagine how she would handle any more, even knowing what was to come for her, the evil her very being was tied to.

He clutched her head tighter and searched the ceiling, as if the answers of what to do, lied within the beams.

Sam climbed into the man who knelt before her, seeking refuge within walls she needed so innocently, so painfully. She didn't know how he knew to come, only that he was here; Sam would never have moved for another, reasons why holding no weight against the truth of it. She felt a deep impulse to push him away, reject the comfort, a learned response to the compassion he bared nakedly and free of obligation, before her.

She had not the strength, nor the desire now, his huge arms and steady heartbeat, the only tangible anchors to the broken pieces, all that was left of her, decaying under the salt of her anguish. Paw was the only man who'd ever held her in this state, and the very thought that she was grateful another dared enter here, consoled her, while equally pulling the tears more fiercely.

Luke felt her hand slide up around his neck and firmly grip it, a silent plea to do what she could not; rise and take her away from Kallik.

In a fluid, breathless motion he slowly rose, turning so her eyes would not see her Paw grow smaller as the distance between them lengthened. Roy followed them into the kitchen, plopping beneath the chair Sam tucked her feet into, her head hanging lower than it ever had.

Luke went to walk away, her trembling fingers clutching his uniform.

"I'm not going anywhere." He whispered. "You need some water Sam."

She let his arm slip from her grasp and swallowed the last of her tears; the hard things coming too soon for her to release more now. She stared at Roy's steady breathing beneath her, her fat, fuzzy anchor; wondering when Creator would take him next. Pondering how long it would be until she was afraid to lose Luke.

She squeezed her eyes shut, as if the action could hide the truth from herself, from him. Sam already had that invasive thought hours ago, only silenced by her insufferable bitterness convincing her how childish it was to be attached so quickly.

Now, amongst the greatest pain of her life, the simple endearment of getting her water, daring to be here, gave her strength to do what needed to be done. Strength, a shield she had always dug from the darkest reaches of herself, now being aided by the sword of another, even if he didn't know it. She sighed a quivering laugh.

She'd never felt such a thing before and could not have found the vocabulary to describe it if asked. Not that she'd ever allowed it. Suppose she would add that to the list of things to ponder, like how her fist hadn't met his nose when he'd shown up. She wouldn't think about it now, maybe she'll think about that tomorrow.

The glass touched the table so lightly, a feather would have marveled at the giant ape's gentleness. Luke knelt beside her and brushed the dampness from her face with calloused hands.

"I need you to drink something Samantha." He wrapped her fingers around it when her head wouldn't lift, and after a minute, finally insisted the glass to her lips himself. "Come on honey, one step at a time." Sam

155

sipped the water he tipped for her. "Finish the glass and I'll fill it with booze next trip."

The slight flicker in the corner of her mouth was enough.

He lifted her head to stare into those lost, wet eyes. "Oh hi." He brushed her curls out of her face. "There you are."

He moved to kiss her forehead, but froze, unsure the affection was something she wanted, or if he even had a place to offer such a thing when he was such a small part of what was going on for her right now.

His uncertainty was stilled when she brushed his nose with her own, her lip quivering under her somber sniffs, before finding his and pressing gently against them.

Luke had never desired to comfort so deeply, something he would have to accept eventually, the fear of it taunting his design. Some designs were flawed, and needed to be reworked, one line at a time. Luke matched her silent cries with equal force, the pressure of her lips drafting a new blueprint right then and there, for both of them.

The warmth of him swam into her, rolling across her with velvet bondage of security. Needing him, that was now his problem, the fact that she hated it, was hers, one long overdue to eliminate. She would learn to need again, need others, friendship, laughter, a purpose; one not created just to keep her spiteful. The refusal of this emotion was her beast to conquer, every journey had to start somewhere. Be brave Sammy.

"Stay." She whispered.

Luke had to control the punch in his gut, gagging it down motionless against her. He moved his lips across hers in a tender promise. They held there for many minutes, Luke allowing her to lead him through her process, communicated what she needed in between encouraged gulps of water.

The gravel declared the arrival of a vehicle, Doc no doubt, and Luke stood up.

"You ok to do this right now? Because I will tell them to wait. You're in control Sam."

Sam nodded and waved him off, he tugged his uniform taught to handle the ugly part of death and Sam slammed the glass down on the counter, startling him.

"You said I got a treat after." She looked so disheveled, so broken down, but a faint smile laid there, a hint of herself returning to her eyes.

"So I did." Luke answered, swiftly grabbing a bottle from their evening together and pouring some in the glass. "I'd say you earned it."

"Fuck you, Deputy."

Luke brushed his thumb over her pained smile, secured his duty belt and met Doc at the door.

~

The timing was shit, but he could hold off for a few days till the old man was in the ground. It gave him more time to execute his plan better anyway, and with the distraction of the town talk and funeral plans, it would be easier to do so.

It killed him to imagine how bad she must be hurting; how little he could do for her. In time she would see that his obsession with fixing the dirty hand she'd been delt in her life was worth it. Those closest to her had lied to her, made her believe things about herself that were untrue, and neglected the pain that was inside her. He took credit for some of that. He himself had his own crimes to atone to yes, but it wasn't as if Kallik would have let him anyway.

Shame about it, but the old man was due, holding Sam back from thriving, racing again, living finally. He would have gotten him out of the way earlier, but he didn't have the heart, not when Kallik had meant so much to her. That was just plain crazy. And he wasn't crazy.

No, he was a man who had to make things right. Now his time would come, to punish the ones who had hurt her, taken her for granted, and he would be left to be the one that she clung to, reached for, and he would do it better this time. He supposed Luke's failure to figure out the obvious culprit of the dog slayings, would have him shipping out soon, and that would be the grand icing on a very detailed cake. He had sacrificed so much for this, all for her. Sacrifices he should have made a long time ago, instead of breaking her heart.

Chapter 17

Shavila had shown up for the Shaw family, what was left of it, giving one of the town's most loved lifers every care and honor he deserved, while humbling Sam to her bitter core. She had never let any of them too close, but every single person in her life had not only been present, but in a way that had Sam feeling as though she had never really been alone, she had just made herself that way out of fear.

Something Sam was certain to pick apart and rectify when she finally dug herself out of the hole Kallik had left if her heart.

It had been a messy time when Kallik was taken from the house he'd built, Sam snapping like a tension wire when it hit her that, once his body crossed the threshold, she'd truly be alone for the first time there. A level of solitude, even her learned boundaries and damaged walls, had not prepared her for.

Luke was strong, but not as strong as a frightened Sam. She'd even bit him, and it'd taken James and Luke both, to calm her down enough to get her to say a goodbye she'd regret not giving, before prying her from that stretcher.

James picked up the dog paw charm necklace that had broken off Sam's neck in the struggle, and laid it across the banister of the porch. That shit head Brad had given it to her, and Sam had always said charm necklaces broke when you didn't need them anymore. Since they had one last job to do before they walked a straight path, James took it as a sign, and left it there for Sam to decide if she felt the same.

Now was not the time nor the place for her to think of any of that now, so on the banister it would stay. It was her right to get rid of it anyway, even if he wouldn't mind shoving it up Brad's ass himself. He might.

After the report was taken by a very distracted Luke, Doc signed off and, along with Fire Marshal Grayson hunt; Tig, Big John, Willow -foot in a cast and all-, Forest, and James, all carried Kallik Shaw out with dignity. Refusing a rolling, clunking exit for a man they all respected and loved.

Star came and helped James with Sam's dogs in the barn, assuring Luke they had it and to stay out. Luke's focus on Sam, he'd chosen to overlook James's oddly fierce refusal to let him in the barn, sighting he didn't have time to introduce Luke on how to do things in there, or the territorial canines, and to stay in his lane.

It was more than tense, but Luke didn't want to cause Sam any more problems, not this day.

Tamar dropped off Vanessa and Charlotte, who had come with food and cleaning supplies, before he and Big John went to build Kallik's coffin to the specifications Sam had mustered out with gentle coaxing from Tamar. They'd be up all night and well into the next day making it happen.

Luke had managed to get Sam upstairs so the ladies could wash all the recliner linens and be certain it didn't seem like someone had just passed in that room. They had snuck up to give her hugs and a run down on what they'd left in the fridge and simmering on the stove, before returning to town.

Luke had walked them to the door and noticed the house was spotless, every room. Even the fires had been stoked.

The only thing out of place was a small photo, the glass of the frame shattered, sitting on the coffee table. He'd seen in on Kallik's lap when he came for Sam, and supposed it'd fallen in the struggle she put up when he'd gotten there.

There was nothing for Sam to do now but mourn, even Roy had the biggest cow femur he'd ever seen to help him chew out the stress of the day. He'd promptly drug it upstairs, refusing to leave Sam's side, but was taken care of none the less.

A symphony of excited yips ricocheted off the cabin's exterior for a few minutes as Luke climbed the steps back to Sam. He smiled weakly out the window, at the sled team running zoomies around the yard, before being locked up. A few moments later, with one swift slap of Star's ass as she climbed in his truck, James drove off for the day.

Willow and Forest had assured Luke he was cleared for the next few days, happily assuming his shifts so he could be with Sam. Luke wasn't sure if she wanted him around that much but thanked them and said he'd let them know if he was coming in. He made sure to promise to pay back their days off asap.

During a rare bout of sleep that kept Sam from staring numbly at the wall, Frank had text her he was coming to be with her. She had limply handed Luke the phone and shook her head, before rolling back into a ball and finding that interesting spot on the wall to get lost in.

Luke knew Kallik had not been fond of Frank, Sam indulging during one of their hours-long talk sessions, and figured Sam needed more time before she let him in the home Kallik built, out of respect for her Paw. Luke responded as Sam, sighting now was not the best time.

159

At the risk of overstepping his boundaries, Luke kept the oddly aggressive and angry tone Frank's response took with her to himself, and simply turned off the phone. Frank may have been a father figure to her when she was a child, but you can't make up for being MIA after arresting her mother, by putting on a cape when her grandfather dies. Frank could deal with that later but he sure as hell didn't need to make today about him.

Luke let Roy out for a final night potty, hauled in wood and locked up.

He'd made his way to the barn prior, thinking he should do the final check Sam always did, finding it padlocked shut. 'Must be some expensive dogs' he thought, hanging his coat.

He sat on the edge on the bed at Sam's back and kneed his elbows. She hadn't said one word outside of the necessary choices one must make after a loved one's death, and he was content waiting for her to decide when she'd speak. Or tell him to get out.

After many moments of staring at the woodstove in the corner, he felt the bed shift and her hand on his back.

"Tell me what you need me to do Sam."

She brushed her hands across his duty belt and landed on his cuffs. "You ever have fun with these?"

"I was thinking you should eat."

"Spill it."

He exhaled a humorous breath. "No. And if I ever planned to, I wouldn't use these. No matter how much I sanitize them, I'm not putting them on a lover."

Sam flopped around to stare at his back. "A lover? That's an ok 'L' word... I guess." Her tone sounded like a disgruntled girlfriend.

He turned to put his forehead on hers. "You. I'm not putting them on you." She rose an eyebrow. "I'll get you your own pretty pair, and save these for all my dirty side chicks, how's that?"

She offered a faint laugh. "You put up with my shit pretty good Deputy." Her palm met his cheek. "Thank you." Her whisper became strained. "I mean that."

"Will you eat something for me?"

The look in his eyes sent her, and even though she couldn't imagine putting anything in her stomach, Sam agreed, on the grounds that strong alcohol came with it.

She managed half a bowl of soup, but the entire glass of scotch, much to Luke's grumbling discontent. While puffy eyed and sore from screaming, her soul couldn't shake the amusement she found in him, still clunking around in his duty belt, boots tight, and how fussy he was. Doting but cautiously avoiding poking the bear, her.

Sam only had herself to blame, she owned it. He did run a risk of getting barked at if he assumed that gear could come off, and supposed it was rather respectful of him to wait for a cue. She certainly had some work to do on her bitter flavor if she wanted this one to stick around.

And boy did he handle her like a pro, even if he thought he didn't know what he was doing.

It pinched her ego to admit, but she could do with Luke taking the lead more often, like he'd done when she was hysterical, because she needed more of that, a lot more, unfortunately.

Truthfully, under different circumstances, that kind of control would have been very, *very* sexy. Even if it stung her pride a bit to admit she needed a firm hand sometimes, too much pride never did do anyone any good.

Sam fought back the isolation impulse, yielding to the urge, and finally coughed it out, painfully.

"I could uh... use some... some comfort." She cleared her throat, as he slowly turned from his kneeled position filling wood stove, to look at her. "If you wouldn't mind. Feel like it. Or something."

She was so cute on her knees in a huge t-shirt, ringing her hands like a kid who hadn't done their homework. He shouldn't, but he just couldn't help himself.

"That had to hurt."

"It was very uncomfortable yes. Shut up."

He rose slowly and sauntered over to her, boots clunking the floor, until she was in his shadow. "Specifications?"

"I guess just..." She fussed with his shirt seams nervously. "I don't want se-"

"That goes without saying." He said tightly, almost insulted.

Sam shook a little.

He was a very good man, and she had no idea what to do with him, or what to say. She'd never asked someone to comfort her before and was certain he would run if she risked what she wanted. But then why did it feel so natural?

She chose the cowards way out, with just a dash of vulnerability to save herself.

"I've never asked someone to comfort me before, I don't know how."

Luke lifted her chin to look at him, her hands instinctively sliding up his chest. "Not exactly my forte either Sam." His thumb brushed across her lower lip.

"Been doing a hell of a job of it all day, Lucian."

He blushed a little. "Let me try a bit harder then, and we'll see if you can spit it out, if I don't get it right. Ok?"

Damn it he was such a good man. The almost six years he had on her was starting to feel like centuries.

161

Her eyes lined with water, and he made a decisive sound, hooking his duty belt on the bed post and ripping his laces off.

Sam sat back on her heels and watched him silently, his uniform folded on the bench, the water starting in the shower, his boxers hitting the floor. Finally, his is silent motions had her shirt over her arms and discarded.

He swooped her up and carried her to the shower and knelt to peel her panties down her legs. She muffled a laugh at his obvious arousal.

"I'm a man, cut me a break here."

"I'm sorry, I'm sorry."

He stood at her back and gathered her curls up, cursing as he bundled them, horribly, on her head.

"Impressive." She teased.

He said nothing, pulled her into the shower, and began feathering kisses over her steaming body, in between massaging her shoulders, and gently washing the sweat and tears from her skin. He turned her to face him, sinking his brown eyes into her green abyss, letting the water pound her back and he kneaded it. He felt the barbed wire softening, knew she was close to surrendering to what she truly needed.

Sam moaned a pleasurable sound and gripped his muscular arms, allowing herself to feel the gentle care she'd never had. It entered her like a missile and hit its target, the final barriers she had left in her heart exploding. She sucked in a breath and squeezed his biceps, unable to swallow the rock. The tears fell before she could stop them, along with any hope of sparing him the mess she knew would scare him away.

Sam buckled into him, the cave crumbling and the words spilling out like a dust cloud.

"I need you." She sobbed. "I'm so scared. Please just hold me."

He slammed the water off and she was off the ground and wrapped around him in a split second. He gripped her thigh and squeezed her back while she cried. Her face buried in his neck, her mouth clinging to his throat, the unbearable heaves vibrating his skin. She tried to suck them down and felt him give a firm shake.

"Don't you dare." Luke whispered. "I have you. Let them come." He stepped out and yanked a large blanket off the dresser, wrapping it around them both before sitting on the bed. "Pain doesn't scare me Sam, neither do you. Let er rip baby."

Luke held her, rubbed his stubble on her forehead, pushed her curls out of her face when she struggled for air, and guarded her like home when she clambered to climb inside his chest. He rocked her slightly when her sobs were childlike and restrained her gently when they breathed ancient, fiery rage. Steadfast as an oak, Luke stayed with her, until she finally shuttered and gasped to a slow, steady breathing.

He laid her down, pulled the covers over them both, pulling her tightly against him. Luke's fingers laced with hers and he buried his face in her hair, breathing in her lavender and pine wilderness.

This was way more than he could have imagined a few weeks in Shavila would bring him, and way more than one woman had ever pulled out of him, and yet he knew. The knowing was not the scary part, but what the rest of the week would bring, was.

Sleep would escape him for a few nights yet.

"This scares me. I'm going to push you away." Sam sucked closer to him. "I just know I will."

"You can try." And *that* scared him.

"Tell me a story."

He thought for a moment, then moved his mouth closer to her ear. He told her a story of an overgrown Deputy, a 'giant ape' some crazy woman had called him, receiving him an elbow in the gut from Sam with a fatigued laugh.

A guy running from his temper, discovering the rampant toxicity in big city departments, and seeing so many drugs on the street, were not for him, even though he tried so hard to do something. How he'd finally run like a coward with his tail between his legs, feeling useless. Seeking stability, calm, routine, an escape, instead of reenlisting in a panic. How he could not define what tormented him until he could; the damage of youth and war combined had made civilian life seem too hard.

He needed a sort of stillness; one he could control. The guilt of feeling like he should have stayed, that he was selfish for not wanting to continue to battle each day. Every arrest was back out on the street dealing drugs before he could blink, making him feel useless, and after serving his country, he wanted less hell than what he signed up for as a Deputy.

The struggle that brought against his ego, his sense of obligation.

That he'd picked the most remote place hiring and hadn't thought much about it other than it was a place to hide, to heal, to die in peace. 'No storms' he'd thought, stable and secure. Then he met this woman, and she was a god damn tornado, receiving Luke another elbow to the gut.

He yanked her closer, whispering how beautiful she was. How she was too short, too unpredictable, and exactly the chaos his broken life needed, even though it scared the shit out of him. That her storm had brought him back to life, and he hoped she'd let him chase it for a while. That he felt like she had been made just for him, had beckoned him here. Her green eyes the green light to find a way to stop running, that being just another guy was enough. He didn't need to save the world, he could disarm.

That he wanted to show her she could too, to please let him try.

Her long, steady breaths, heavy body, indicated she was asleep. How long Luke didn't know, but he meant everything he'd said, and he'd say it again until she heard him.

"Because he was obsessed." He whispered sleepily. "A snow fairy with a pistol for a mouth, had done what no artillery or threat had ever done."

Luke's eyes shot open a few hours later, the sound of footsteps outside pricking his militantly trained ears. He carefully slid from under Sam and leaned over the window and scowled curiously, his hand resting gently on his gun.

Bradley Oliver was rubbing his hair, pacing back and forth by the porch. He went to set a pot of flowers down, hesitated, walked some more, rubbed his wet face, shook his head. He paced a few more times before finally setting the flowers down and jogging out of sight down the rugged road.

"I'll be seeing you later." Luke sneered.

~

In the chill of the morning, Frank waited on the porch at Luke's request. The fact that the deputy wouldn't let him in the house, becoming a nervous twitch in his lip.

He hadn't set foot in that house -short of to get his things- since he'd taken Elizabeth Shaw in over 15 years ago, something Kallik had made sure of. Still, being kept out now, by someone who had only known Samantha a short time, was more than insulting.

He tried to muster up some understanding as footsteps scuffed towards the door. Frank knew Sam had loyalties unparalleled to her grandfather, and that he'd earned some of her coldness, it had been the norm between them for years. Yet what place Luke had earned beside her was a mystery.

Frank wondered if she knew that Deputy Lucian Rose had been investigating her, when the door finally opened.

Sam looked tired, defeated, but oddly calm and secure. Frank shifted on his feet and held up the flowers he'd brought.

"Three men have brought me flowers in the last twenty-four hours." Sam stepped outside, in Luke's shirt, Frank noticed. "I'd have a big head, if it didn't take someone dying for it to happen."

"I know you didn't want company, but I needed to make sure you were ok."

Sam rose a brow.

"I never stopped caring about you kid." He cleared his throat. "But I've got flowers now, and a hug if you want it."

Sam took a deep breath, finally closing the gap between them and accepting his embrace.

"I'm so sorry kid. I know this was an awful blow." He pulled her back to cup her face. "I know you're never gonna forgive me for backing off after I took your mom in, but I wish you'd let me be here for you now."

Sam took the flowers and went back up the stairs. "I might Frank, if I thought you were doing it for me, but it won't fix anything. I will always care about you, but I don't need you. You taught me not to."

"Damn it Samantha, I got you away from an addict!"

"And left me, instead of being the dad you lied and said you would be. You were obsessed with my mother, and once she was gone, I didn't exist."

"You are a part of her, I will always love you kid."

Sam nodded. "Only because of that." Her face soured. "Jesus why are you bringing this up now Frank? We have hardly spoken for years. It's done." She shook her head. "You're a good man. Thank you for the flowers."

"Is Luke a good man?"

The man in question was at her back before Sam inhaled the breath it took to speak, the screen door slamming behind him, Roy at his ankles.

"Time to go Frank. You can talk this out another time, but she needs compassion and support right now, not someone trying to use her anguish to make amends." Luke shifted Sam beside him to clear a path should he need it. "I respect your place in her life, and your rank Sir, but you need to carry your own load for now." He gestured towards Franks patrol truck.

Frank tugged his pants up and nodded. "You're right. I'm a bit emotional myself, my apologies. I mean that. Let me know if you need anything kiddo, I'm good for it. I'm sorry about Kallik."

Luke watched Frank drive away before turning back to the house.

"A good man?" Sam shook her head as if blown away. "So far, I'd say so."

Luke smiled and took the flowers. "Vase or trash baby cakes?"

"Vase. I love white roses." Sam rubbed her tired face. "That was awkward I'm sorry. It is always like that. You never really get over a father figure arresting your mom and skipping out on you."

"You two seemed pretty ok in the office."

"Dead puppies Luke. It breaks me up. Even though our relationship will never be repaired, I do care for the man, and a small part of me craves a father from time to time." Her eyes dampened. "And I don't have Paw anymore, so now I suppose Frank abandoning me back then, has some fresh pain to it." She rubbed Roy's fat head, gagging her tears back. "I'll just add it to the list. Not my first rodeo."

Luke drew her in close. "Mind if I stay off that list?"

Sam used his neck to pull herself up to kiss him. "You have more coffee waiting for me when I get back in, and you won't be."

"You sure you don't want some help in the barn? I'd like to-"

"No." Her tone, harsh quickness, showed on Luke's face. "I could use a few minutes alone before I go approve the coffin."

Luke watched her round the house with Roy on her side, a pit forming in his stomach.

Chapter 18

The funeral would be in two days. Luke had fielded phone calls, let Charlotte and Vanessa in a time or two to exchange dishes and clean, waving off Sam's assurance they didn't have to do any of it. James came by once to help with the dogs, Sam taking over the duties fully out of need for distraction. He gave her a huge hug, and surprisingly, shared a laugh with Luke, clapping him on the back in thanks for being good to 'His Sammy'.

Willow and Forest had covered for Luke as promised, but still took one of those nights to slip away and get Sam hammered on the porch, Luke wrestling her spaghetti limbs to bed just before the sun rose.

The day of the funeral, Luke suited up. Frank, Willow and Forest, all needed to be in civilian attendance more rightfully than he did. Sam said it was better for her that way anyway, she had months to prepare for this emotionally, and would be stronger if he wasn't at her side. Luke understood and went about his day shooing moose out of the road and fielding minor tourist issues.

Judging by the lack of locals about, half of Shavila showed up for Kallik. School was closed, and so was the general store and bar. After Luke simmered down some less than understanding tourists in front of the store, he headed over, standing by a far tree and out of sight.

The coffin was wood burned in Kallik's native tongue and had a grizzly bear on the top. The rumored early Spring had come, but it still took a backhoe and a good operator to get that hole in the ground. Kallik's old fishing grew, those still alive anyhow, had just placed some memorabilia on his coffin and the crowd was starting to scatter.

Sam smiled and gave hugs as they dispersed, a pile of flowers building beside her. Darleen and Frank gave a wave as they drove by, and Big John walked away last to wait by the machine to fill it in, before he headed to the bar where most of the town would gather to remember.

Luke was unsure if Sam wanted to go, but his shift was over in two hours, Frank would be clocking in, so he'd go with her if she wished.

He watched her, so still, staring at the hole her grandfather now laid in. The muscular strong woman who faced bears and chased mountain lions for a living, looked so small, so alone, even as Roy laid dutifully at her feet, cute bow tie and all. Her curls were black as night, moving with the faint breeze along her lower back, hands trembling in her pockets.

He wanted to go to her, heeding her request causing an outright war in his intestines.

Luke had buried many soldier brothers, stood by and served uniformed stranger's final walk, had even attended for a fellow fallen officer, but had never watched someone he cared about mourn. He only hoped he knew what to do when the noise died down, and it was just another day. Because while it would be for others, it wouldn't be for Sam for quite some time, and he had no idea what he was doing.

Sam stared at the bear on Paw's coffin, or what could be seen between the dirt thrown in, native offerings, and flowers.

She had been prepared for this for a very long time, and yet she still thought he may just get out laughing, like he did when he told her a fish was already dead and it flopped like hell in her hands, slapping its tail in her face when she'd picked it up. She smiled, a silent tear dropping down her face.

Paw had always told her fish stories, but the bear stories were her favorite. How he and her father Liam, in nothing but their underwear, had run out of a tent and chased a bear away from their smoke rack, only to have that bear turn tail and send them screaming for their lives. Another time, Paw had thrown a fish to a bear blocking the shore he needed to pull up on, and it had led him to drinkable water, leaving him be for the night until he was rescued in the morning.

There was also a bear rug in her living room, a story more frightening, that left her mother saved, Sam in her belly, and her father grateful to his own. He had come home to Kallik offering prayers of respect, for the animal he had to kill, to save his son's wife and unborn child.

The stories changed over time, to dreams.

Sam loved that Paw and she were strong bears conquering a mountain together in his visions, a strange bear always watching from the shadows. It never made sense to her, but she never cared. She had her Paw, and they were surviving together, the strange outside bear mattered not. She always figured it was her father in spirit, and that's why its fur was so strange to the terrain.

Sam loosed a heavy wind from her tired lungs. She would keep climbing, both of them in spirit now to guide her. She blew Paw a kiss and pulled her curls into a messy explosion on her head, done with being pretty for the day.

"I love you Paw. Thank you for being everything for me. You were all I needed old man, and you did better than anyone could have. I'm going to be ok." She patted Roy's head. "Let's go home."

Sam's peripherals caught movement. Swiftly, she snapped around, Luke's back silently strolling from the far-off tree behind her, getting into his truck and pulling away.

Big John thumbed towards Luke. "Strange bear, that one." He gave Sam a gentle smile and turned on his machine to fill the hole.

She huffed a laughed. "Yea he is."

As they began to walk away, Roy trotting beside her, Sam suddenly stopped and whirled around to where Luke had been, breathlessly blinking back the water gathering in her eyes.

"Strange bear…" The wind kicked up, pulling her from all sides. Sam spread her arms and looked up to the sky as the breeze swirled around her. "Well played old man. Well played."

~

The bar was full of well-dressed locals and love. Big John had Kallik's favorite music playing, and although it wasn't a fan favorite, everyone was more than happy to sing along to Gordon Lightfoot and tell stories of Kallik popping them on the heads for smoking weed and repeating his fish stories.

James was more than happy to take a bow for having the 'hugest nuts' for daring to knock boots with Sam, when every other boy in school had been scared shitless of Kallik's Baleen blade skills.

The memories flowed, a joyful celebration of life.

Sam shoved James into Star's awaiting arms and waved them off laughing, accepting one more beer from Big John.

"That big deputy of yours gonna talk to anybody or just stand there looking scary?"

Sam flicked her eyes to Luke, who was leaning against the wall with a hard eye on Brad. "He's just giving me space, which I asked for." She took a long pull from her beer. "He is also on duty hun."

Big John leaned over the bar, it protesting under his weight. "Not with you he ain't. So don't take too much space, because by the look on his face, even a good man can be tortured by doing what's asked of him."

Sam blushed and lowered her head.

"He's it, isn't he?" Sam lifted wet eyes to his, and he patted her hand. "Lean the hell in kid, I'm glad I did, even if I didn't get ya, it was worth the shot, cuz I never would have known otherwise, and that is an unbearable thought aye?"

"Indeed." Sam swallowed hard. "You're a good man, John."

"Shut the fuck up Sam." He gave her a wink and lifted jovial arms to friends as he made his way across the bar.

Sam turned to face Luke, downing the rest of her beer as his eyes met hers under the brim of his hat. He looked so pissy she stifled a giggle.

He had been such a good boy all day, and he clearly was not happy she had asked his to keep a distance. But he had, without a single gripe. Gave her the space she asked for, respected her, but still stayed close, because he needed too. She'd be a damn fool to not adore the shit out of that, or the sexy man attached to it.

Sam leaned back on the bar and crooked a finger at him, biting her cheeks to hold the smile forming. The joy he tried to school out of his face, had flashed just long enough for her to catch it.

Big bad deputy, I see you, Sam thought.

Luke lifted from his lean and walked over to her, his mass blocking out the light above her. Everyone they knew was in that bar, and Luke wasn't sure how she needed him to be, or if she was ready to blow the lid off the sauce can that was their a very hot attachment, when it had only been rumors thus far.

His question was answered as the weight left his back foot, her hand yanking his duty belt against her.

"You know, my boyfriend is a Deputy too. Maybe you know him? Big guy, kinda frigid, really sexy."

Luke clenched his jaw, red heat rushing his face. "How drunk are you?"

"Two beers Deputy, I'm square." She reached up and touched his gritted jaw tenderly. "Ashamed of me Officer?"

Like hell.

Luke tilted his head, lowering to claim her mouth, clutching her body close as if she had been on another planet all day. Sam lifted and opened for him, his gentle tongue flicks and firm hands a declaration of his failing sanity, a blaring truth he pulsed into her with zero reserve.

He wanted everyone to know he claimed her, and she could feel it rushing through his flexing arms. They were slowly, tenderly lost in that sweet kiss, when an eruption of whistles and whooping exploded in the bar.

They both chuckled in their kiss before breaking away to face the onslaught.

"Atta way Sammy!!" Willow lifted his beer clapping.

"Hey!" Tig hollered. "What kind of station you running Chief!?" The locals exploded and more jabs flew. "Oh wait he's not Chief yet guess he can make out on the job huh?!" Charlotte jumped on Tig's back and bit his ear to shut him up, much to the delight of their audience.

Luke lowered his hat to cover his eyes and turned his red face back to Sam. "Guess you can't take it back now hmm?"

"Wasn't planning on it, Bigfoot."

Luke lifted her chin and brushed his lips across hers. "I'm off in an hour." His voice was so deep it echoed in her bones. "Text me if you want compa-"

"I want." She smiled. "Warnings no longer apply to you Deputy, just show up." She smacked his ass and headed to the door.

"You tamed the beast man." John gave Luke a wowed look.

"I sure hope not, my guy." And Luke meant it.

He wanted her wild and just the way she is, always. That is how she'd gotten inside him, and unfortunately, that was what she needed to be to survive what was coming for her, in less than twenty-four hours.

He'd had a meeting with Detective Scott earlier in the day, and his heart ached with the thought of what this woman was going to have to carry, after what she had just been through. He only hoped she would forgive him for what he must keep inside now, so he had a chance to help her later.

~

He loaded up the gas cans and went over his final plans. Tonight, would be as good as ever, he'd waited long enough, and Sam would find comfort in the closure this brought for her. Sam would be home and recovering from the day's events, and most of Shavila would no doubt be closing down the bar or too drunk to notice any out of the ordinary activity from a local. The long days were here, but later was better, then the fire marshal would be delayed to act, hopefully.

He covered the cans and walked back to his other vehicle, resigned in his choice. The fucker deserved it for the way he hurt her, and she needed to be shown that he himself, still cared. Then she'd let him in again. She'd be free of the weight and race again, when all of it came tumbling down on the one who deserved to fall for it. She'd forgive him for how he'd hurt her. He put the dog paw charm necklace back in his pocket and began the rest of his night's delusions.

Chapter 19

Luke decided to test the theory and open the door without knocking. The house was silent, urging him to drop his bag loudly to alert Roy he was there, so he wouldn't get bit. The dog knew him by now, and liked him well enough, but he protected Sam like no other, and Luke certainly did not think startling him was a good idea.

When no clunking, fat feet sounded, he took a couple steps and peered in the living room, Roy's head on the arm of Kallik's recliner, his body curled as tight as his lard would let him, in the seat.

"Awe buddy." Luke knelt by the recliner and loved up his ears. "I know pal, it'll be ok."

"Everyone says he my dog, but he loved Paw more than me, I think."

Luke turned and almost fell back on his ass. "Jesus Christ Samantha." He took his hat off and drug his hand down his sharp features. "What are you trying to do to me?"

Sam was backlit from the hall light, casually drinking water as if she wasn't stark naked before him. Her hair was in two loose braids framing her breasts, spiraled tendrils draping in her face, dusting daring green eyes that were more dangerous now than he'd ever seen them.

The shadows silked over her tone and wrapped around her curves, emphasizing the very body that had broken him, and she absolutely knew what she had. The little dip in her hips that guided his eyes to the feminine swell of her belly was the thing ancient artists were known for painting, demanding he crawl on his knees and beg for the sweet death she offered.

He shifted, but didn't rise, the desire to crawl to her, almost paralyzing him.

"I haven't been able to walk around naked in years." She headed to the kitchen. "Sue me."

Luke turned to look at Roy. "Don't eat my corpse dude." Roy harrumphed annoyed.

Luke hung his hat and duty belt, clearing his chamber and tossing his gun in his bag before he walked into the kitchen. He found her cruelly bent over in front of the stove, pulling something out that he refused to shift his eyes off her, to identify.

"Samantha, if this is a test." He grunted down his shaky tone. "I'm about to fail." He slid his hands around to grip her stomach and back her into his painful arousal. "Horribly."

She pressed into him. "I was always... *aggressively*... distracted in school."

Copy that.

Luke spun her around and lifted her on the counter, ripping his uniform shirt off before stopping a breath from her mouth. He gathered her braids and pulled her head back, brushing his lips against hers, releasing a guttural sound from his depths. Her thighs fluttered around his hips, her hands exploring beneath his undershirt, a content sigh entering his mouth before he dove on hers.

He was rough and demanding, her tongue consenting to his brutal need. He had been so good to her, so gentle, a generous lover, so caring and kind, so damn patient. More than any man could have been so soon. Sam wanted him to be none of those things right now. She needed Luke to need her in a way that he couldn't control, and he was almost there.

That mind of his was reeling, she could feel it. Questioning all the things, she herself, was plagued with.

"Time means nothing." She ran her tongue over his sharp jaw line. "You either know in five minutes, or you know in five months." She rubbed her cheek on his throat. "I know *now*, and I no longer fear if you don't."

He stared into her truthful gaze, the vulnerability dwelling there with a fuse about to spark. The blast could destroy him or save him. Wouldn't change that he knew the moment she barreled around the side of her house with pure hatred in her eyes, that she was a drug he'd never get out of his system. Like water for life, that could drown you. Wind that obliterated walls, while promising to never let you hit the ground, and this was dangerous ground.

"Think later." She cupped him through his pants, squeezing. "You have been so patient, so gentle with me... I need you to turn that off tonight."

He growled, biting her bottom lip. "So be it." His voice was dangerous, lifting her off the counter and pushing her back down on the kitchen table. He released himself and slammed her knees apart, driving into her readied need.

Sam's arms flew above her head as air violently left her throat. She gripped the table's edge as Luke drove into her mercilessly, his dark brown hair falling into his piercing stare. He bore into her eyes, indulging himself in her reckless abandon as he rammed into her, gritting his teeth, his fingers painfully squeezing her thighs to be certain she felt every inch he gave her.

She arched her back and cried out for more and he delivered, pistoning into her with everything he had, relishing in the water that gathered in her eyes.

"Lucian…"

His name escaping her lips almost sent him, but he was no fool, and had handled himself before he came over.

"You're in for a long night baby." He grunted out, before he leaned over her, grabbing her hands to continue his feverish bucking with the table as leverage. He bit her neck and rolled his hips deeply. "What do you need Sammy?" He pressed himself to the hilt, ripping a surprised squeak from her. "Tell me what you want."

"Everything you've got." She gasped out. "Claim me."

Jesus this woman was going to kill him.

He pulled her up and spun her around, shoving her feet apart and pressing her chest to the table. When he felt her entire body relax, he hesitated, watching her fingers curl around the edge of the table, a rapid realization sweeping over him.

He made her feel safe, and she was surrendering, her blissful face a picture of relishing in its newness. He clenched back the water pooling in his eyes and ran his hands up her spine, back and forth in worshipping acknowledgement, before he rifled into her. His fingers were gripping her hips so hard, her skin flushed up between them, causing her to cry out as he worked. He felt her begin to rise and pressed his back to her, holding her face so he could watch her go.

Her release was beautiful, her cheeks rolling against him as she writhed on the table, her throat vibrating under his grip with her pleasured sobbing. She slickened them both so much he almost lost his load, slowing himself to make sure he had enough left in him to answer her pleas again.

He brushed the hair from her face, placing a comforting hand under her tabled cheek before kissing every surface of the other.

"I want to make you do that over…" He glided in and out slowly. "And over again."

He pulled her to standing and pressed her back against him, her body curled just enough so he could finesse her pulsing desire as he spoke.

"I want you Samantha, just the way you are." She whimpered as he pressed as deep as he could go. "You are mine."

She came again, her nails ripping into his neck as she buckled against him, weeping in ecstasy. The man she needed had kept her skillfully stimulated, and the words were exactly what she'd asked for, and too much, all at once.

She went limp and he swooped her into his arms. Sam curled into his chest gasping for breath as he kicked off his boots and pants, briskly taking her upstairs, after he'd squatted down to grab his gun.

His strength was astounding enough, but something about this giant cop hauling her upstairs with a gun in his hand, sent heat to her core and pulled a giggle from her throat simultaneously.

He dropped the magazine out and clunked his weapon to the bedside table. "Safety first baby girl. I don't leave it out of reach." He put her on the bed. "And I'd rather you weren't either."

Luke braced his hand on the log headboard and leaned over to kiss her. She seductively explored his mouth, a familiar clanking sound sending his hand snapping to her wrist, halting her. She was quick as a snake, his eyes falling on his wrist just as the cuff locked around it.

"Always watch the other hand, Deputy." Sam smirked at his hardening lines.

"Cops aren't a fan of being the ones in cuffs sweetheart."

Oh he was so pissed, and Sam was eating it up like candy.

He yanked his hand, now cuffed to the headboard. "Where's the key Sam?"

She slid off the bed and backed towards the wood stove. "On the dresser." She began to slowly release her braids, Luke reluctantly sitting down to face her, his hand tense against the restraint. "You're awfully cute when you're mad."

"You won't think I'm cute when..." Shaking her curls free distracted him. "When I rip this headboard apart... oh fuck." He jerked his cuffed hand.

Sam had grabbed a second set and began to saunter towards him, rendering him silent as he came to full attention. She slinked up his thighs, pushing him back on the bed and throwing his legs on it.

She worshipped every inch of his skin as she made her way up his body, finally grabbing his other hand to join its restrained partner.

"You're not cuffing my other hand Sam."

She slid her wet center over his swollen lust and his head fell back. "God damn it." He bit, the other cuff slapping into place. "Where the hell did you get these anyway-"

Her lips plunged firmly to his, devouring his words. "Shut up Luke."

Sam massaged his shoulders as her lips explored his skin, flicking and kissing every part of him, giving special attention to the bear paw tattoo that sung to her. There was no part of his body she hadn't gently teased or romantically caressed by the time she felt the tension finally ease from his body.

Luke watched her make love to every part of him, realizing too late she was doing so. She was worshipping him in every way, no threat imminent to deflect, the damage was already done, and this woman had written promises on his body as if carved in stone. She had surrendered over and over, her body, her sorrow, her fears, and now she begged him to let her claim him.

Time is nothing, he repeated in his head, and he knew. Luke knew. He'd be addicted to her for the rest of his life. He let the tension leave him and surrendered to the one thing that finally broke him, the wilderness whispers of a wild woman.

Sam ran her tongue across his bottom lip, taking it with her as she backed down his body, holding his bewildered stare as she slowly slid herself down on his swollen need. His fists flexed and released, his breathing shallow, air left him with a nervous laugh, the tingling in his skin making it impossible to gather himself.

Her eyes never left his as she moved, rocking and rolling in smooth waves, pleasuring him with her body in the most erotic way he'd ever experienced.

He followed the firelight over her body as her arms lifted her hair, her hips grinding him slow and steady, her own pleasure radiating off her skin. Sam's head fell back, gasps of joy and sobs of bliss making her chest rise and fall with his own exasperated breaths.

She was lost with him, and he knew he would never see anything more elegant for the rest of his days. He lifted his hips, rewarded with a curl of her lips and deep moan, her thighs beginning to quiver around him, her assault hardening. Her hands slid down her body and Luke felt himself about to lose it.

"Get these off me." He gritted.

Sam reached up and pushed the tiny button on both cuffs.

"Trick cuffs-" His hands slammed around her face. "You are fucking evil."

"Definitely." She clawed his chest and began to work him wildly, the bed rocking with her force, the sounds of her pleasure filling his mouth and shattering his final reserves.

He clutched her face and bared his teeth, feeling her clench around his imminent explosion.

"Lucian.. I…" She sobbed the words silent, before screaming euphoria into the roaring growl of his violent peak.

They burned together. No longer a ship battling the waves, no longer a soul seeking shelter, they created the storm, their bodies fusing together to let the lightning strike, and the thunder roll.

Luke pressed her down on him, pulsing his heat into her impassioned tremble, tasting her mouth and feeling the telling salt burn out of his eyes. This was the second time she had melted away his hardened shell, pulling tears from him simply by being everything she was. She had made love to him, poured everything out of her, and reached the darkest depths of him in the process. He would not hide them, a tear reaching his ear as she sat up on quaking arms, to meet his face.

Sam watched the tear leap from her eye and give her secrets away across his cheek, to mingle with his own.

Luke opened his mouth to speak.

"Later…" She trembled.

"Ok baby." Luke closed his lids and pressed his forehead to hers. "That's a good 'L' word."

Chapter 20

Detective Harley Scott paced her hotel room. She had tracked his movements, and Sam's for good measure, for the past few days, most revolving around the funeral preparations and actual burial, if not mundane tasks.

She had all the paperwork and almost everything was in place, yet if this suspected action was not halted before its execution, the results could be devastating, the worst of it landing on a person who had nothing to the detective was here.

Harley threw her glass against the wall and stared out the window as the sun finally hoovered on the horizon, signaling night had fallen upon the endless sun season.

She could smell it was close, the days given to Sam, out of courtesy and now, she was certain, stupidity, on her badge's part, had risked much. Her informant had lit a rocket under what was just a mild dog snatching investigation-one quite below her paygrade-throwing it into a full-fledged homicide investigation, with more seemingly pointless moves and tabloid pages than a bad movie.

If the suspect hadn't shown signs of making another move, she had nothing but speculation and the word of her informant, and given the suspects clean record, hardly enough to gain a warrant to search his property, something she knew would tell her what she needed to know. She'd already searched the barn during the funeral, without a warrant and in desperation, finding exactly where Sam fit in the equation, and what to do about her.

It was a delicate dance between waiting for probable cause, while simultaneously being quick enough to keep him from succeeding, less more lives lost.

Harley grabbed her badge and zipped up her boots. It may be a risk to the final draw, but it was time to pay Samantha Shaw a visit.

~

It was as dark as it was going to get, and Sam knew she needed to finalize plans with James for tomorrow evening, feed and settle her dogs in for the night.

They had been neglected a bit the past couple days and could use a rip around before she fed the massive man next to her, a selfish sliver hoping it'd fuel him for another round of mind-blowing sex.

She muffled a chuckle and kissed his arm.

Sam had a boyfriend for the first time in fifteen years and felt like a foolish little girl, endlessly horny to boot. She was grateful she still had the stamina to enjoy it, after truly resigning to never letting someone get close to her. She heard the weight of her sigh and shook her head, knowing she was in deep, with mild alarm that she didn't care.

She'd kept people at arm's length to hide her desperate need to be loved, enough, wanted. The only one she ever believed genuinely did was dead, but truth be told, she had hoped Luke would too, before Kallik's last breath had left him.

She couldn't blame the loss, no, only her reckless abandon, wholly her own desire, to let Luke in. She didn't know what it was about him, but he had done it, so it didn't matter. She would face his back if he walked away, and then she could truly be the icy bitch she'd created to protect herself, but for now… maybe…

Sam rolled over to look at Lucian's smooshed face on the pillow and laughed. Ok then, let's try this open arms thing, not just with him, with those who kept trying too.

Take Vanessa and Tamar up on dinner. Try to teach the dog training courses Star had suggested. Open a real rescue and do it right. Maybe it would feel good.

A low howl sounded from the barn.

No part of her wanted to get out of that bed, the man wrapped around her a warm sanctuary one would never wish to leave. The dogs, however, knew it was dinner time, and Sam reluctantly groaned out of the bed.

Her thighs were bellowing their soreness as she jumped into her holey jeans.

"Can chase a bobcat up a mountain and ya beg for more." She hipped her hands, offering her thighs a disappointed look. "But ride the hell out of built man and yer crying wolf."

"If that was a ride." Luke gave her a side eye. "I'd really like to see how you f-"

"Do not even complete that sentence, Lucian." She barked a laugh. "You pig."

The sex-drunk man stretched and sat up slightly, the blanket falling down to tempt her with his beautiful lines.

179

"You know, cops aren't too fond of that word." He crooked his finger at her. "Come make it up to me."

She flashed him her chest before offering a middle finger. "Gotta feed the dogs, especially Roy." She winced. "He hasn't been eating well since… anyway I won't be long. We should eat dinner."

"I will." Luke licked his lips. "But you are dessert."

Sam's knees buckled.

No matter how hard she tried to keep her sharp wit, this man was crippling her with every move he made. How good he was with his mouth aside, the tenderness he gave her through those days of mourning, were a glimpse into who he was at his core.

His eyes twinkled at her, and she felt a heavy rock take seat in her stomach.

Hours ago, they'd cried in the throes of love making, and here he was, being a smart ass, light and playful, knowing she would push him away and lock up in self-preservation if he mentioned it.

No, Sam thought. We just went over this. You must try.

She straddled him and sweetly kissed his lips, slow and sure. "Lucian Rose, you can have whatever you want, for as long as I'm breathing."

He fisted her hair and buried his face in her neck. "Then live forever."

She giggled at the stubble tickling her neck, hopping up to slip into her boots. "Dogs first big boy, then dinner, then we'll attack the F word."

"I'm gonna help." He went to get up. "Then maybe I'll get the really good F word when we're done."

"No!" It came out sharp, hardening his face. "I'm sorry, I uh, need a few minutes alone anyway." She smiled nervously, trying to gather herself. "That romp was, a bit intense ya?"

Luke glared under his lashed. "What's in the barn Samantha."

She paled, and by the look on his face, Sam knew he'd noticed.

Damn it. If she had gotten rid of those puppies before Paw had passed, she would only have had to keep him out of the back stock room for a few damn days.

She had one last hoorah and then she'd walk the line. She didn't want to lose him right before she gave up this law bending obsession for him.

Her insides went sour. He had been interested in her file when they'd met, the fact sending a sudden bolt ready to poke her cloud nine.

What if all of this was so Lucian could get information of her, turn her over.

She took a step back. "Why are you with me?"

Luke got the memo and stood up, holding the blanket around his middle. "No. Don't do that."

"Then start talking Deputy, because I don't know why you give a shit other than-"

"Enough!" He shouted, causing Sam to angle towards the door. "Damn it you are so impetuous with your assumptions, you never let anyone finish a damn sentence!

Luke exhaled his temper. "I am here for you, not a case." He tried to make himself look smaller at her guarded stance. "It's just a little odd baby, ok? James kept me out too. Can you blame me for asking?"

Think fast Sammy, you have an out.

"Luke, you're being a nervous cop. Of course, he did. J knows my dogs. I have a sled team of rowdy ruckus wolf breeds in there, caged or not, that don't know you. That's all." He wasn't budging. "Roy almost ate you and he's a fat mutt. How about a proper introduction when I'm not starving, and it's not their feeding time? I have no issues with that." A Lie, but it bought her some time.

Luke's face softened, sitting down he ran his hand through his hair. "Sorry Sam, I'm used to golden retrievers and shit. Didn't really think about it like that."

Sam tried to keep the relief from showing in her body. "I'll be right back, and we'll eat." She paused at the door. "Don't ever yell at me like that again."

"Let me get a word in before you slam up your glacier walls and I won't."

She snapped her mouth shut, thinking better of biting his head off, remembering she had to try.

He wasn't wrong, she got defensive and mean in a blink, something he picked up on very early, and clearly wouldn't tolerate. While that left room for good communication and would force her growth in a good way, her rough edges might cut through it brutally.

So, while the make-up sex might be great, when the arguments came, they were going to be ugly unless she learned to gag down accountability well, something she didn't like much.

Sam slammed out of the house without Roy, all the reasons why you don't rush into things busting out of the 'Be Brave' box she'd put them in.

He was good for her, and it was scaring the shit out of her.

Luke jumped into his pants and downed the water by the bed. Nervous cop or not, if this was going to work, he needed to know he wasn't falling in love with a criminal.

Growls and yips pulled him to the window, where eight dogs were losing their bloody minds creating a tornado around the house in between play-fighting and leaping up on a laughing Sam.

Damn those dogs were huge. So was her smile.

She loved dogs so much, you could see it in every part of her movements, her eyes, even when she yelled at them to behave there was adoration in her tone.

Luke hung his head and shook it. He didn't want to know; damn it he didn't want to know.

He was about to drop it, for now, when he saw Sam pull out a phone he'd yet to see, and start typing away, before letting out a high-pitched whistle as she walked back to the barn, a pack of hungry teeth on her heels.

He sat on the bed and steepled his hands on his brow. "Son of a bitch."

Sam stared at the map while the caged dogs ate their dinner, four tumbling puppies finally vaccinated and ready to go, right outside the door.

Thankfully, she'd had one taker, a nice family in Yukon, and James was ready to rock tomorrow.

She only hoped the delay with the funeral hadn't put any more risk to the dogs she was preparing to liberate.

She checked the food bins next to her desk and sighed. She would have preferred to have rehome these puppies before holding more, but James said he may have a spot for them right away, and Sam was praying by tomorrow he confirmed it.

She didn't know how in the hell she'd feed them all, let alone keep Luke out of here long enough to-

Sam turned her head to see Roy standing in the doorway of her office.

"How did you… oh hell." She turned her back, knowing what was coming, before Luke stepped behind her best boy. "Traitor." She mumbled, her voice already shaking.

"He'd make a good cop." Luke's voice mirrored the militant tone he'd taken on duty, and it sent her body to a tremble.

She wasn't afraid of anything, or him for that matter.

No.

She trembled because she could feel her heart breaking apart, along with the world she'd so foolishly thought she could have. She felt nauseous and palmed her desk, lowering her head to take a deep breath.

Couple the dog's meals with Roy's presence; they hadn't given two blinks about the tall man that had just walked past them, sounding no alarm. She may have had a chance if she kept him out of here, but there was no explaining the giant map on the wall beside her, nor the trail of her hits, marked like a beacon of guilt.

He walked up behind her and looked at the map. "Tell me this is an art project."

The gig was up.

He had no choice but to arrest her, and it sent a wave of emotion coursing through her that she'd never felt before.

That map showed every place a dog had been stolen from, and every place she'd scoped out, even if she hadn't needed to execute the location. Which was which didn't matter, it was done.

"You know better." Sam murmured weakly.

He loomed behind her, his eyes dancing over the map.

She didn't need to look, she knew he was putting it all together, so she stood there, and waited, begging her legs to hold, give her a final walk of dignity when he drug her out of there in cuffs. He had no reason to hide this for her.

Despite what was said, what was shared, they were so new, and he was an Alaskan Deputy with a code to follow. If the last thing she could give him for being there for her, seeing her, showing her she was worth it, even for such a short time, was making sure he didn't lose his badge over this, so be it.

She'd go down for James, and this man who had brought her to her knees.

Sam stood up straight and exhaled, Luke's heat on her back.

"Those puppies…" He tapped his finger on the exact place she'd taken them from. "You rode through that storm across the lake to get them almost two weeks ago, the same night Brad's pups were taken?"

"Yes. Different breeds, I didn't hurt his dogs."

"I know god damn well the breeds and that you didn't. But you risked your life, for dogs!?"

"I'd do it again."

"Of course you would." He punched his finger on Bradly Oliver's house. "What do these marks mean Sam?" She said nothing. "Sam god damn it, what do the X's mean, verses the circles?" She swallowed hard, the tears coming. "Sam, I need to know, this is bigger than you."

Her breath hitched.

She didn't know what that meant, but given that she was being interrogated, she just shook her head. She'd tell it all, put it on record, but she was not going to have Luke do it. She couldn't bare it.

"James helps you, doesn't he?" Silence. "And if I'm reading this correctly, you have lifted over fifteen dogs in the last year." Sam clenched her jaw, her heart disintegrating inside her. "Alright then. That's all I need." He slid his hand down her right arm and grabbed her wrist.

She sucked back a sob.

"Samantha Shaw, you have the right to remain silent, anything you say, can and will be used against you in the court of law."

He whipped her around and backed her into the wall, his face a force of rage she had never seen. "So don't you dare say a god damned thing until I'm fucking done."

He lost the temper he kept so well hidden, and violently.

Luke grabbed Sam's burner phone and shattered it against the wall before careening back around and flipping her desk on its end.

Her hands slammed to her mouth as she slid further back on the wall, sinking to her feet, Roy growling in front of her as the Deputy raged.

Luke drug his hands across the map, tearing it to pieces and cursing. Feed bins tumbled down, her laptop met his powerful fist, and every obscenity known to man flew from his mouth, the barn an eruption of snarls and howls.

He heaved with his back to her for a beat before releasing a long exhale and slowly turning to her.

"I have to leave." He made huge strides to the door.

"I know." Sam buried her face. "I knew you would."

He stopped, keeping his back to her. "I said I had to leave. I didn't say I was leaving you."

She peered up at him. "I don't understand."

Luke fisted his hands at his side. "Neither do I." The large barn door made a deafening sound as it slammed shut.

Luke threw his bag in the truck, his hands shaking. He had to calm down before he made a choice.

That woman in there had him wrapped around her finger and had also committed robberies that had made the papers many times over. She should be in cuffs, and why she wasn't, was what he needed to figure out, before he decided ultimately, if she would be.

He gripped the steering wheel and screamed.

He didn't think he could put that woman in cuffs, but damn it what was he supposed to do? Lose his job? For a woman he hardly knew? His heart thudded otherwise.

Time did not dampen the love he felt for her, and he knew it.

He'd ignored all the signs because of it, telling himself what he wanted to hear so he could have her. He fucked up everything, and now he had to decide if he could live with it. He was about to pull away when headlights blocked his exit.

"Bad timing Detective." He snarled, slamming out of the truck and meeting her nose to nose as she got out.

"Back off Deputy." Detective Scott nudged him back. "I just want to talk to her." She noted his disheveled appearance. "Rough night?"

"Private property. Get out."

"Went in the barn, did you?"

His brows lifted, taking a step back. Harley brushed her front off, as if he'd gotten 'barn' on her, and smiled.

"I've already been in there. Ah Listen." She lifted her hand to silence him. "For her safety, I needed to know, or I couldn't pull the trigger I need to pull, and soon, or this could get worse. Luke, she was out of town when all those dog deaths occurred."

"I'm aware." He bit. "And she is not capable of hurting dogs." A questioning look held his face, demanding her clarity.

"That's not my case, it's yours. But what's in there, adds to the circumstantial evidence and backs up what my informant said, and that is all I care about. However." She gave him a serious look. "There is evidence in that barn proving her crimes, and every single one of the locations she's stolen dogs from, has gone up in smoke at varying times, since I arrived here."

"As in arson?" Harley nodded, sending Luke's eyes darting around in calculation, finally pinning the Detective with dagger like sharpness. "She was with me, short of the funeral, which half of Shavila saw her at."

"That too I am aware of." She tilted her ear towards the symphony of canine yips coming from the barn. "Doesn't change the four puppies in there matching the description of the ones lifted in Anchorage, now does it?"

Every muscle in Luke's massive body bulged. "Stop pussy-footing around detective and get to the point, I have shit to do."

A muscle ticked in her jaw. "Do not make me the bad guy here and watch your pay grade. I will do my job, and you will do yours." She tugged her suit jacket tight. "Based on that map in there, you know as well as I do there are two locations the next hit could be." Luke clenched his fists. "She may not have set those fires, but someone who knows what she's been doing, has, at every location she's hit this past year."

Harley lowered her voice and stepped closer. "Deputy, he has been trying to keep eyes on her to see this through undetected, which leads me to believe after he hits that mark on the map, her house could be next if his already questionable emotional state snaps. He's obsessed. Profiler thinks he wants to take everything from her so she runs to him."

"I can't have her no one can." Luke murmured as Harley concurred, sending his military training to school his entire body into a professional lockdown. "What is the next move Detective?"

"I have to locate the suspect. He has eluded me this past night while you've been dicking down a person of interest." Luke bared his teeth and Harley grinned in warning. "I need you on the beat by the morning. If what we assume is correct, he's going to execute this within the next day or so, the policy on the house has just finalized."

Luke filled his lungs and held, wrestling the contents of his stomach down.

She followed his head as it snapped to the side in anger, lifting a pair of handcuffs. "You do it or I do. It is the only way to ensure she doesn't get hurt Luke. She'll forgive you someday."

Luke made his badge visible on his hip and reached out for the restraints, heat rising to his face in a whirlwind of emotion he was failing to hide.

Sam jolted to a stop when she noticed them.

"You manipulating, lying sack of shit!" Her voice shook under the weight of his betrayal, forcing her feet to run to the door, Roy growling behind her.

"Samantha…" Luke knew his words would be futile. "You need to listen to-"

She spun around at the door. "Tell me how the world has suffered by me saving them!? No good deed goes unpunished huh!? While the ones who abused them are walking around gathering more." She sucked back a sob. "How low can one person go to snag a case?"

The pain in her eyes incinerated every inch of Luke's fortitude.

"I hope it was worth it Deputy Rose." Luke clenched the cuffs and took a step towards her. "Get off my property cop, and come back with a warrant." She slammed the door, a devastating scream seeping from the cabin walls.

"Luke."

He snapped his head to Harley. "Your tactics leave something to be desired, Detective."

She lifted her chin and grabbed her door. "As do yours, but time is of the essence." Detective Harley Scott's face washed in an expression that sent Luke to pause "Then again, as it pertains to Samantha Shaw, well…"

Her fingers brushed across a weathered photo of a combat dog on her dash. "That's not my case, now, is it?" She gave him a wink and drove off.

~

Stupid moron passed out off more booze than a man should drink in one night, he thought. Serves you right to go up in smoke with it, you mourned nothing but the fact that you weren't there for her, that you made her cope alone, you selfish prick. He tossed the gas cans back in his truck, hidden back in the trees and lit a smoke, taking a long pull.

"Damn old friend, how I've missed you." He inhaled deeply again, dropping the cherry on a thin black line. The trail began a slow, painful crawl towards the house. "I'll be long gone by the time you burn, and just as surprised as everyone else."

He nodded and let his truck slide back silently in neutral. "It is done Sammy. The wrong is put right now, and I'll be waiting to hold you through it."

The ember crawled towards its gas-soaked destination, a team of sled dogs shaking and stretching, waiting for their daily run.

He watched the truck bubble and hiss as it sunk into the lake, as Shavila rested, minutes away from waking to sirens, chaos, and all the wrong things, put right, finally.

Chapter 21

Detective Scott walked into Frank's office like she owned it, grabbing herself a cup of coffee before he could mention she could stand to knock.

"Help you Detective?" He looked exhausted, dirty, a file in front of him. "You don't normally come in on the night shift, ain't much going on tonight."

"Can't sleep." She mused. "Curious where we are in the case of course… my patience for the sentiments of this town's recent loss have run their course, naturally." She leaned over to peer at the file. "What you working on?"

Frank abruptly slapped the file closed, clearly aggravated. "Stolen truck report. Not your concern."

The corner of her mouth curved. "Touchy this late, are we? Long night?"

Frank leaned back and laced his fingers on his belly. "We just buried a well know local and half the town was drowning in booze from three pm on, what do you think?"

Harley aimlessly stirred her coffee. "Tragic. Any more leads on the dog nappings?"

"I already told you." Frank bit. "We got nothing, and not a trace on the guy who covered his tracks in flames either. Its gone cold. So why don't you make yourself useful and figure it out so I can finish this report. Your presence here has been less than helpfu-"

Willow slammed into the door in a panic as the first siren pitched out from the distance. "Frank, fire, it's bad."

Frank stood up, his inquiry drowned out by the Detective's coffee cup splattering on the floor as she whirled towards Willow. "Where!?"

"Bradley Oliver's house."

~

Luke sat on the porch for a long while, his hands clutching the cuffs to the point of pain, as Sam cried inside. The door was locked, he'd tried it.

He knew he should do more, hell he was about to break a window to get to her, but -his lack of relationship skills aside- the guilt conflicted him. Not the fact that she'd done it, or that he knew. No.

Luke had made a conscious choice to get close to her, fully aware she was likely breaking the law. It was that selfish, reckless choice to ignore it, that swallowed him. Some perverted self-centered part of him, hoped it would all just fizzle away, so he could have his cake and eat it too. He'd fallen for her so fiercely, that the facts in front of him seemed expendable.

What's more, he couldn't stomach how many officers pocketed drug money on busts, broke the law themselves when it suited them, made excuses for those close to them, even planted drugs to arrest someone they disliked -all things he'd witnessed- and yet he was expected to haul this woman in for taking abused dogs and finding them better homes?

It threw him completely. He stomped his boot and tossed the cuffs into the dirt.

It was all so twisted. Marijuana growers doing twenty years for a damn plant, when rapists were getting five to seven years, only to rape another the second they got out, and how many more they didn't get caught for.

No one's lives were ruined, no therapy needed, for the abusive owners of those dogs, hell even murderers got less time that someone who wrote bad checks sometimes.

Luke glanced at his badge.

Damn it he loved his job. He wanted to do good things, the blatant corruption leading him to a small town in Alaska, where doing the right thing suddenly seemed corrupt in itself.

He rubbed his jaw, noting the silence from inside. It was his case, and the odd inflection in the detective's voice left him to ponder, the hint that he was in control of how this ended, as long as Scott got her murder suspect.

He never saw himself as a crooked cop, Sam not hesitating to call him out on taking justice in his own hands not only as a soldier, but looking the other way so James could fill Brad's mouth with the knuckles he deserved. None of it was right, technically, but neither was a putting a woman who rescued animals, to no gain of her own, in cuffs.

Not just any woman, his woman. This broken cop on the steps, was in love with that raging storm on the other side of that door.

Luke stood, and set his badge on the banister, before getting ready to kick the damn door in. Not the cop, but the man who loved her.

Sam flopped on the recliner, her face swollen from crying, too defeated to count the minutes until Luke, or even worse, Frank or the twins, showed up in full uniform to haul her in.

She'd lost Paw, and now, on the brink of walking the line, ready to do things right and stop rebelling against things she needed to stop being angry about years ago, was about to lose everything else.

She clutched Roy's head, fearing what would happen to him, this house Paw built, her sled team that she loved with all her heart.

Not all of it. The overgrown bastard that had just used her, held her heart too.

She knew she should hate him, and she did, but that did not dampen her heart's ache. She had known long before one was supposed to, that he was it for her, even when everything in her said, to keep him away. The risk was there, she could not deny it, and had selfishly made the choice to let him get close, knowing it could cost her.

She sighed and elbowed her knees, her curls flowing wildly around Roy, his wet nose nudging the broken photo of her father on the table.

Sam grabbed it carefully, the frame splitting, glass cracked. "Sorry Dad. Maybe it was best you didn't watch me grow up. I'd have disappointed you." And edge fell off the frame to her feet as Sam's eyes pooled again.

She sniffed and began to remove the photo. "I'll reframe ya Dad. So you're safe till I get out of the slammer." Her eyes narrowed on the folded edge. "What the hell?"

Sam lifted the flap, her eyes widening at the full scope of the photo she now held. Her breathing hitched, choked and sucked inside her.

Younger or not, there was no mistaking the eyes of the man who stood next to her father. He stood there, ready to go out on the ice with her daddy, the last day he was alive. She had no idea he'd ever known him; her father Liam made a jovial face and pointed at the man next to him, Frank.

Sam flipped the photo over, the words slicing her open.

'The one who came back, is her father. We will be a family. -Your Frank'

Sam clapped her hand to her mouth and shot up, running to the sink and dry heaving into it.

Paw had always hated him, and he was with her Dad on the day he died. Her mother said she got the photo from one of 'Liam's friends' as a gift at the funeral.

Sam stumbled back against the sink as a rapid realization took her feet from under her. No. She looked nothing like Frank. She had a native tint to her skin and shape to her eyes, Frank was whiter than her Irish mother, no.

The green eyes and curls were her mother but damn it, this black hair was her daddy's, her Paw's. Paw would have told her, wouldn't he? This had to be a sick joke, or a drug fueled scribbling...

Her mother's addiction, Frank's presence, the echoing words of their fights, came flooding into her traumatized brain, causing Sam to clamp the sides of her head.

"This is your fault Frank, I'm sick because you took it too far!" Her mother had screamed. "You made me need this!"

Sam had been too little to understand, but as her head spun, her life's truths that she had blocked out, buried, flashed before her with aching clarity.

"You're obsessed! I told you I loved him!" The argument before Frank arrested her mother, sent Sam hurling into the sink again.

She'd shot up and destroyed the house, Paw dragging Sam out to fish.

"She will never be yours Frank! I'll tell everyone!"

"I'll lock you up if you so much as speak a word of it, Elizabeth!" Frank had bellowed. "I warned you this would happen! You did this to me! To him! You two timing hussy!"

Sam had panicked and pulled away from Paw, grabbed her mother's purse. Found the drugs, her mother subsequently trying to yank them from her little hands, sending it raining on her. Her mother had slapped her, and Frank had her in cuffs before the first tear left Sam's eyes.

Paw had simply given Frank a firm nod and taken Sam to get cleaned up. Paw had let Frank come get his things, and while he'd allowed Frank to see Sam occasionally, he'd never let him across the door jamb of that cabin again, the visits fading to nothing when Frank hard started dating Darleen.

This was a bad movie and Sam had just opened pandora's box.

Sam clung to Roy on the kitchen floor, her breathing rapid. She knew she would be taken in, she'd broken the law, and she would go. She didn't know what this meant, or how much of it was true, but if there was a possibility Frank killed her Daddy, her sweet Paw's only son...

Abandoned her after the fact, didn't fight for her, prove she was his to see her... He'd ruined her life for nothing. For vengeance over a woman he was obsessed with.

Sam grinded her teeth as more rushed through her. Only one man could have gotten passed Brad's security to steal those dogs, besides her, and it was Frank. She'd given him the access code when she had him come get the rest of her things when she left Brad.

That's why Bradley thought she'd taken his dogs... He hadn't changed the code after she'd left, always hinting she'd come back, turning it to torment when she didn't. It made sense how he managed to pile them and burn them on Brad's lawn undetected as well.

Nobody could have pulled that off, and he barley did, as that random ankle injury was no doubt the bite Brad had mentioned his dog took out of somebody.

Sam spun slightly, Roy leaning his big body against her for strength.

Frank's sick obsession with her mother, and her, whether she was his biological daughter or not, had destroyed her life and the lives of so many dogs, for what? What was he trying to do? Sam stood and gripped the sink.

He had strategically kept the suspicion on her, so he could do it. Hurting the things Sam loved the most? Was he punishing her for being angry with him for abandoning her? For not loving him like a father?

Dogs were the only thing Sam loved, Paw the only person, except… Oh god. Brad. Frank knew she had loved him, deeply, and he had hurt her. That's why he hurt Brad's dogs; the Iditarod leads and his puppies.

Sam clutched her stomach. Frank was hurting anyone and everyone she loved because she hadn't loved him. He was going to pin this on someone she cared about. Eliminate Brad or, she shuddered, James. Sam rubbed her face, trying to find logic. This can't be. If he hurts Luke…

"No." She rinsed her mouth out and locked her spine. "My father went down, my mother went down, I'm going down. Then so the hell is Frank Brown."

Boots on and gun strapped to her thigh, she gave Roy a big kiss. "You're my best boy. James will make sure you're ok buddy. I'm not letting him, or Star, go down for being my friends." She hugged him deeply. "I'm going to fix this so nobody else gets hurt. Thank you for standing by me pal. You're a good boy. The best boy. Forgive me."

Sam opened the door, narrowly dodging Luke's boot. "Going for excessive force or what asshat, Jesus!!"

Luke palmed the door jamb to steady himself, looming over her. "That's the second time you've called me that."

"You deserve it. Get out of my way."

"Samantha, listen to me for a damn minute."

Her head snapped to the horizon. "What the hell is that?"

Luke turned. "Oh fuck."

"I used to stare at that spot every night." She palmed his chest. "Luke, that's Brad's house."

He grabbed her arm. "Get in the truck."

She yanked free. "Like hell."

"You need to be safe!"

"Since when have you cared, you asshole! You used me to find your clues!" She let out an angry sound. "Broke my damn heart is what you did! Go to hell Sherlock!" She peeled out in her Bronco, shooting rocks into his shins.

"Son of a bitch!" Luke spun to grab his badge off the ledge, before running down the driveway and leaping in his truck.

The familiar sound of a gun hammer locking back sent Luke's hands up.

Frank sat up in the back seat. "You made this too easy son. Nice gun by the way." He nudged the back of his head with the barrel. "Get out. You're about to be the reason Brad set your girlfriend's barn on fire, and I'm about to have a very busy evening writing reports."

He shot Luke a cruel grin in the rear-view mirror. "And comforting my baby girl."

~

Sam skidded on to the road that led to the bluff where Brad's million-dollar home sat, her truck barley stopped before she leapt out, making a beeline for Brad.

He was yelling at the Fire Marshal to save his dogs, all hands focused on putting out the east side of his house that was in flames.

"Brad son, I know, but I need you out of the way!" Fire Marshal Grayson Hunt was filthy and scattered.

Chaos was erupting around them as volunteer fire fighters, including Willow, Forest, Tig and Big John, scrambled for water out of half frozen pipes, the tanker not yet arrived. Tamar was feverishly directing boaters away from their vessels, the risk to much for them to attempt to move them.

"We barely got you out son." Grayson hollered. "We'll do what we can, but these flames need to be out or the whole dock could go up!" He whistled to Detective Scott, who was intently scanning the spectators. "Keep him back detective."

"Those dogs deserve to live!" Brad snapped, moving his fit body at the speed of light towards the kennels.

The back lot that held Brad's dogs was heavily smoking, but not yet lit, the Gazebo next to it threatening its imminent combustion.

Sam took off running, Detective Scott slamming into her and restraining her. "Don't you dare."

"I loved that man, and Frank knew it." Harley stilled; she knows. "I can't let him or more dogs die."

"You don't need to fucking die either." She pulled out her cuffs. "So be it." The first cuff clapped on Sam's wrist.

"Detective! I took the dogs in Anchorage. And more." Harley froze a moment, and it was all she needed.

Sam dropped low, and took off towards the kennels, one cuff loose on her wrist.

"Sam wait!" James grabbed Detective Scott's arm. "Where the hell is Frank?" He snarled at her.

James had been made aware of the situation and had been keeping tabs on Sam for safety while they waited for Frank to make a move. It was risky, but Luke's distraction made it necessary.

James's loyalty to Sam unparalleled, he'd agreed to help, on the grounds that Sam or Star didn't go down with him, and he got a plea deal on the charges; ones he would claim to be his and his alone.

Scott shook her head. "I don't know, I ran out with Willow as soon as I heard, thinking Frank was on my heels, but I have an idea. If he was planning on pinning this on Brad or you, he'd have to give a damn good motive. Which means, if he isn't here-"

"Samantha's dogs." James panicked. "Where's Luke?"

"If he is where I think he is, this just got worse."

"You should have brought more agents in. What the hell do we do?" James took a step towards the flames his best friend had just run in to, torn between going after Sam and saving her dogs.

"James, I need your help." She gripped his arm firmly. "What would Sam want you to do?"

James bit his words. "Save her dogs." He fisted his hands. "And the man she loves." He spun to the detective. "Well, she's shit out of luck, because Luke would want me to save her." He ripped his jacket off and tore out towards the flames.

Brad was yanking and kicking the kennel doors, coughing violently when Sam slid into him and began to join the effort. The dogs were drooling and fighting to get out. Brad did a double take on her and she smacked him.

"Thank me later idiot! Why won't these open?" Sam ducked as debris fell from the roof, sparks flying.

"Padlocks!" He coughed and pointed. "I didn't want them hurt like my babies!" He kicked panicked. "They're too hot to touch I can't-" He thrashed about. "I can't lose my babies Sam, they're all I have!"

Sam reached for her gun, Brad grabbing her. "No! Don't kill them you monster!"

She shoved him back, and one by one, walked deeper into the flaming kennels, firing the locks off and releasing the dogs.

Brad cried out and herded them towards the opening, James blasting past him.

The last dog was limp, Sam jumping in to lift it as a piece of roof came down, blocking kennel door. She screamed in pain as the heat flared, covering the dog with her body.

"Sammy!" James hollered. "Sammy god damn it answer me!"

"Here!" She coughed, kicking an opening. "The back!"

James slid down to the small hole. "Give me your hand honey now, she's coming down!"

Sam shoved the dog through the hole. "Take him!"

"God damn it Sam!" He yanked the limp dog out. "I can't carry you both! He's gone."

"TAKE HIM!" She pleaded. "He can make it!"

"Sammy honey please." James reached in for her, his body too large to fit through. "You're my rock kid, come to me please. PLEASE!"

"You're my best friend James, I love you." Sam was struggling to breathe. "Take him, take care of Roy."

Brad hauled James back and-lean enough to fit-dove under the debris, yanking Sam's legs towards him. "You always were a pain in the ass." He rasped, coughing as he hauled her close.

He shoved her towards the hole and James ripped her through it. Sam kept her hand on Brad, pulling him through as James bellowed under the weight of both of them, collapsing on his back.

James growled up and hauled up the limp Iditarod champ, and the three of them ran like hell as water singed and hissed, causing the kennels to collapse as they tumbled to the ground outside it.

From the time Sam had pulled up to the moment she tumbled on the grass, less than ten minutes had passed, but it felt like hours.

A coast guard helicopter had come in, and medics were on them before they could blink.

Brad rolled over and grabbed Sam's hand. "You... Sam..." He slid closer to her. "Samantha. Thank you." He began to cry, as a medic hauled him back and snapped a mask on his face.

Sam managed a middle finger before the mask came over her face and she fell back, Brad steaming his up with a hefty laugh.

"God you're a bitch." He chuckled.

"And you're a piece of shit." She choked out.

"I know." He laced his soot covered fingers with hers.

James was shoving back medics, declining help, on his knees next to Sam, moving her hair and patting her down.

"You ok Sammy huh? Ya? You're alright ya?" He gagged back tears. "You're alright honey?"

She fisted his hand, his calloused palm swallowing hers. "Where's my damn gun?"

James launched his head back laughing. "Thank God."

The medics had astounded looks on their faces as they pulled the mask off and sat her up, giving her an all clear, demanding she hit the doctor in the morning for a follow up.

James yanked her into his chest and squeezed. "All that damn bounty running has you in some ridiculous shape, you crazy kid." He sniffed and coughed. "God damn it you scared me, Sammy."

"I'll work on it." Sam smiled through glassy eyes. "I'm working on it."

The smoke plumed and filled the sky, beginning to steam as it settled under the water, half of Brad's house in ashes, the kennel destroyed. Red and orange jackets, as well as many helpful locals, were running around shuttling bottles of water, dog crates and helping Star administer medical care to the struggling canines.

Medics had managed to stabilize all but two of Brad's sled team, and James held Sam closer as she watched Brad cry over their bodies.

She knew then, as he'd run back to his certain death to save them, watching him cry hysterically over the ones he'd lost, that he had known Sully would pass on that course, gave her one last run, knowing it's what made the dog happiest.

Yes, he ran his dogs too hard, but he didn't abuse them, race dogs often race themselves sick if you didn't reel them in. The vet said Sully had gotten to something toxic, racers had been known to poison as a way to cheat, and that even if Sam had got her to the vet, she wouldn't have made it. Sam had stayed angry because she should have been holding Sully as she passed, knowing Brad had distracted her to keep her from watching her baby die.

It was not the right thing, and her broken sled was proof he was still a piece of shit in many ways, winning more important than helping her through the loss, but he wasn't a dog abuser. No man in his thirties, built like that, with all the money in the world, sobs over dogs like he was doing right now, if he hurt them intentionally.

Horrible with women, yes, but Brad loved his dogs.

Sam sighed into James's gentle rocking. One more thing she needed to let go of. Her anger was her responsibility, and she needed to chip away at all the resentment for things that happened to her. They were not her fault, but damn if it wasn't her responsibility to live better than the legacy, they laid upon her.

Luke.

What she'd done was her fault. Her crimes were her own, and she had to give Luke a chance to speak, before she added him to a list of people to hate. He was an officer of the law, and she had known the risks, having been the only one of the two of them, with the full picture, when they'd started this relationship.

Accountability was a bitch, not Sam's favorite thing, but she had to try.

Sam shot up and looked around, her eyes falling on the Detective marching towards her. Although she didn't need it, looking far worse than she felt, James helped her soot covered body to its feet, minding the scratches on her arms.

"I will tell you whatever you want to know," Sam lifted her chin in strength, "but I would like to see Deputy Rose first, if you don't mind."

"You and me both, princess." Harley checked her gun. "But we have a situation, one that cannot leave this circle, or lives beyond your boyfriend's could be at risk. You understand?"

Sam took a step forward. "Where is Frank?"

Harley slammed the magazine in her gun and Darleen cleared her throat behind her.

"When the fire started, he headed up your road." Darleen's voice was trembling. "I'm sorry Sam I-"

"Sentiments later." Harley quipped. "Darleen has been an informant for many weeks leading up to my arrival here." Sam flicked her eyes to Darleen's hanging head as the detective continued. "I'll fill you in later, but long story short."

"I know." Sam gritted. "I'll fill you in on how I know, later as well. Where the hell is Luke?"

Harley tilted her head. "How good of an actress are you?"

Chapter 22

Luke heard Sam's bronco pull up the driveway and slowed his breaths as best he could. He'd be grateful to see her alive and uncuffed, assuming he may not live through this, but would have preferred she wasn't at risk to the Chief of Police's current psychotic tendencies.

As he knelt there, cuffed in the middle of the barn, helpless to do much with a gun to his head, he only hoped Sam would know the truth and be able to get herself away from this asshole before he did something to her.

"Oh dear, we have company." Frank sighed. "Guess she'll just have to understand the why's, before we follow through with the how's, huh?" He nudged the barrel to Luke's head, receiving a dark glare from the man who'd have him in pieces if he wasn't at gun point. "Hate to burst your ego before you die son, but she's gonna wonder why you couldn't manage to overpower an old fart like me, and that's certainly going to affect your sex life anyway."

"You're no hero." Luke spit. "Coward."

Frank hauled the gun across his face as Sam rounded the corner.

"Sorry pups been a long day I-" She palmed her chest in surprise, lunging towards them. "What the hell are you doi-"

"Ah!" Frank put his gun to Luke's head. "You do anything, and I'll pull self-defense so fast your little head will spin."

Luke spit blood on the ground and took her in under lowered lashes.

She was covered in soot, a few holes in her leggings and a little scratched up, but her hair was pulled back and she was alert, wits sharp. She must have run in that fire after those damn dogs. He smirked a little, of course she did. Damn he was ever blown away by this woman, utterly smitten.

Luke stiffened slightly, averting his eyes from the slight bulge in her boot, one easily missed unless you had a militantly trained eye to see it. She never armed herself there.

She knows, she's ready for something.

Luke began to check the perimeter, being sure to keep his head still.

It was so hard for Sam to see Luke like that. Even on his knees, damn that man was proud and strong, still a massive force to be reckoned with. His chest breathing deep and steady against his muscle shirt as he stared at her, the heat in his eyes. He was worried, but he didn't know her that well yet. And she had back up.

Once she got him out of this, she'd have to ask Luke how that potbellied sucker fish, got him at gun point. She pulled her eyes off the dog charm necklace around his neck, controlling her grimace.

Frank was a sick man.

"Easy Frank, what are you talking about?" Sam slowed but kept moving forward. "What's going on? What'd he do?" The barn was awfully quiet, and Sam noticed all her dogs were gone. "Where are my dogs, Frank?"

"Back run. Luke got himself a nice bite on his arm helping me move em." Frank nudged his head towards the photo on the floor. "And I think you know my sweet girl. Noticed you found my little gift to your mother." He flicked the gun against Luke's head. "I wasn't going to hurt this one, but the opportunity presented itself." Sam stepped closer and Frank lifted a second gun on her. "I am doing this all for you, do not make me ruin it."

"Samantha." Luke's voice was gentle. "Baby please. Stop."

"Baby?" Frank laughed. "Boy you had him in deep."

"I certainly did." Sam grinned widely; Frank had just walked her into this better than she could have hoped for. "But you know what they say, best way to get away with it, is right under their noses." She hipped her hands. "Guess you taught me that, Daddio."

Frank's eyes welled and he lowered the gun he had on her, holding firm the one to Luke's head.

Sam shot Luke a wink when Frank wiped his eyes.

Luke bit the smile down from his cheeks. That's my girl.

"Dad…" Frank sighed. "Damn I waited so long to hear that. You aren't mad honey?"

"Well." Sam rocked her hand. "I'm a little pissed about the dogs, that was a bit excessive." She softened her sooted cheeks and swooned slightly. "But Brad's demise wasn't. I helped, made myself look pretty good, and covered your sorry ass. I have questions of course… but nobody has ever gone to such lengths to show me how much they love me. Brad deserved it."

Detective Scott had briefed her on dealing with this level of psychopathy, and she only prayed how she shook on the inside, wasn't apparent on the outside.

Frank glowed. "Yes, my girl, he did."

"Brad hurt me so much." Sam pushed tears to her eyes. "I only wish you'd had let me help."

She took a step to the side, and Luke shifted. She was lining Frank up and damn it, he was going to help.

Frank yanked Luke's shoulders up and dug the gun into his temple. "Move again pretty boy and you're done.

"Wait! No!" Sam cleared her throat; she'd almost lost her cool. "Is that necessary?"

"He'll talk." Frank's eyes caught movement outside, anger flashing across his face. "You're a deserter like your mothe-"

A shot rang out and Frank dropped, his shoulder hit. Luke rolled out of the way as Frank shakily lifted his gun to him, bellowing with nonsensical rage.

"You belong to me Sammy!" Frank suddenly fell back violently with another shot, Sam shaking from her kneed aim.

Detective Scott, Willow and Forest rushed into the barn, Sam frozen in place, her breath stilled in shock.

Luke got to his knees just as Willow was kneeling beside Sam, reaching up for the gun Detective Scott had given her.

"Let go Sammy." Willow said calmly. "Put it down my friend, so the detective can cuff Frank safely." He palmed her back. "You have to lower it now Sam or I have to get physical with you. Please honey. It's over."

Sam trembled, the panic riding on her quivering lip.

"Samantha." Luke said softly, sitting back on his heels, watching her tears fall as she looked at him. "Give Willow the gun baby. You're ok." She began to shake harder, Willow about to engage and disarm her. "I love you, Samantha." Luke whispered. "I have you. It's over."

Sam dropped the gun and clambered across the dirty floor, throwing herself around his neck.

"Bullshit asshole. I have *you*." She buried her face in his neck. "I thought you were dead before I got here." She rifled kissed all over his face. "I thought I lost you. Oh my god I was so scared." She sobbed into his collarbone. "I *am* so scared. What the hell! Why did he do this?" Her fingers dug into his skin as the shaking took over. "I'm so scared."

"You get to be. You saved my sorry ass baby. Damn you are-" Luke fought with his cuffs. "Somebody get these fucking things off me please!?"

Forest ran over and uncuffed him as Willow and Detective Scott hauled Frank to his feet. He was barely conscious, with Detective Scott's shot in the shoulder and Sam's shot in his forearm, but they managed to shuffle him up to put distance between him and a very tapped out Sam.

Forest clapped Luke on the back to make sure he had Sam well enough for now, before dialing for the EMT and jogging out to assist.

Luke gathered Sam and stood, wrapping her around him. "You are the most incredible thing I have ever seen."

He claimed her mouth, both of them in a panicked frenzy, devouring each other as if the other would disappear, her tears smearing soot all over his face.

He dug his fingers into her thighs. "I meant it Samantha. I love you, and I don't give a shit how crazy that sounds. You get me?"

"I'm still mad at you for keeping this from me." She inhaled his neck deeply. "So mad."

His hand fisted her hair, forcing her to look at him. "I accept." He sniffed her. "I do not, however, accept that you smell like a god damn boy scout camp."

She buried her face laughing. "I'm mad, don't make me laugh."

"Too late, I'm off the hook."

"Like hell." She whimpered.

He hitched her up higher with a grunt. "Fair enough."

Detective Harley Scott cleared her throat, pocketing her hands as Luke let Sam slide to her feet.

"I suppose." Sam swallowed hard, eyeing the cuffs on the detective's belt. "I have to go in now because-"

"Well." Harley interrupted. "This had been quite an evening, for a boring small town. I will need both of you down at the station to give reports as soon as my boss hits the train platform in the morning. I'll be taking a brief statement now of course." Sam and Luke exchanged a glance as she twirled around. "Pretty clever, Frank planting those puppies in here to make it seem like Brad was doing this all this out of spite, your history is indeed, well known."

Luke raised a brow at her smug face.

Detective Scott shrugged. "Might have worked too, with that big policy Brad took out on his house, if Frank hadn't gotten selfish and tried to add Deputy Rose to his body count." She blew out a breath. "Attempted murder of an officer? I'm gonna get a damn good pat on the back for this one. I'm just glad he didn't get around to lighting this place on fire. No water to be had at the moment." She gave Luke a sarcastic look. "Oh, I suppose you still having a heartbeat counts for something Deputy."

"Thanks?" Luke gave her a wary look.

"I'll need your report on this as soon as possible Luke. Frank has a large paper trail of dog nappings to cover, and oh.." Harley snapped her fingers. "Darleen needs to sign off on the dates Frank hid those pups into their garage." She grinned at Sam. "Which she is more than ready to do." She clapped her hands. "Well, I have shit to do. Get that report in Luke." She went to head out.

Sam rubbed her head. "I don't understand, I…"

"*You...* need to find a new hobby." She winked and pulled her jacket tight. "Thank you for your assistance, Ms. Shaw. That will do." She raised her voice when Sam went to speak. "You know, this town could use a dog rescue, you think?" She rapped the door jam and slipped out.

"What the hell just happened?" Sam felt the smoke she'd had for dinner turn in her stomach as the adrenaline slipped away. "Why would she do tha-"

"I think." Luke pulled her into him. "You have absolutely no idea what she's talking about."

Sam gagged down her smart-ass retort with his warning glare, shrugging in grateful and indescribably humbled defeat.

"Understood Officer."

~

Reports were taken, made, and filed. James handed over the puppies as evidence, a shelter in Anchorage promising to find them good homes. Sam begged to keep one, and after proper photos were taken, she tucked it in, excited to hand it over to Denali when things settled down.

Darleen had submitted copies she'd made of the love letters, pregnancy and Frank's diary weeks prior, all to be submitted as evidence for Frank's trial in the murder of Liam Shaw.

James had come to help make sure the dog team was fine, sharing a private conversation with Luke that ended in Sam's ape man giving James a bear hug, he looked rather awkward in, followed by a firm handshake. Safe to say they would be on an even playing field after Luke ponied up the beers James said he owed him.

After Doc had seen to Luke's bite on his forearm, Sam asked him to take blood from her to be sent in for a DNA test. Sam was given antibiotics to ward of any risk of infection in her lungs and scratches, then scheduled for another round of checkups by the medics in town for three days from now, to ensure her lungs were clear.

She was assured Brad was ok, by Doc, and again, he refused to charge her for the antibiotics, settling for her to run off the next bobcat that sniffed around his house instead.

As the morning began to approach, Charlotte would not take no for an answer, barging up the driveway declaring Vanessa would not go back to bed until Charlotte had hugged Sam herself, and called her to let her know she was in one piece.

By the time the chaos winded down, it was nearly dawn, Luke and Sam having a zero-fun shower and passing out, Roy obnoxiously sprawled out between them. Just as well, Sam was still reeling with confusion, guilt and a bad case of shock, touch was not her love language on the best of days let alone in this state.

She had spoken to Luke for a bit, cried hard in the shower, and knew she had more to work out, asking him for space when he got up to handle his reports in the morning.

Sam watched him drive away, sliding down against the door, a solid introvert's sob fest long overdue. It had been the worst week of her life, and she did better alone, at least she had convinced herself of that as she wept.

~

Darleen wiped her nose and tried to steady her hands as Frank hung his head in front of her, cuffed to the bed of the hospital; Anita's looming, protective presence on the back wall, mirroring Detective Scott's stance.

"Why'd you do it Darleen?" He didn't bother to look at his wife.

"Same could be asked of you Franklin." She slammed her palm on her thigh. "I am your wife, and you didn't think what this would do to me. So you look at me old man, you owe me that much." He lifted his head, tired, filthy, stripped of his uniform, bandaged and disgraced. "You will remember the face of the woman who loved you more than anyone, that you lost because you couldn't have the one you killed for."

She took a deep breath. "I did it because I can only swallow so much. I knew you would never love me the way you loved Elizabeth Shaw, but I was grateful to have you, the one I always wanted, and I was a good wife to you Frank." He dropped his head again. "But I could not in good conscious, allow you to parade around this town in that badge once I found that diary. Those letters." She blew her nose and made an angry sound. "I know I shouldn't have read it, hell I wish I hadn't. But you killed that girl's daddy Frank, on the off chance she was your child."

"She is my daughter! Elizabeth was in my bed more than his!" He growled, Anita and Detective Scott both lifting from their wall leans at his aggression. "This wouldn't have happened if you'd let me be close to her."

Darleen huffed a pained laugh. "Blame me if you want Frank, that's the least of the pain I'll carry. She didn't want you around long before you asked me to dinner, and you did not even verify she was yours! You could have told her, asked her for a DNA test!" She grabbed her hair. "This whole thing is deranged! An indulgent waste for nothing! So much death and loss, for nothing! I simply tried to help you let go and stop chasing an old flame. It wasn't right Frank." She pointed a finger. "The way you watched her at school, tracked her call logs in Anchorage, that's sick obsessive behavior!"

Frank fisted his hands.

"Darleen." Detective Scott warned. "Remember what we discussed."

Agitating a deranged man was not good, in cuffs or not, and he still had a long ride to Harley's department that she had to see him through.

"Let's wrap this up." She ushered.

"My issues with Sam were only how she spun you up so, and nothing is worth letting a woman get close to a man who killed her daddy, and went about doing what you did. You hurt her more, and she's been through enough. I did the right thing, even if I am losing the man I love because of it." She stood up to leave.

"You gonna be alright Darleen?" The pain in his voice showed there.

"She'll be just fine." Anita took her arm. "And so will Sam."

Detective Scott escorted them back to the station, before finalizing the false stolen truck report Frank had made, phone calls to get it pulled out of the water, and the stack of papers for her boss, in what was no longer Frank's office.

Darleen's eyes welled when she saw Luke lumber through the door, a finished file in his hands, and flowers he promptly placed on her desk in front of her.

"Oh you big goon." She reached over the call center to clutch his face, rubbing his wrapped arm. "You ok honey? Oh Lucian I'm so sorry."

"You have not a damn thing to apologize for Darleen." He tapped the file in clarity. "Not a damn thing, you're and angel among demons, ma'am."

Darleen sniffed as tears fell and nodded. "She's going to be ok now. I won't be right about it for a while yet, but I won't ever regret it." She waved Luke off and turned her face into Anita's chest.

"Chief Rose." Detective Scott motioned him to enter the office with her and her boss. "If you please."

"Not Chief yet, Detective."

The head of the FBI sat back, lacing his fingers. "I beg to differ son."

Chapter 23

Samantha didn't see anyone for over two weeks. She managed a text or two with Luke, mostly answering in emojis and keeping her distance, still angry, still confused, frightened by how much it terrified her seeing him squared up to be executed. Losing Paw caused a war, between her need to be loved and her fear of losing it; A battle she was unprepared to have reignited in her already broken state.

She had decided not to see Frank, refusing his repeated and, according to Detective Scott, volatile requests. The story had been laid out for her well enough, nothing he could say could fill the gaping hole not having her father had left, or the destruction and pain he'd caused others, robbing her of proper mourning over Paw to boot. There was no room for his explanation, nor did she want it.

She chose to forgive herself for not seeing his deterioration, the signs, it mattered not. The last paper she signed was to be certain no mail from him would ever arrive. She would go in again when questions needed answering, trial weeks if not months away, but for now, she mourned, recovered, healed.

She ran her sled team on wheeled sleds, many times on the Spring growth, though the air still chilled the skin. Sometimes crying, sometimes screaming, sometimes just staring off into the wilderness lost in thought. The exercise was good for them and helped her anger ease.

She even let all eight of them in the house for a movie night, something Roy thoroughly resented, cursing her choice while she cleaned up behind them the next day, laughing.

She let Roy sleep in her bed, his own adjustment to Paw being gone apparent in his leech-like behavior.

Brad was in a brand-new land yacht on his lot, overseeing the rebuild and refusing to yield. He'd sent Sam Sully's collar wrapped around a pot of daffodils, in response to her giving him the charm necklace back with flowers for the loss of his dogs. She'd never be comfortable with him again, but a peace had been restored, and she was happy for it.

205

The town had gone silent with tourists leaving in a fright, only to pick up again about a week later, the sun and fishing beckoning.

Sam had ordered Roy a dog bed that was waiting at the post office. Since Luke was officially being sworn in as Chief today, she thought now was as good a time as ever to give Denali his puppy, hide in the back and quietly support the man she painfully missed, before picking it up. Noting her comfort snacks and wine stock getting low, she supposed she had hid long enough.

She sent Sal a text to make her hold her own word to leave the house and managed to put eyeliner on and do her curls, deciding it felt good to feel decent for the first time in weeks. Sam placed the puppy on the seat of her Bronco next to Roy, his face less than pleased.

"Oh hush pal, he's on his way to make a teenager really happy." She pulled a weathered note in her wipers into the cab and let the truck warm up.

Mildly losing my shit over here.
I understand but I miss you .-Luke
Ps. Still love you, in case your ears chose to ignore that part.

"Smart ass." Her head hit the back of the seat, listing to meet Roy's low grumble. "Yea I know. He's a good one." She threw the truck in reverse. "Let's go get him then."

~

Sam made a mental note to thank Vanessa for texting her about Luke's ceremony and tried to control her salivating, as she slinked discreetly through the tiny Town Hall.

Luke was in a brand-new uniform, one far too nice for the everyday nonsense of a small-town cop, fresh tight cut under his hat, and he had clearly been working out his frustrations at the gym, because he was nicely swollen for the mere two weeks, she hadn't seen him. The Chief was testing the integrity of that uniform and her knees.

Damn he was delicious. It almost deleted the image she had of him about to be killed, almost.

She shook the memory away as she slipped along the back wall with her hood up, Tamar mercifully giving her a silent hello and subtle hug, compassionate to how overwhelming her day will become once the locals know she's finally out and about.

The Town Hall held the ones who knew Luke, Tig and Big John right up front, Willow and Forest in the chairs next to him on stage. A few officials from the big office off the island, and a good number of locals simply here for the free snacks, listened to the expected script and appeased when applause was needed.

Sam slinked down a bit when she caught Luke's eyes scanning the crowd. She didn't want him to think about her, just be in the moment. She blushed when those dark brown eyes snapped on her. She should have known; damn special ops eyes can find a needle in a haystack.

The wink Luke sent Sam, heat rising to her face, all but confirmed she was hopelessly his, while also causing the old woman in front of her to fan herself. Amusing them both to no end.

She was here. Luke leaned back and fixed his hat, fighting to keep the thrill from altering his face in front of a hundred people. He needed that, her, like some sort of support beacon, a secret sign that he still deserved it, even though sometimes doing the right thing meant skirting the line.

At least in Shavila it did.

You didn't need to lock up a man for being a little drunk in public, if he wasn't a risk to others, just let him sleep it off in a cell, give him coffee in the morning. Local kids didn't need citations, they needed to get brought home in a cop car and embarrassed straight. You don't need to tow cars here; you need to help the old woman get the broken down clunker home.

And you didn't need to haul in a woman who had only hurt herself, for the love of dogs.

Luke would uphold the law when it was necessary, but this wasn't the big city, and he was really falling in love with Shavila and the amazing people who kept this community going.

His community. His.

Especially one pack of black cats on the back wall about to light his world on fire, again.

Willow let out a whoop when he accepted Sergeant, and Luke rose. After the obligatory verbiage and pinning, Big John jumped up and shouted.

"Way to go Cheechako!"

The officials were none too pleased by the antics of the crazy little town, but Sam was warm all over as the clapping commenced and she slipped out the back door to her truck.

She had to try; her heart had loved every rock in this town, long before she ran from it, chasing something even she didn't understand. She had become a cop because she wanted an out, and the power to do what she was now planning to do the right way.

She glanced at Star's printed packet on nonprofit rescues, sitting in her cab.

Sam loaded the groceries she needed, laughing wildly as Denali leapt across the street, pissing off a driver who had to slam on his brakes, and skidding into her truck.

Luke watched the woman he loved glow as the teenager spun around with his new puppy, the joy it brought to her face was something he would hold on to on her darkest days, remind her.

She handed his mother bags of puppy pads and food, exchanging words with a very attentive Denali about care and training, no doubt.

Anita bumped his hip. "You look so good today I might just fight her for ya."

Luke smirked. "I wouldn't recommend."

He couldn't peel his eyes from Sam. He'd missed her so much, his heart clinging to the hope she'd let him near her again, that she wasn't too broken to try, to trust a man again.

Sam caught his longing gaze across the street, flashing a small smile and nudging her head towards her road, before she got in her Bronco and drove off.

"Nobody is gonna miss ya for a few minutes." Anita brushed off his badge and straightened his collar. "Go get her, Chief."

Sam sat on the porch waiting for him.

She owed him a show of how much she longed for him, the truth. While she had needed this time to wrap her head around what had happened, she had missed him, and never wanted to be away from him that long again.

A hive of bees swarmed her stomach as he pulled up. Far more than they had the first time she knew she would lay with him, the respect he had shown her when she needed space, making him all the more enchanting.

The uniform helped. She was not above that shallow fact. He rose so sharply, so sexy, out of that patrol truck, she thought she was looking at him for the first time.

"God you're beautiful." He quipped, slamming the door and looping his thumbs on his duty belt.

"Funny." Sam brushed her butt off. "Was thinking the same thing about you Chief."

"Thank you for being there. I didn't expect you to and-"

"I love you, Luke."

He muscled down the lump in his throat her words brought. Finally, he knew for certain, and it took every ounce of control to be the strong man Sam had showed him she needed, and hold steady in the moment.

She craved someone stronger than her, and that was a tall order to say the least. A man who could let her not have to be strong anymore. It was in him, but he'd already proven he wasn't above crying beneath her, and the terrified look in her eyes, the longing, the questioning... well he was about to.

"I do. It's so different than I thought it would be. God so much I do... and I... I'm sorry I just, don't know how to do this." She wrung her hands. "You make me weak, and I don't like it, but its good, to be weak for someone, I think. And it's right, right?" She looked up and blinked back tears. "Your temper scares me, but so does my own, and not as much as that god damn image of you about to be killed does. Luke It scared me so much."

Her mouth trembled, but he held steady, listening to her bleed her truths, how hard it was for her to bare herself this way. She was destroying him in the most beautiful way.

"I don't want to need you, but I do. I can't stop feeling the hole inside me seeing you on your knees. I love you, Lucian. I hate it. Ugh!" She stamped her foot at the tears forming and searched the roof above her. "Thank you for being there for me, for understanding my screwed up...uh... I need you to be stronger than me and hold my feet down sometimes... That's not fair to ask but..."

She rubbed her face frustrated, afraid. "You are something I never knew existed, the way you treat me... I don't know how to deal with it... You deserve... Look, I will be fine without you if you don't want-"

"Sam."

She looked down at him, a tear releasing in spite of her efforts.

"Come here."

She hesitated and he tilted on his back foot, that sexy stare looming under his trooper hat.

"Come.here.Samantha."

Please Creator let him demand her always. She needed that grit, that refusal to back down from her fight. Sam scuffed her feet towards him, and he yanked her to her toes, a startled chirp escaping her lips as they hoovered close to his.

"I hope you enjoyed your solitude sweetheart, because I'm not going anywhere." His mouth crushed hers, the searing heat of him igniting every frostbitten part of her. "I love you Sam."

He nipped and tasted, lapping up the tears she rained against his passion. "You stay right here." He whispered on her tongue. "Right.Fucking.here." He ordered. "I'll be back up here the minute I'm off duty, and I'm going to make love to you until you believe me." He planted her on the porch and fixed his uniform.

"Right.Here." He thrust his finger to the ground before he made long strides to his truck and drove off.

~

Sam had kept her promise, as Luke pulled in to keep his. Well, sort of. He leaned on the door of his truck, shaking his head as she careened out the door messily and planted her feet on the steps, her legs shaking in anticipation.

"Tsk Tsk." He slammed the door. "I said stay put."

"I had to feed the dogs." Her tone had attitude, until his chiseled mass loomed under darkening eyes, marching towards her like a cave man. "And I made you dinner..." She stammered.

He made her feel like she was the most important thing in the world, while simultaneously meek and vulnerable. She relished in the gift of being able to be such things, be free from being strong. She needed him to be firm and demanding, aggressive in his love, refusing to let her run from what she so desperately wanted. Divine femininity releasing like a flock of doves that would never be shot down.

He had read her perfectly, and she bit her lip as he picked her up, saying nothing, slamming the door behind him.

"Guess we aren't eating first." She giggled as he hauled her upstairs.

"Shut up Samantha." He threw her on the bed. "When I get back, you better be naked."

She ripped her clothes off and was crawling back on the bed when he tromped back in, wine in hand, and a bottle of lotion.

"I think you should get the pampering, being made Chief today and all."

"Sam." He struck a match and lit a bundle of candles by her bed. "Shut.Up."

She pressed her lips together and folded her hands in her lap. He was never like this with her, no one was, no one dared, and it was thrilling. It's as if he knew she would make light of what she'd said, toss out jokes to avoid the weight of it all, and he was having none of it.

Sam had a tongue like a razor, and he'd already been more patient than she'd deserved, so gentle and caring, that he was making it clear, he could, and would, force her to listen, to face her feelings, and to let someone else call the shots. The blissful lack on control her offered made her core ache in need.

Lucian Rose was perfect for her.

Luke stripped to his jeans, laid Sam face down with a warning grunt at her protest, and began to massage the lotion over her back. Her groans of delight confirmed his assumption was correct.

This woman, while possibly had dealt with her mind, was holding all the stress and trauma from the past few weeks in her body.

The fact that he doubted any man had taken the time to massage her, also aided his decision, as did Charlotte in picking out a scented lotion Sam wouldn't bitch about. Lavender was a safe bet, but Charlotte swore the rosemary and citrus would have 'desired effects for relaxation and stimulation'.

She's said it a bit too loud, but Luke was grateful for her anyway.

He did not spare any part of Sam's body from his hands, making sure the tension eased from every square inch of her.

When a deep exhale sunk her into the bed, he was satisfied, and began his next attack: Normalcy.

"So, the locals have a baseball game every year huh. You play?"

Sam sighed into the mattress. "I will if you want me too." She would do just about anything he asked at this point. "I did once, but usually just help prep the bats. It's a really fun day."

Luke grinned silently. She was right where he wanted her.

"I brought us bats. Big John said you'd know what to do with them." He felt her body chuckle under his thighs, reminding him he was controlling a raging erection, miserably.

"Oh, he would. I'm the best bat prepper there is." She let her fingers curl around his denim. "You're in for one good time, babe."

There it was. No jabbing pet name, not his real name, just a calm, normal term of endearment. Like they always were, and always will be. A security and comfort she better well get used to and was long overdue. He felt her tense slightly when she said it, promptly lowering his chest to her back, clasping his hand gently around her throat.

"Felt good, didn't it?" Her entire body melted into the mattress in surrender, acceptance, and she nodded. "Get used to it Samantha." He turned her over beneath him, his thumb dragging the tear away. "I love you." He whispered. "It's scary as shit, but that doesn't change it, does it?" She agreed silently. "I'll take your shit well enough, but tonight, I want to take your love, and I want you to take mine, and don't you run from it."

"Lucian…"

He made love to her, claimed her, worshipped her. Their bodies rolling and tumbling together in sweet abandon, neither of them holding back, both on them refusing to dampen the powerfulness of it. There was passion enough, always had been, but Sam moved on Luke like he was the only man allowed to see her, unveiled her soul and cried out his name under the firm grip of his hands, marveling in the ownership of it, his delicate dominance of her darkest fears.

Luke pulled her close, every inch of her body he could muster against his, rolling into her, he filled her ears with his triumphant release, clutching her so tightly until every ounce of him was spent inside her. When his head stopped spinning he lifted to watch her bare chest pant for breath, sliding his hand down to cup her stomach.

"I know you said you don't want them, but in a few years, if you don't hate me by then." He squeezed her delicate flesh, before rubbing her tummy tenderly. "You'd look so sexy swollen with our babies… I think this is a great place to raise a-"

She kissed his mid-thirties, hormonal clock silent, and he lowered his hand, working her up again.

"Oh my god, no I can't." She began to writhe under him, the sensitivity too much.

"Can't what baby?" He kissed her as she squirmed, his fingers expert in their marksmanship. "Can't come for me or can't carry our babies?" She gasped for breath and clutched him. "Tell me you will." He begged, driving her to the brink. "Say it my love."

"Yes!" She arced violently, screaming into a sob, the orgasm blinding her, his tongue sucking the air from her mouth. "Oh my god." She curled into him and cried, everything that ever haunted her, dissipating in his arms.

"I have you." He wrapped himself around her. "And I was just kidding about the kids."

"Fuck you, Chief." She sobbed a laugh.

He laughed and squeezed her tight. "There she is."

Chapter 24

A few tourists aside, the local crowd let out a massive cheer as the frozen bat Big John swung blasted into pieces as he cracked one over the elementary school fence.

Denali bolted around the plates, John looking quite the spectacle jogging his massive frame behind him.

Sam scowled at her all too pleased man, across the way in the men's dugout. She'd shown him how to freeze the bats for the best explosion, and when it was decided it would be men against women this year, he'd done what a good teammate would do, and froze all their bats using her method.

"Snake." Charlotte bit. "You trusted him too soon. That dick must be good."

"Too good." Sam smiled. "But not good enough for me to give it all away."

"You are my favorite devil, Sammy." Charlotte slapped her on the ass, lifting a bat thick with ice. "I'll get us on base."

"What the hell is that!?" Tig slapped Luke's chest. "You too busy training the new deputy and holding out on us Chief?"

Luke watched as Sal lugged a cooler out from behind a bush, Denali giving his mother a look of defeat. Sam opened it, plums on white smoke assaulting the dirt, sending Luke a middle finger.

Luke took off his baseball cap and rubbed his head. "I think we're about to lose guys."

Charlotte and Sal both got on base, impressive explosions from both, when Vanessa stepped up to the plate, bunted and filled the bases.

"Ah hell." James mumbled. "The only class Sam liked was science."

The men shoved and verbally assaulted each other about critical information, as Sam pulled on thick gloves and lifted a steaming bat out of the fogging cooler.

"With how big you are," Big John took a long pull from his beer and nudged Luke, "you ain't never gonna live this down."

"None of us are." Luke hipped his hands, the side of his mouth curling at Sam's focus.

The crowd began a low chant, slowing rising in volume as the ball flew. 'Swing-it-Sam! Swing-it-Sam!'

"She's worse with a bat than her fists." James shook his head, already defeated.

"You're telling me asshole!" Big John balked, the rest of them lurching in laughter.

Forest tried, bless him. The pitch was fast and hard, but Sam made it rain glitter and glacial shards as she blew the bat apart in one strong swing.

The crowd had chosen, and as the girls ran in and began to jump all over themselves in triumph, the men handed their bets over to Denali.

"Told you not to underestimate women guys!" The teenager ogled his wad of cash. "I know cuz my mom is the toughest lady ever! Add Sam playing this year? We never had a chance!"

"You're wise beyond your years kid." Luke shoved him off and they all went to grovel to the champs.

~

They pulled up to the bar to celebrate, Sam in a rare social form that Luke almost didn't want to burst. But he felt he ought to let her make up her own mind.

"Wait." Luke started.

Sam stopped the door from closing, a questioning look on her face.

"This came in for you today, thought I should tell you." Luke held up an envelope, from the paternity DNA testing labs.

Sam loosed a deep breath. "Nah. I'll look at it later. Today needs none of that!" She soaked up the proud look on his face.

She was living lighter, and Luke looked forward to enjoying it with her for the rest of his life.

Sam loved up Roy's head and closed the Bronco door. "Come on babe! You owe your woman a beer, loser!"

Luke watched Sam run up and jump on James's back, her best friend hauling her in, surrounded by the lot of folks he now called his friends.

He popped the letter open and read, wanting to prepare himself for any support she may need. Exhaling a heavy breath, he tossed it on the seat, Sam leaping into his arms at the bar door and kissing him deeply.

"I love you, Chief Lucian Rose."

"I Love you, Sam."

Roy settled his furry head on the letter, and resigned himself to sleep until his parents returned, the results resting under his tired jowls:

Samantha Shaw
DNA Paternity results: 99.98 Accuracy
Mother: Elizabeth Shaw; Maiden name O'Reilly
Father:
___Liam Samuel Shaw___

Coming soon from C.K. Haworth

The WHISPERS Collection

(Title TBA) *Whispers:*
Contemporary FBI romance full of suspense, mystery, and wit.

And more…

C.K. HAWORTH'S FIRST VAMPIRE SERIES

The Morganthe Vampire Clan Trilogy (Book 1 in 2023)

Please note: All of C.K. Haworth's series are longer, more intense novels, than her collections/stand alone works.

Links C.K. Haworth's social media/newsletters/sites:
linktr.ee/c.k.haworth

C.K. Haworth

Made in United States
North Haven, CT
26 April 2023

35884354R00136